THE
LAKE
HOUSE

A.J. RIVERS

The Lake House
Copyright © 2022 by A.J. Rivers

All rights reserved. Without limiting the rights under copyright reserved above, no part of this publication may be reproduced, stored in or introduced into retrieval system, or transmitted, in any form, or by any means (electronic, mechanical, photocopying, recording, or otherwise) without the prior written permission of both the copyright owner and the above publisher of this book.

This is a work of fiction. Names, characters, places, brands, media, and incidents are either the products of the author's imagination or are used fictitiously. The author acknowledges the trademarked status and trademark owners of various products referenced in this work of fiction, which have been used without permission. The publication/use of these trademarks is not authorized, associated with, or sponsored by the trademark owners.

PROLOGUE

UNKNOWN PERSPECTIVE

The man put the phone to his ear and waited for her to pick up on the other end. Calling her was always tense business, and in this case, even more so, because of the news he would have to give her. That old saying about not killing the messenger didn't always apply to her. She had no problem killing messengers—or at least, she had no problem ordering their deaths. He supposed that was one benefit of being at the top of the food chain, so to speak.

The phone rang a third time, and a tiny flicker of hope rushed through his stomach, that his upsetting news would be delayed by a day or so. Maybe she was traveling.

Maybe she's dead, he thought, grinning at the thought of her lying in a pool of her own blood.

He looked around almost guiltily, as if someone might have overheard his internal thoughts about the big boss. For all he knew, and given her eyes and ears on everyone and everything, maybe she had. He didn't like to think about that, though. Not with a view like this.

Readjusting his grip on the phone, he moved to the window and looked out over the bright, colorful houses and buildings artfully arranged against the placid shore. It was the best place he had ever lived. In all the years of working his way up the ladder of power, all the years of building trust with her, he had only been mid-level in the organization until last summer, when she'd finally promoted him to top-tier ranking and had allowed him to set up shop on the shoreline of Greece. The Mediterranean weather and the view of the endless blue sea fit him. He breathed deeply of the salty ocean air. It smelled like success. Like he'd finally made it.

Keeping that success was not always easy, though, and he knew it could all be wiped away if this phone call went sideways.

The fifth ring. He pulled the phone from his ear and his thumb hovered over the disconnect button.

But to his dismay, there was a click from the other end of the line. His heart clutched in his chest and he rammed the phone back to his ear.

"This better be good news. I've had a bad week, and I don't need more bad news."

He cleared his throat and dabbed at the small beads of sweat along his forehead. They hadn't been there a few seconds earlier. He trained his eyes on the water. "It's Elizabeth."

"Elizabeth? As in that American who can't keep her nose out of my business and works for the US Government?" Her tone was clipped.

He could imagine the tightness at the corners of her mouth, the hard set of her icy eyes. "Yes. Elizabeth James."

"I thought that problem was being taken care of."

"It is, uh… it *was*." He could hardly form words over the dry lump in his throat.

"*Was*? Tell me that means our Russian friend was successful in South Africa and this *Elizabeth* is not a problem any longer."

It wasn't a question; it was an order, but unfortunately one he couldn't follow.

"Our Russian friend is dead." There, he'd said it. It was out and there was no taking it back.

Silence from the other end of the line.

He could feel the heat of her anger boiling across the miles, across the ether to singe him.

"He injured her before he was killed, though," he rushed in, in an attempt to fill that silence that felt so threatening. He leaned close to the lavender on his balcony and inhaled deeply of the highly fragrant aroma. He had to stay calm.

His superior was unimpressed. "Fix it, or the next death will be yours. This is your job and your life we're discussing now. I don't want her injured; I want her *dead*. Do you even know where she is now?"

"Our intel says she most likely went back to the United States."

"Most likely, but you don't know for sure?"

"No," he admitted, dreading the next bit of information he had to spill. "And there's something else."

"Don't make me guess. I'm not into playing games."

"Ash Patterson. In the US. Do you know him?"

"Why the hell would I know him? Does he work for the organization? Is he one of mine?"

"He's Cornbread Mafia. The Southeastern faction that supplies us and delivers goods sometimes. We do know for sure that he gave information to the FBI about part of the organization."

"Has it caused the kind of trouble from which we can recover, or is it the other kind of trouble?"

"Recoverable damage. We, of course, are in the clear for now. What do you want done with this Ash Patterson?"

There was a considerable pause of silence, in which the only sound was that of her fingernail tapping against one tooth. He'd seen that particular tic only twice, and both times, someone died horrifically not long after.

"Even if you have to go to America yourself and fix this, I want it fixed immediately. Find this Ash Patterson, and whoever he takes orders from—the next person up the food chain—and you make an example of them. Don't make me spell it out, but I want the US factions to understand when they see them that they best not screw with me or the same will happen to them. Do. You. *Understand?*"

He nodded fervently, as if she could see him. "I do. I do. Don't worry another minute about this. I'll get it fixed." The sweat ran down his temple and his stomach turned. No amount of Mediterranean air or lavender would calm the storm inside now.

"If you don't, I don't need to remind you what will happen."

"No. Ash Patterson and Jack Kearns will be made into prime examples of your far-reaching power, ma'am."

She disconnected and he held the phone out, looking at the flashing timer until the screen went dark then he took a deep breath. He didn't need a reminder. Not at all.

CHAPTER ONE

Desiree walked into the living room of the small apartment and flopped on the couch, leaning against Jonathan. The phone was pressed to her ear and she laughed as she listened to Akira and Cai describing their latest live-action role-playing session.

"I don't know how you two can stand being out there in the woods for a week, living rough and wearing all those layers of thick costumes," she said with a shake of her head.

Jonathan nudged her and laid aside the Xbox controller as YOU ARE DEAD flashed across the television screen. "Are they going to be able to go with us?"

Desiree shrugged and held up a finger, waiting for a break in the chatter so she could ask again. "Hey, are you two going to be able to come with us to the lake for a month, or do you have too many LARPing engagements?"

Jonathan nuzzled at her neck just below her ear, making it difficult to concentrate on the phone call. She pushed him away, stifling a giggle as their friends discussed the month-long vacation at the lake.

"Where did you say it was at?" Akira asked.

"Bumbee Ridge in County Crider, Maine. We found the cabin online. I sent you the info yesterday about it, but I guess you were hanging from your toenails in a tree or something," she said, laughing.

"Ha-ha. Garnomorphs don't hang from their toenails. We have nests in the trees and we sit in them and wait for unsuspecting players to come by so we can shoot them with our stun bolts and take their health and energy bags."

"Whatever floats your boat," Desiree said, rolling her eyes dramatically for Jonathan.

He flapped his arms, imitating a chicken silently, and Desiree punched the mute button on the phone. "Stop it. It would hurt their feelings if they knew we were laughing at them."

"Oh, they can take it. Kind of comes with the territory."

She glowered at him and shook her head. He gave in and went back to playing his video game.

"So, can we put you guys on the reservation?"

"Are you driving us up there?" Cai asked from the background.

"Jonathan's driving. He knows Maine. Remember, he grew up there." Desiree smiled at him.

"We can go, then. Who else is going, anyway?" Akira asked.

"Awesome," Desiree said, giving Jonathan a thumbs-up. "Trevon and Nova said they were definitely coming, and they would buy all the beer we could drink while we're up there. BB and Kalen are in, too."

"Oomph," Akira muttered.

"What?"

"Kalen and BB?"

"They're part of the group, too. Just because they're single guys doesn't exclude them. What's the deal?"

"Oh, nothing. Except that they'll be spending all their time trying to pick up girls from the local scene. They'll have strangers in and out of the house in a constant stream. You know how they are."

"We will just have to lay some ground rules for them, then." Kalen and BB weren't so bad. Most of the time, anyway. Sometimes, they could be obnoxious. Well, mostly BB was the obnoxious one. Kalen just sort of followed along when he was feeling left out because he was the only other single guy in their group.

"Alright," Akira finally relented, sighing as if she didn't believe the guys would follow the rules no matter who made them. "Hey, when do we go? What are the for-sure dates? I have to schedule around the vacay or risk losing our spots in the community."

"You mean they won't let you be Garnomorphs if you don't tell them you're going on vacation?"

"Nope, they won't. We've worked the entire season to be upgraded. I don't want to lose my rank and have to start out as a Chiprand again. That sucks. The only power they have is that they can blend into their surroundings. Slightly. And steal from other players, unless the other players make them dead."

"Okay," Desiree said, halting the lesson in live-action fantasy role-playing. "We have the cabin from July 1st until August 1st. We'll leave the night before so we can miss the worst of the traffic."

"Two weeks from now. Okay. See you guys tomorrow at Bernie's for some beer, hot wings, and a few games of pool, right?"

Desiree grinned. "You bet. See you at seven."

She turned to Jonathan. He was insanely focused on his video game. Some violent, gruesome fantasy horror game that she didn't understand and didn't like. "They're in, too."

He nodded without looking at her as he maneuvered his character away from what appeared to be some sort of gigantic zombie wolf creature. "Looks like we'll have a full house."

"A full cabin, you mean," she corrected him, standing and heading to the kitchen.

"Trevon and Nova said yes, too, right?" he asked, calling after her but still focusing on his game.

"Yes. Everyone is coming. It's our last fling before we have to start *adulting*, and they're all in for that."

"Who's bringing the weed and the bong? Trevon?"

"Nope. They're going to supply beer and liquor. You don't smoke, so why do you care?" She peeked around the corner from the kitchen.

"I might this time. Like you said—it's our last fling before adulthood proper begins."

She knew he wouldn't. He never did. He always said he was going to try it, and then he always backed out at the last minute, using his sleeping pills as an excuse. The sleeping pills didn't affect his drinking with the rest of them, though, and sometimes, he got plastered right along with the best of them, sleeping pills or no.

"What are we contributing?"

"Definitely not the Xbox," she muttered.

"You don't think they'd enjoy playing while we're *on vacation?*"

"If you take that thing, we're getting divorced," she announced.

"We're not married," he countered with a laugh.

She stepped back into the room with two sandwiches and a bag of chips. "And we won't be if you take that damn thing on this vacation. I want to enjoy our time with each other and our friends. Just think, we'll all be going in different directions after this. Who knows how long it'll be until we see them again. If we ever see them again."

"Oh, we'll see them again. It'll just have to be a lot less often, I guess. Damn it," he groaned. The words YOU ARE DEAD flashed on the screen again and he finally tore his eyes away from the television. He took his plate and kissed her. "Thank you."

"You're welcome," she replied, settling back with her own plate.

"And, I won't take the Xbox." He smiled and goosed her knee.

"Good, because I was kind of looking forward to marrying you next year." She held up her hand and let the sunlight from the window glint off the small diamond on her ring finger.

"You just don't want to give up the diamond. That's really it, isn't it?" he grinned.

"I thought I was doing such a good job hiding that."

"Nope. I can always see right through the act. You just stay with me because of my money." He sighed heavily. "I'll take it, though."

"Whatever gets me in your bed, right?" she asked, laughing and enjoying their goofy banter.

"Yep. And I thought I was doing such a good job hiding that."

She shook her head and continued laughing. They had a great relationship most of the time, and that was what she wanted when they went to the cabin. She was under no illusions that life would still be easy and fun after they married and started their lives together. It would be full of hard times, and she wanted to have this one summer to always be able to look back on, to hang on to. It should be filled with wonderful, fun memories that would last all of them a lifetime. And no one ever made those kinds of memories if there was an Xbox involved. She was glad he wasn't going to take the console. It proved that he really did care about her. More than anyone else ever had.

CHAPTER TWO

T HE CABIN WAS ONE STORY TALL, BUT WITH THE SIXTEEN-FOOT vaulted ceiling with skylights over the living room and kitchen, it felt huge. The bedrooms were along the outer edges of those two main rooms. There were five bedrooms, which was perfect for three couples and two singles. Desiree smiled and wrapped her arms around Jonathan's neck as they stood in the center of the house.

"It's perfect," she smiled, kissing his cheek.

"And it's ours for a whole month," he replied, kissing her on the lips and grabbing her butt with one hand, giving it a firm squeeze.

"Hey, hey, you two go find a room," Trevon cut in, holding his hand up to block them. "We don't want to see any of that shit, man." He grinned despite the harsh tone of his words.

Giggling, Nova ran up behind him and clapped him on the ass. He jumped and laughed. "Don't you get started, too, now."

She shrugged. "If ya can't beat them…"

"No. Absolutely not. It's too early in the day for all that. I think I'm tired from driving."

Nova rolled her eyes as they passed Desiree. "Such a drama queen."

Trevon turned to glare at her over his shoulder. "You try driving for twelve hours, through two major wrecks and detours, and dealing with all the damn tolls. You'd be tired, too."

Jonathan nodded. "I'm tired, too. I think we should all just take the day to get settled in and recover from the drive. We have lots of time up here."

Akira and Cai came in grinning and wide-eyed. "Wow, this place is great," Akira marveled.

"And we're not tired from driving at all," Cai added. His crooked grin said he was considering ribbing the drivers some more, but he didn't. The heated looks that landed on him probably changed his mind.

"Good. That means you and your girlfriend can go to town and pick up lunch for all of us, right?" BB asked as he walked in the door.

Kalen came trailing in behind him, looking as he always did—as if he were slightly confused but okay with it. "Damn, town was a few miles back. Why didn't anybody think to stop on our way up?"

"Because we hadn't discussed it beforehand," Nova told him.

Kalen waggled his cellphone at the group. "Communication is key in any—"

"Shut up," three of them replied in unison.

He slid his phone back into his pocket. "All of you know I'm right."

Nova threw a couch pillow at him. It whacked him upside the head. He laughed and picked up the pillow.

"If we're going for food, everybody's getting cheeseburgers and fries except for Nova; she gets a plain burger because of her lactose intolerance. No one else gets to order different," Akira announced, dropping her bags on the sofa and floor in front of it. Cai followed suit and held out his hand for the car keys.

BB and Jonathan both offered their keys. It took Cai about three seconds to decide he would rather drive Jonathan's 2019 Honda than BB's 1993 manual-transmission Chevrolet Beretta.

"Bring back some beer, man," BB said, putting his keys in his pocket.

Cai shook his head. "Trevon and Nova are buying the beer. We brought a little Chinese sweet leaf for later," he said, the corners of his mouth curling up and making him look like the Joker from Batman.

"You know there's no such thing, right?" Kalen asked.

"It's our special stash," Akira offered. "We only smoke it when we win a big battle."

Jonathan chuckled. "LARP battles?"

Akira smiled and nodded. Desiree poked Jonathan in the side and shook her head at him.

"Fine. Go get the food, and after we eat, Trevon and Nova can run out for the alcohol," Desiree said.

"Or, I could ride with them and get it now," Nova offered.

The group made sounds of agreement.

Trevon shrugged. "I'm not going anywhere except right here in this room. That bed is my destination for the next couple of hours."

"Yeah, yeah, sleepyhead," Nova admonished him playfully as she planted a kiss on his cheek. "Rest up."

She went with Akira and Cai as the others waved goodbye and set about unpacking their things.

It was going to be the perfect summer vacation. Desiree hadn't had a perfect summer anything in a while. The previous year, her summer vacation had been ruined by a hurricane. The year before that, she'd had a broken ankle. The one before that, her mother had been dying in the hospital. She tiptoed and gave Jonathan a peck on the lips. He had been eyeing BB, and she was afraid the old tension would crop up and cause a problem for them. If she could get over the whole Banks wanting to date her situation—which she had laughed off more than a few times—she wished the two guys could get over it; just drop it and let it die.

Banks Becker wasn't the type of guy to let anything go, though. He could hold grudges longer than anyone she'd ever met, and Jonathan was right behind him in second place for that award. Back before she and Jonathan had cemented their relationship and their place within the group, Becker had wanted to date her. He thought she deserved a better man than Jonathan. The two men had come to blows once. It was a drunken brawl, but it had been bad enough to upset everyone for a week. As the months turned into years, Banks would have occasional girlfriends, but they never lasted more than a month or two, and then he was single again and Desiree had to be careful how much attention she paid to him or he would take it the wrong way and make a move on her. She hated feeling uncomfortable around him, but she couldn't help it. If they were ever left alone, she made sure to find some excuse to get out of the situation pronto.

Akira was worried about him bringing a steady stream of local girls around, but Desiree kind of hoped he would find some nice girl in the area who would spend the summer with him. It would take a lot of pressure off her, and would surely cut down on arguments with Jonathan.

"Come on," she said, turning Jonathan toward their bedroom. "Let's go get our stuff put up." She pulled him into the room. "Might have some time for fun before they get back with burgers and beer." She winked and bit her lower lip seductively.

"Not with him lurking outside the door," Jonathan grumbled, jerking his chin in BB's direction.

She pushed the door shut with the tip of her shoe and glared at BB as he stared at her from the other side of the living room. Why couldn't he just stop it? Why couldn't he understand that she loved Jonathan and would never go out with him?

Men were so obstinate sometimes that she thought she would never understand them.

"We'll be quiet, then," she said, still trying to lure Jonathan toward the bed.

He shook his head. "I'm just not in the mood, Des. I'm tired as hell from all the driving, I need a shower, and I want to rest before everybody starts kicking up their heels this evening."

Chagrined, she nodded and dropped onto the edge of the bed. "Sorry. I wasn't really thinking about all the driving you just did. But to be fair, I did offer to drive the second half of the way up."

"I didn't want you driving, though. You know what they say about women drivers."

She nodded. "Yeah, if a woman is driving, the family is thriving."

He laughed as he stripped off his shirt and headed for the bathroom. "Not hardly. Women drivers, no survivors." He puckered and made a kissing sound as he disappeared into the bathroom. "Be out in five."

"I'll be right here," she replied, looking at their bags and really not wanting to put the clothes away right then.

She had plenty of time to get to the bags. The bed was really comfortable and soft and inviting as she sat there with the sunlight washing warmly over her legs. It would be fine if she just laid back and took a little nap until Jonathan got out of the shower.

Or until the food and beer gets here, she thought with a smile as she laid her head on the thick pillow.

CHAPTER THREE

Cai and Akira brought a small, black shoulder bag out of their room and set it on the coffee table to unzip.

"Is everybody ready to party?" Cai asked, dipping both hands into the bag.

The resounding response was affirmative. Everybody was more than ready to start partying away the month. There were no neighbors at the lake. Desiree had asked Jonathan about the empty pool house that looked more like a guest house, but he had no answers. It just seemed that no one had rented it. Lucky for them, anyway. At least they didn't have to worry about disturbing anyone while they partied.

Cai brought out enough marijuana that it caused a gasp to ripple through the group.

"Oh my god, Cai, how did you even get that much? That must cost a fortune."

"Don't worry about it," he replied coyly. "I know some people who got me the hookup. This is the good stuff."

Nova tilted her head. "Are we sure that it's okay to have here?"

"I looked it up. It's legal in Maine for recreational use, for up to a certain amount. But trust me, by the time the cops even think about coming here, this shit will be long gone. Or, at least, most of it will."

Akira punched his arm and glared at him. "Language, Cai."

He gave her a confused look. "What did I even say?"

"Shit, Cai," BB said, leaning forward to snag a lighter. "You said shit."

Akira shot him a hateful look. "Really, BB? Language, please. You know cursing is a sign of a seriously low IQ, right?"

BB held his arms close to his chest, clapped his fingertips together repeatedly, and made sea lion sounds. "Then, I'm totally screwed, right?"

Akira threw a pillow at him and turned back to the bag, pulling out the grinder to prepare the first round. Everyone else laughed. Even Cai had to fight the urge.

Nova dragged the cooler into the living room. It was half-full of ice that was beginning to melt, and there were dozens of beer bottles poking up from it. "Come on, guys. The sun is dropping and we have yet to crack open the first beer or light the first bowl. If we're doing this, let's do it."

Trevon pumped his fists in the air and stood, giving a whoop as he grabbed a beer and held it aloft, letting the water drip on the floor and run down his arm. "You heard the lady," he announced and tossed the beer toward Kalen, who fumbled to catch it before it hit the hardwood floor.

Trevon and Nova passed out beers while Jonathan manned the stereo system. There were soundbars all over the huge living room, mounted on the walls and up in the corners. He picked something with a chill, yet refreshing beat, and slowly faded it up so it sounded like they were surrounded by the music.

When Desiree turned her attention to the table again, Akira and Cai had set out a few glass pipes and bongs for everyone to share. They were all in the shape of characters from their LARPing games. She chuckled.

Akira handed her a pipe that was bright pink and in the shape of a forest fairy reclining on a flower.

"Seriously, Akira?" she asked, looking at the pipe.

"What? She's the queen of the Forest Folk. Lots of magic. Powerful," Akira said, nodding solemnly as she passed the small grinder to Desiree for her to fill it up.

"I have to suck on her *toes*?"

Akira grinned impishly and nodded.

"Seems like someone has a fetish to me," she grumbled.

Jonathan got the music levels where he wanted them and then he plopped down next to her. Akira tossed him a joint, but he declined, placing it on the coffee table. "If I smoke, I can't take my sleeping pills later. You know that."

Akira looked from him to Desiree, who shrugged. "Okie-dokie, party pooper. Have it your way."

"Man, are you pulling that shit on us *again*?" BB asked, shaking his head as if disgusted.

"Yes, Banks, I am. Is that going to be a problem for you for the whole month?"

BB glared at him and gripped his beer tight enough that his fingertips turned white. "It might be, man. It just might be a big damn problem."

"Hey," Akira snapped, stepping into their sightline. "Stop it. Both of you. And watch the nasty language. I hate that. BB, smoke. And leave Jonathan alone. We're here to have a good time, not argue over stupid stuff all month long."

Kalen immediately turned to BB. "Hey, can you help a guy out?" He held out the pipe and weed.

BB looked at him in disbelief. "You still can't pack your own shit?"

Kalen shook his head. "It's always either too tight or too loose."

"Such are a man's lifelong problems," BB remarked.

"Come on, guys," Akira said, throwing her hands up in the air. "*Act* like you're not hopeless pervs at least for the first few days. That's just gross."

BB chortled and took the pipe from Kalen. As he packed the pipe for his friend, he kept staring across the room at Desiree. Several times, she shifted in her seat, trying to put Akira or Cai in the line of sight, but each time, Banks moved so he could still stare at her. It would only be a matter of time before Jonathan noticed, and that would cause more problems. Jonathan would be the only one not smoking, and therefore, he would be the straightest one there. He always saw and noticed way too much when they partied, and Desiree was beginning to wonder if it had been a mistake to include BB.

∽

By one-thirty in the morning, only BB and Cai were still functioning. They were playing a card game on the coffee table when Nova finally laid her head over on Trevon's thigh and fell asleep. Everyone except Jonathan had fallen asleep in the living room. He had gone to his bedroom after taking his sleeping pills.

Nova lay half-conscious until the music turned off and the guys finished their card game, and then she welcomed the warm embrace of total darkness and peace. She floated down into that warm, comfortable abyss and let it hold her like a mother holds a child. It was a good decision to do a group vacation. She was glad she had joined the little group. It was rare for her to fall asleep with a smile in her heart, but that first night at the cabin, she did just that.

And then there was an odd noise. It wasn't the total silence of the warm abyss. It was something different. Something that felt dangerous, even.

Nova struggled to break out of the fog of sleep and pull herself upright on the couch, but the bonds of sleep were heavy.

The noise again. Her brain interpreted it as a clink-scrape. Nothing in her repertoire of easily-accessible memory matched that sound, and it scared her. She struggled harder to wake.

As she opened her eyes in the darkness, fear settled over her, prickling her skin. No one seemed to be moving around at all. Light, occasional snoring came from the direction of Jonathan and Desiree's room. Everything else was silent, but she knew she had heard something out of place. Otherwise, she would still be sleeping.

Then a long *shhhhh* sound came from Jonathan's room, and his snoring ceased. Nova sat bolt upright on the couch, beads of perspiration popping out on her forehead. Someone was in the house with them. Everyone was accounted for in the living room except Jonathan. Even Desiree had fallen asleep there. Nova silently scooted to the edge of the bed and strained to hear any sounds. Nothing. But someone had shushed Jonathan, and that someone had not been any of them.

After a few minutes of dead silence, she had convinced herself that she hadn't heard anything, but she couldn't lie down and go back to sleep either.

Easing through the muddle of sleeping friends, she made her way to Jonathan's door. It was completely open. Had he left it wide open like that? She couldn't remember, but it would have been out of character for him. Peeking around the doorway, she let her eyes roam over the room. The only person in there was Jonathan stretched out flat on his back on top of the covers with both hands over his head. No wonder he snored so much.

She timidly poked her head into the room and gasped as the curtains over a window fluffed upward. Slapping her hand over her mouth, she watched as the curtains moved in the breeze again. Why had he left the window open when they had the central air on?

Shaking her head, she moved to the window, flipped the curtains back, and reached for the window. She stopped. There was no screen in the window. It faced the front of the house where they had approached earlier in the day. Nova couldn't remember seeing a window that had been missing a screen. She stuck her head out the window and squinted at the ground only a couple of feet below. There was no screen there, so maybe it had been missing all along and she hadn't noticed.

The surroundings were totally black. The only light anywhere was from the sliver of moon in the sky and the thick smattering of stars. The scant, silvery light danced on top of the ripples in the lake. Other than that, there was no light, ambient or otherwise, anywhere on the property. Complete isolation.

A shiver traced her spine, and she pulled back inside the house, pushed the window down quickly, and turned the lock. As she stepped out from the curtains, she wanted desperately to wake Desiree or Trevon and tell them what she had heard, but it wouldn't do any good. They were sleeping under the influence.

"They won't believe me, anyway," she muttered as she made her way to the kitchen. She sat there until sunrise, unable to get comfortable enough to even think of dozing off again.

As she had half-expected, no one quite believed her story, and they laughed.

"You are such a scaredy-cat city-dweller," BB teased as he poured himself a cup of coffee. "You'd think you never went camping with us or anything. How did you survive those camping trips?"

"Because nothing happened on those trips to scare the crap out of me. That's what I'm trying to tell all of you. Something was going on in the house last night that shouldn't have been. It freaking scared me."

Akira rubbed Nova's shoulder as she passed by for her own coffee. "We had all just smoked a massive amount. Maybe that had something to do with it."

Nova shook her head. "Whatever it was, it shushed Jonathan, and he stopped snoring."

Desiree locked eyes with her, and Nova nodded. "Seriously. I know what I heard and what I felt."

Desiree nodded and looked slightly concerned as she glanced around toward her and Jonathan's room. "We'll keep an eye on everything. Try not to worry."

Nova sighed. None of them really believed her, and now she would be the butt of their jokes for the whole month. She wasn't paranoid. What she heard had nothing to do with smoking and drinking. What she felt had even less to do with any of that. Someone, or *something*, had been in the house with them the night before, and they couldn't convince her of anything else.

CHAPTER FOUR

"YOU SURE YOU'RE NOT HUNGRY?" AVA ASKED FOR THE FIRST TIME. Sal took a deep breath and squeezed her eyes shut for a moment. Ava waited. The trip to Wyoming had been an unexpected left turn in the kidnapping case they had been working, and a far cry from their home base in Fairhaven, Maryland. It didn't help matters that Ava and Ash were the only ones on the team who were seemingly unaffected by the sparse, bare, middle-of-nowhere surroundings. The rest of the team despised it, and they didn't care to let their disdain show.

Sal opened her eyes, forced a tight smile, and finally relented. "Okay. Let's go in and get something to eat. God knows how long we're going to be out here. Might as well get used to the boot-kicking country music that seems to be playing everywhere around."

Ava grinned and opened the door. "We could be going to Saddle and Spur for lunch."

"No, we absolutely could not. I would rather have whatever fast-food drive-thru there is out here than go where there are half-naked women in cowgirl outfits as servers. Nope." She shook her head and stepped into Jake's Steaks.

Ava followed her with an amused grin. She kept it to herself, not wanting to further annoy Sal or the rest of the team.

Metford, Santos, and Ashton were already seated at a table near the side windows that looked out to absolutely nothing. There was a paved road and a flat expanse of windblown dirt, rock, and scrub trees, and somewhere about a million miles away was the horizon. It was like looking into forever out there, and it was very deceiving because if Ava turned her head and looked out the other side of the restaurant, there were mountains just piled on top of each other, crammed into the landscape and competing to see which one could grow the densest forest. It was a confusing place, and one in which Ava understood someone could *get lost* if they so desired. It might take weeks to track down Grandma Loretta and her four-year-old granddaughter Lumen.

"Hey, boss, I thought you weren't coming out," Metford called over as they took their seats.

Sal nodded. "I know how much misery loves company, so here I am."

"It's desolate," Santos added, nodding out the window that overlooked the Big Nothing.

"I kind of like it," Ash countered mildly, with a wistful look on his face as he seemingly compared the two opposing views of the land.

Sal blew air between her lips and shook her head. "Could we order already? I have a ton of paperwork to push through on this case, not to mention I need to coordinate search efforts out there." She pointed out the window to the mountains and then dropped her gaze to the menu. "Does anyone have any new leads? Where the hell is this loving, little, old grandma and the baby?"

"I thought she was like four," Metford said. "That would make her a toddler, right? Or is my info wrong?"

Sal let her hand thud to the table. "The *kid*, Metford. Is that better? Since when are *you* so technical about anything?" She gave him a burning look and then looked at each of the others in turn, letting her glare rest longest on Ava as if accusing her of being at fault for them all being in Armpit, Wyoming. "Well? Anyone? Anything to add to the case? Or have you all been just wandering around town getting the lay of the land and making friends?"

Ashton cleared his throat and waved for the waiter. "Everything I've got leads me to believe that Loretta Schmidt and her granddaughter Lumen Fischer are in an off-grid location somewhere in or near Jackson

County. I'm running a search to find any structures out that way they might be utilizing as shelter."

"Great," Sal said. "At least one of you has been putting in some effort to get this solved."

Chagrined, the others, including Ava, lifted their menus and pretended to be absorbed in the reading of it.

If they all continued to grumble and be grumpy as bears the entire time they were in Wyoming, Ava thought she would need counseling by the time they returned to Fairhaven.

"So, I know this isn't anyone's top pick for a place to have to search for someone who obviously doesn't want to be found, but it could be worse," Ava attempted after the server left.

Santos barked out a laugh. "Yeah, right, if we were having to search through the New York City sewer system, maybe."

Ava pursed her lips and took a deep breath. "I meant that we could have absolutely no idea where they were. We could still be sitting in Fairhaven twiddling our thumbs and trying to *guess* which direction she went."

"Might be better than actually being out here," Metford grumbled under his breath. "Of course, we could be in the Louisiana swamps. That would be worse."

The conversation took a turn toward discussing the wildlife in the swamps versus wildlife in national parks like Grand Teton National Park, Jackson Hole, and Yellowstone. Ava was glad to have helped steer the conversation away from their frustration. At least they were giving their griping a rest. Sal remained mostly quiet as they ate, and she seemed to want to be anywhere but at Jake's Steaks. Santos tried to pull her into the conversation, but Sal was having none of it. She even pulled out her phone and started working at one point—something she hated anyone else doing.

"Well, it looks as if we have the local tracker and his five bloodhounds at our disposal for the duration. He'll meet us tomorrow at the 'cop shop' in Jackson. His words, not mine." Sal put her phone away and looked at Ashton. "Will that work as a meetup point for tomorrow?"

"Sure. I'll refine my list of likely places tonight and have a starting point for the foot search by morning. My bet is that she has a place she feels safe out near Taylor Mountain. Maybe even on Taylor Mountain."

"Why do you think that?" she asked.

"Because there's dense forest in spots. Lots of dips and peaks, and we all know it's easier to hide in the dense ravines and valleys of a mountain. There's fresh water from Snake River through there. Lots of room to raise crops and smaller livestock like rabbits and chickens, even pigs for food. It'd be a good off-grid location."

"How do you even know all of that?" Metford asked.

"Yeah, you don't go hiking or adventuring," Santos added.

Ashton shrugged. "All you have to do is use online satellite maps and you can fly over almost anywhere to have a look."

"You could zoom in and search for structures that way, too, right?" Ava asked.

He shrugged again. "You could, but there could be newer structures out there that weren't picked up when the last satellite image was taken."

"Our best bet is to show pictures around, talk to the locals, and find out if anyone has seen these two," Sal said as she finished her lunch. "Even out here, I daresay they would stick out, and they had to pick up supplies somewhere. Traveling light across the country would be smart. Getting supplies in Jackson would be smart, too—less distance to have to transport the goods. Everybody be up and ready to head to the *cop shop* at six in the morning. We have to be there by seven or the guy might change his mind." She waved to the server, ready to pay and get out of there.

"We could just use the PD's search team if he changes his mind," Metford pointed out.

"Nope. They don't have dogs, and we need dogs. He's a tracker, and we need a tracker, too. I want him, so be up and be ready to leave at six, Metford. Got it?" Sal snapped.

He held up both hands and nodded. "I'll be there. With bells on."

Sal stood. "Leave the bells and the smart mouth in the hotel. I don't want to deal with either one." She tossed twenty-five bucks on the table and passed the server without a word or even acknowledgment.

"Wow. Someone's in a *bad* mood," Santos observed. A hushed nod in agreement passed through the table.

Ava nodded. "She hates it out here probably worse than either of you. Keep your gripes to yourself tomorrow, and let's just try to clear this up as fast as humanly possible so we can close the case and get back home."

"Agreed," Santos nodded. "I don't want to be in this dump a day longer than necessary."

"Amen, sister," Metford said as he put thirty dollars on the table and stood. He smiled at the server. "Hey, man, keep the change. Great steak, by the way."

Ava and Ashton paid with cards, both leaving hefty tips. Ava was a little embarrassed that the server had heard what they had been saying about the place he called home. It had to have bothered him, but he had remained polite, if a bit red-faced, throughout the entire meal.

Hopefully, a huge combined tip from the team would make up for a bit of the rudeness.

CHAPTER FIVE

Cai hooted in laughter as Akira ran to the end of the dock to jump into the lake and then froze, pinwheeling her arms and squealing, rooted to the spot instead of leaping in the air.

"I can't do it!" she yelled, clenching her hands into fists. She turned to give Cai a scathing look. "It's not funny, Cai."

He covered his mouth with one hand and nodded as he bent forward laughing.

Nova ran past Cai. She whooped and threw both arms into the air as she jumped off the end of the dock. The splash was tremendous, and Akira squawked as the water splattered her.

"Now, that's how you're supposed to party!" Trevon yelled. He ran and did a cannonball into the water to the left of Nova. They laughed and twirled into an embrace and then parted to get out of the water again.

Banks turned up his beer and drained the last of it, nodding as the couple got out of the water. He turned to Kalen. "You know, if you'd let your skin tan a little, you wouldn't have to sit in the shade slathering that goop all over yourself. Unless you just enjoy stroking yourself." He laughed and tossed his beer bottle toward the sand.

"Hey, not everybody wants skin cancer later in life, BB. I can't help it if I was born with less melanin than anybody else here. I don't *tan*. I *burn*. Then I'm miserable for a week, peel, turn pink for another week, then I'm back to blinding white."

Banks scoffed and flapped a hand at Kalen. "Whatever, pansy."

Kalen turned away, shaking his head. "I don't even know why I hang with you."

"Because you'd be a lonely loser if you didn't. What would you be doing right now if you weren't here?"

"Not getting insulted."

Banks laughed and stripped off his tank top, kicked off his sandals, and gave a war whoop as he ran down the center of the dock and leaped into the water.

Cai joined Akira to stand at the end, looking over the water. He slipped his arm around her shoulders, and she smiled at him.

"It's okay if you're afraid of the water, babe," he said.

"Aw, thanks, Cai." She laid her head on his shoulder. "You getting in?"

He shook his head. "Nah. Who knows what kind of monsters live under that water, buried in the silty mud at the bottom just waiting."

She moved so she could look directly at him again. "Waiting?" She stepped to the side, moving closer to the edge, and looked down.

"Yeah. Waiting." He shuddered and shook his head again.

Akira giggled and hugged him. With the suddenness of a snake-strike, she pushed off the dock hard, and they both tumbled toward the water.

Desiree snorted, taking another swig of beer. They had been drinking for hours, and they still hadn't eaten. Kalen and Trevon were in charge of the grill, and they had made no move to put the burgers on.

Banks slicked back his hair, which had gone from dirty blonde when dry to dark brown when wet. His green eyes sparkled with mischief as he swaggered toward Desiree and Jonathan. He'd been a little too rowdy all morning, and Desiree hoped he wouldn't start anything with Jonathan or she would have to deal with the fallout for the rest of the day.

"Hey, Des," he called out, letting his eyes roam over her bright orange bikini top and down to her denim short-shorts. "I'm liking this new tanner you. That orange really looks good on tanned skin."

"Hey, man," Jonathan said. He shook his head. "Keep your eyes in your head and preferably off my woman."

Banks held up both hands and grinned. "Fine, fine. I'll just go count the exotic, bright flowers on Nova's suit and compliment her fine mocha self." He made an hourglass shape in the air with both hands. "Trevon appreciates that his girl looks good enough to get compliments."

Desiree dropped her eyes to her feet and tucked hair behind her ear. Why did BB have to be such a prick? Did he really think she would go for him if she and Jonathan broke up? She was glad that she wouldn't have to deal with him being around after their vacation. It was, thankfully, the last time she would ever have to endure his bullshit. After they left the lake, it would just be her and Jonathan, and they could move on with their lives. Get a fresh start. That would be nice.

Banks walked toward Nova and Trevon. "Hey, my man, you ever gonna put on those burgers? Or, is it like with your woman here, is another man gonna have to take the reins and show you how it's done?"

Trevon laughed raucously when Nova waggled a finger and shook her head at Banks. "Not even in your wildest, wettest dreams, white boy." They all fell to laughing.

Everyone except Desiree and Jonathan. He was glaring at her. He looked her up and down. "So, you happy he noticed how tan you got?"

Desiree sighed. "Jonathan, don't. I didn't instigate that, and you know it."

"Do I?" He motioned at her outfit. "Flaunting yourself in front of him, writhing and wiggling while he was watching... that's not instigating?"

"What the hell? I was dancing. There's music, weed, beer, it's summer, and we're on vacation. Excuse me if I thought we were supposed to have a good freaking time." Suddenly, it was too hot, too humid, and the alcohol she'd consumed rushed to her head. The wave of nausea that followed was harsh, and she took a step back, arming sweat from her forehead.

"Wow, I call you out on your shit, and look at you breaking a sweat. That tells me that you and ol' Banksy there have some chemistry. Of course, I didn't need this little exhibition to prove that, did I? He practically foams at the mouth every time he looks at you. What have you been doing for him to act that way, I wonder?" He tossed a half-full beer bottle to the grass by the dock.

"Screw you, Jonathan." She turned to walk away. The woods to the side of the property called to her. There was plenty of shade, and with the breeze blowing, she thought it would be a nice walk. Maybe it would cool her temper.

"Maybe I don't like sloppy seconds, Des," he called after her.

She turned to see that everyone except Kalen had heard the remark. The shocked looks on their faces infuriated her. Not at them, but at

Jonathan. How could he be so cruel and still claim to love her? Why did she have to fall in love with him, anyway?

With tears stinging the backs of her eyes, she shook her head at him and then turned away. She wouldn't even give him the satisfaction of a response to such a statement. He'd just called her 'sloppy seconds.' Was that even forgivable? She didn't know.

The world spun slowly on its wobbling axis as she tried to regulate her breathing. The woods would help. She could take the long scenic route back to the house and sleep off the beer and weed. Then she could make up her mind whether she even wanted to forgive Jonathan for his stupidity.

Stepping into the shadows of the tree line, she took a deep breath. The air was at least twenty degrees cooler in the dim forest, and the sound of the blasting music from the dock was muted after a few steps. The overwhelming humidity dissipated as a cool breeze rattled through the thick canopy. Birds dipped and flitted from tree to tree. Squirrels skittered behind rocks and up trees to chatter angrily at her as she passed.

The forest was nice. A lot nicer than keeping company with Jonathan and BB. Desiree stopped and looked up through the branches of an enormous pine. The needles jittered in the breeze, and sunlight filtered through in fits and starts to spackle the entire world below.

"Just be present in the moment," she whispered, closing her eyes and reaching out to touch the rough bark.

Something moved behind her. It was obviously out of place. Not a normal forest animal that belonged there, and definitely not a squirrel.

She spun, sucking air in sharply through her nose. Her gaze darted, trying to find the abnormal shape of whatever was stalking her. There were too many moving shadows, bushes, tree limbs, and too much deadfall rattling. Her ears strained to hear the odd movement again, but there was nothing but the normal sounds of nature. That didn't stop the pit in her stomach or the sweat that trickled down the center of her back.

When she turned around, the trail wasn't as prominent as it had been before, and she had trouble seeing a clear exit. The forest was closing in around her, and her heart kicked into overdrive. Panic was terrible and it would get her into trouble. She had to hold it together. The woods weren't that big at the edge of the property, as long as she stayed on the flat part, which she had. The exit had to be close.

Trying to pace herself and force her legs to walk and not run, she inhaled deeply through her nose and out through her mouth. Maybe she'd heard nothing more than a raccoon or some other mid-sized critter. Maybe even a dog.

Just as she had convinced herself that she had no reason to be afraid, the sound came again. It was the sound of something walking on two feet instead of four, of steady footfalls against the forest floor. Her heart skipped two beats. She bolted into the forest, veering sharply off the skinny foot path and into thickets. The farther she ran, the more often she heard the sound, and then, she heard nothing but the wind in the trees again. She'd lost whomever it was.

But then she looked around and realized she had lost the path entirely. Her stomach grumbled and whimpered. It might take her hours to find her way back to the house. Hours wandering through an unfamiliar wood and being tracked by who knew what. Wanting to cry but too exhausted, Desiree turned in the direction she thought was the right way and started walking as quietly as possible. Keeping her senses keen, she moved from tree to tree, taking time every few steps to look behind her. After several minutes—it could have been ten, or it could have been sixty, she wasn't sure anymore—she decided there was no one following her, and she started to relax.

She leaned against a tree and breathed deeply. The fine hairs stood up on the back of her neck as the acrid aroma of stale cigarette smoke filled her nostrils. It was a familiar smell from her childhood when she would climb onto her father's lap and watch TV before bedtime on Sunday night—the only night the bars weren't open in the little town. Her father smoked like the proverbial freight train, and that stale smoke smell had been a permanent part of him, sticking to his clothes, hair, and on his breath.

Squeezing her eyes shut, she breathed in again. The wind picked up, and the smell was strong. No denying someone was out there with her who had been smoking. Her eyes flew open and she turned to scan the forest. The wind changed direction and swept the odor away, leaving her unsure of its origin.

None of her friends smoked cigarettes. The occasional vape, sure, but not cigarettes. That was as distinct a smell as marijuana, and she could never forget it. It flooded her mind with good and bad memories of her childhood. Her heart raced, and she plodded clumsily forward, away from the direction of the smell. She couldn't wait around to see who was out there with her.

Rounding a large boulder, she stumbled, caught her balance by grabbing onto a tree, and gasped for breath. As she started forward, she heard running feet, and she screamed as she turned, stumbled, fell sprawling to the ground, and brought up her arms in front of her face.

"Rah!" Banks landed with one foot on either side of Desiree's legs.

Startled, she kicked, catching him in the groin. He yelped like a kicked dog, grabbed his wounded manhood through the gaudy Hawaiian swim trunks, and toppled to the dirt beside her laughing and choking.

"You idiot asshole!" she screamed, pummeling him with her palms as she struggled to her knees. "What the hell is wrong with you, BB?"

"Jeezus pleezus, stop hitting me, Des," he groaned, laughing a little less. "It was a joke."

"You're an *idiot*!" she screamed at him, standing on legs that felt like hot rubber.

"Guilty as charged," he replied, trying to stand, but still holding his crotch. "God, remind me to never jump-scare you again."

"Your nuts will do the reminding," she fumed, striking off at a determined gait.

He cackled like a lunatic. "You're not kidding. Hey, hey," he said, trotting to catch up. "I'm sorry. I really didn't mean to scare you that bad. I just wanted to walk back with you. You know, spend some time with you when Mr. Big Man wasn't standing watch like a sentinel or some shit."

"Not a good idea. You've caused enough trouble. I just want to go back and crawl in bed for a while." She kept walking and didn't look at him. He had some gall being so persistent when he obviously wasn't wanted.

"I could keep you company."

She stopped and turned on him, holding her hand out. It planted firmly against his chest and he grinned. "No, BB. You need to leave me the hell alone. You don't have a chance. You *never* had a chance. If you screw up what I have with Jonathan, I swear…" She let the words hang in the air along with the implied threat.

He held up both hands and chuckled dryly. "Hey, if you think that's something so special, I won't mess it up for you, but just know that I believe you deserve a hell of a lot better than Jonathan Williams. He treats you like shit, and you take it."

She gave him a sharp, short push and shook her head. "Stay out of it. It's not your business, BB. I love him, and you have zero chance with me. Give it up." She waited to make sure her words had hit home, and then she turned around and started walking again.

"I wish you'd give it up. Just once, and you might change your mind," he said, but not very loudly.

Desiree thought he was unsure of his statement, and that was a step in the right direction. At least he wasn't being so damn cocksure of himself anymore. Not where she was concerned, anyway. Now all she had to worry about was whether Jonathan had noticed BB going the same way she had. If he'd noticed, it would be a cruddy evening, and likely a cruddy rest of her last vacation before she had to start adhering to the regulations of a real adult life with all its responsibilities and social mores.

Some vacation this was already turning out to be.

CHAPTER SIX

BY MIDNIGHT, THE GROUP OF FRIENDS HAD MOVED THE PARTY indoors. Cai was sunburned, but not as badly as he could have been if Akira hadn't insisted on coating him several times with Kalen's sunscreen. By six in the evening, Cai was already totally wasted and dozing in the shade of the hoary old elm in the side yard. Akira didn't mind, though. She had a lot of thinking to do about… *everything*.

She and Cai had been together since high school. Junior high, if she counted the year-and-a-half they'd spent as 'best friends.' They had both known the relationship was more than just best friends, but neither of them had even tried to make it official until high school.

Now, she looked toward a future with him. She'd never even had another boyfriend, but was that so bad? She didn't know. How could she know? Nova and Trevon had met in college. End of their freshman year, and they'd been together since. Jonathan and Desiree had been on and off since the beginning of their sophomore year of college. All of them had been with other people, even Cai. He had cheated on Akira only last year, but she had forgiven him almost instantly.

She couldn't imagine being with anyone else, and she was terrified of being alone. Single was not in her vocabulary. No one else shared her passions in life.

The music was too loud by half-past twelve, and she only wanted to go to bed, but Cai wasn't having it. He had recuperated well enough during his several short naps that he thought it was a good idea to get blasted again.

"I'll roll it for you," Akira told him with a smile.

"Thanks, babe," he said, dropping onto one long couch and pulling his feet onto the cushion beside him.

Opening the box, she took the baggie with the weakest blend they had brought, and she rolled him a mosquito leg joint. He didn't need more, but if she allowed him to do it, he would roll the strong stuff, and she would be lucky to get him awake by noon the next day. Careful not to inhale, she lit the smoke and passed it to him.

"Must be the good stuff," he said, referring to the skinny roll.

She raised her eyebrows and pursed her lips into a smile that committed her to neither truth nor lie.

Jonathan stood abruptly and walked to his room, slamming the door. Desiree covered her face with both hands and flopped back in her oversized chair. Akira went over and sat on the arm of it.

"Hey, trouble in paradise?" she asked.

Desiree groaned. "Yeah, thanks to one unnamed troublemaker." She shot BB a heated look.

"Ah, yeah. We all saw that on the dock today. I'm sorry. Is there anything I can do?" Akira thought Jonathan had overreacted and that he had taken his anger out on the wrong person, but she also knew it wasn't her place to say anything. It wasn't her relationship. Besides, Jonathan and Desiree were known for their volatile relationship. They were always arguing over something, and it always seemed as if that something might spell the end of their years-long relationship. But it never did. They were just high-drama people. Akira preferred the way she and Cai handled their drama—in the LARPing community and in the field.

Desiree shook her head. "No, but thanks. I have a splitting headache, so I think I'll just hit the sack. Maybe he'll sleep it off. He drank more today than he has in two years. It was probably the heat, humidity, and alcohol that set him off today."

Akira clamped her mouth and nodded. No, it had been his crappy attitude and his jealousy that had set him off. He was insecure, and he took it out on the person he was supposed to love the most in the world. That's how Akira saw it, at least.

"Alright, then. See ya tomorrow," Akira said, going back to the couch with Cai.

Desiree nodded and smiled before turning away and plodding toward her room.

"Hey, Trey!" Akira yelled over the music.

Trevon sat on the floor with his back against the chair between Nova's legs. He was kissing the inside of one knee with his eyes closed.

"Trevon!" she yelled louder.

He raised one hand and tried to sit as he pulled his eyes open a slit and grinned at her. "Yo?"

"Turn it down!" She pointed toward the stereo.

He gave her a thumbs-up and then flopped back against the chair again, taking up his position between Nova's legs. He made no move to press the volume button on the remote control in his lap.

Akira huffed and went to the stereo, cranking the volume down so it was barely audible. Her ears rang, and she felt the beginnings of a headache at the base of her skull. Cai was nodding in the corner of the couch and BB and Kalen were playing poker at the kitchen table. They both looked sloppy drunk, and she decided it was time to get Cai to bed before the good day and night turned bad.

She helped Cai to bed, stripping him to his underwear. Crawling into bed, she tossed the sheet over them and snuggled into her pillow with her ears still ringing and feeling as if she were in a tumbler every time she closed her eyes.

A loud thump-scrape caused Akira to sit up in bed and hold her breath. Cai eased up right beside her, finding her hand in the dark and giving it a squeeze.

"You heard that, right?" she whispered.

"I did. It came from over there," he whispered back, pointing toward the window to their right.

She nodded as a sickly cold sweat popped out on her forehead and the back of her neck. Peeling the sheet back slowly, she swung her feet over the edge of the bed. "We should check it out."

Cai was right beside her in one smooth and silent movement. He nodded and held his finger to his lips. They stood together, Cai slightly in front of her and holding a restraining hand against her stomach as he moved toward the window. She crept along behind him, ears and eyes straining to catch any sign that someone might be in the shadows.

The curtains blew inward and they both jumped. Then the chilly air swept over them, taking Akira's breath momentarily. They moved closer to the window, and Cai grabbed the curtains. He yanked them aside, and the window was standing open. Akira put out a hand and waved it back and forth. There was no screen.

"Wasn't there a screen before?" she asked.

He shrugged. "I'm not sure. Can't remember." He poked his head out the opening and looked around. "No screen out here, so maybe there wasn't."

Akira laughed and covered her mouth as she looked at their door. It was closed. She was sure she had left it cracked a few inches when they'd gone to bed. She had a thing about leaving the bedroom door open. Closed felt too claustrophobic, like anyone could be hiding on the other side, and wide open always felt too vulnerable and exposed. Every night back home, she made meticulously sure to leave the bedroom door open only barely a crack. She wasn't sure where the fear had come from, but it had persisted as long as she could remember.

"What's funny? Who opened the window?" Cai asked, confused.

"I bet it was Nova," she said as if that explained everything.

"Why would she do that?"

"Remember, we made fun of her for getting scared last night?"

It slowly dawned on Cai's face and he smiled. "Oh, yeah. So, this is how she pays us back."

"Right," Akira said, grinning with relief. "We'll wait an hour and then go in and open their window. Repay her in kind." Akira covered her mouth and laughed. It was going to be an ongoing prank, she thought, but it was fun and harmless. It would add a bit of excitement to their vacation. Maybe it would even turn into something that they could all remember in sharp focus afterward because God knew that much of the rest of their stay at the lake was going to be only a blur.

An hour later, she and Cai tiptoed into Trevon and Nova's room, fighting the urge to laugh, and slunk silently to the window. As Cai pushed the window up, Akira held the curtains and kept an eye on the sleeping couple. They were both snoring as if they had been asleep for hours even though Akira knew better.

The window squealed and Cai froze, looking wide-eyed at the bed. The snoring didn't even slow down. Akira motioned him to hurry it up, and he quickly raised the window, grimacing as it squealed loudly.

The snoring stopped, and Nova's breathing seemed halted. Cai gently lifted the curtains from Akira's hands and let them drop. Akira waited for the couple's breathing to become normal again, and at the first sign of returning to snoring, she turned to the window and pulled the curtains shut. There was a screen in that window, so it wouldn't be nearly as scary when Nova and Trevon found it open, but it would still work.

She and Cai eased out of the room, leaving the door barely shut against the jamb. They ran back to their room and fell into bed laughing.

CHAPTER SEVEN

Ava and Sal parked in front of the sheriff's office in Jackson. It was smaller than small, and Ava imagined it was very under-funded for the vast expanse of land they were in charge of.

Sal sighed and looked down, running a hand over her hair. "I really want to be done out here."

"I could take the team and go with the tracker if you would rather work here in town," Ava offered. The prospect of getting out in the woods and doing some gritty fieldwork appealed to her. It would be a good opportunity to brush up on her leadership skills, a good opportunity to bond with the team, and maybe most importantly, a good opportunity to get away from her boss's constant griping.

"Let's just see what the sheriff has in mind and how many warm bodies he has to help out." She didn't wait for a reply; she just threw the door open and got out.

Ava stepped out and looked back to the other SUV. Metford dragged himself out and eyed the super-small town with disdain. Santos didn't bother looking around. She adjusted her sunglasses and caught up to Sal. Ashton stepped out and inhaled deeply, and immediately broke into a coughing fit followed by three loud sneezes.

Metford turned and scowled at him. "Man, if you make me sick—"

"I'm not sick, Metford. It's allergies, alright?" He dug in his pocket for nose spray and used it.

Metford stomped away, shaking his head at Ava. "Allergies out here but not back home where there's more pollen... *everywhere.*"

"Maybe he's allergic to your bad attitude, Wayne," Ava shrugged, though she said it in a light enough tone that Metford appreciated the joke. A Chevrolet long bed truck rumbled past her, kicking up dust that set off another of Ashton's coughing episodes. He fanned the air and headed for the sheriff's office.

The truck was practically twice as old as Ava, a relic from the seventies. It sported four different colors of paint and a Plexiglass back window. Four droopy, barking bloodhounds moved around in the bed, and one sat on the passenger seat with his head propped so that his snout was out the window.

The driver looked about as friendly as a honey badger. Ava regarded him quickly. He was in his late fifties or early sixties, stout, with greying scruff on his face, and salt-and-pepper hair that looked in serious need of a trim or a brush where it stuck out from under the badly worn John Deere cap.

Metford whistled low and patted Ava's shoulder. "Sorry, you're on your own with this one," he said as he trotted toward the door of the sheriff's office to join the others.

"Thanks, Metford."

He gave her a thumbs-up as he ducked through the doorway.

Ava decided to greet him. She headed in his direction and the door swung open. The man inside leaned out and coughed, then spat gruffly on the ground. Ava stopped, her stomach crawling up her throat.

"You the one needs the dogs?" he asked in the gravelly voice of a lifelong smoker.

Ava nodded. She held out her hand. "Ava James, nice to meet you."

He looked at her hand but made no move to shake it. "You're a cop?"

She shook her head. "Not quite. FBI agent." She left her hand extended.

"Levi Kemper," he said, stepping past her extended hand and pulling on gloves. "These are my dogs. Best trackers around. Maxie is up front. She's the matriarch, the mama to the rest of these brutes."

Ava smiled. The dogs seemed amiable enough with their wagging tails and doggy grins. "How long have you been training them?"

"Maxie is twelve, and I trained her parents, too, so about twenty-five some-odd years." He whistled and the dogs lined up, sticking their heads over the tailgate so he could snap the leads to their collars. "Harry said y'all are looking for some old woman who kidnapped her granddaughter. That right?"

Ava cleared her throat and nodded. "We think they're hiding somewhere out there," she said, pointing toward the mountain range. "Living off-grid."

"Not exactly gonna give Sherlock Holmes a run for his money, are you, honey?" His laugh was sarcastic and dry.

She gave him a smile that hid a dagger. "It's agent or just Ava, not honey, if you please." Ava's temper threatened to flare, but she held it in check.

He shook his head. "I don't please. You're a woman. A *young* woman, at that. My opinion is that when a young woman becomes an *agent*, she's just setting herself up for failure. Y'all women are supposed to be at home, taking care of the home and the damn kids, not out here traipsing around chasing criminals like a man. You're not built for that kind of shit, but somebody decided to put it in your heads that a woman can do whatever the hell she wants." He pointed at her and cocked one eyebrow. "Just because they said you could don't mean you should."

Ava glared at him. She couldn't engage in an argument about a woman's place in the world, she couldn't set him straight and tell him it was the twenty-first century, not the Dark Ages; all she could do was bite her tongue and fight the urge.

He let the tailgate down. "Might want to move away, little missy. Got to let the dogs have a bathroom break."

Ava didn't immediately react because she was still in some bit of shock over his rude comments.

"Course, if ya want shit on your shoes, just stand right there like a statue. Don't matter to me." Levi let the dogs run to the end of the leads, and Ava shuffled backward as they ran for her.

"Levi, don't you let those dogs shit in the parking lot!" Sheriff Monroe yelled as he stepped off the sidewalk with the FBI team close behind.

"Easier to clean up off the pavement, Harry. 'Sides, ain't nobody driving through here."

Ava and Sal exchanged a look and Ava joined the team.

"I like him," Metford said, nodding toward Levi.

"Good, you can join Ava on the tracking team," Sal announced with a tight grin.

"What about me, boss?" Santos asked.

"Tracker team. Ashton, I don't want an agent in the hospital from an allergy attack, so you're here with me. We'll help canvass the town. Find out if anyone's seen Grandma."

"Come on, Levi, get these dogs loaded up and over to Taylor Mountain," the sheriff said, motioning at the dogs with disgust.

"Taylor? Why we starting there? Shouldn't we wait until after you're done canvassing?"

Sheriff Monroe shook his head. "Andy Breckenridge saw a little Subaru wagon heading off the main road there just last week. Not a local."

Levi shook his head. "Not in a Subaru. Might've just been a tourist."

"Nope. He said it had a Maryland tag, but it wasn't hesitating about taking turns and heading into the mountain. Like the driver knew where they were goin.'"

Levi nodded and put the dogs back in the bed of the truck.

"They've asked around a little bit over the last couple of days," Sal told the team. "They're seriously under-funded, and there are only two full-time deputies and the sheriff here. The part-time deputy has been out by herself knocking on doors." She shook her head.

"The place is a smudge on the map," Santos said. "How many people could possibly live here?"

"Five thousand, eight hundred, and ninety-one, according to the last Census report in 2020," Ashton informed her.

"Almost six thousand people?" Santos turned in a circle. "Main Street has two freaking red lights. How could so many people live here?"

"Because the county is big, and most people don't live anywhere near town," Sal explained in a tone of annoyance. "Scattered around far and wide. This, team, is true rural living."

Santos and Metford groaned in unison.

Ava, Santos, and Metford followed the sheriff toward their destination. It was a longer distance than Ava had judged. The lack of hills and topographical diversity between the sheriff's office and the mountain range made it seem closer, she suspected.

They parked in a wide, clear area to the left of the main road. A lightly graveled, badly rutted road ran toward the mountain on their right. Somewhere far off in the distance, the steady snore of traffic came to Ava as white noise broken by the occasional semi hitting its jake brake.

Sheriff Monroe stepped out of his cruiser and adjusted his belt, sunglasses, and plopped a hat on his head. "This is the road. Andy said the Subaru was pretty clean, so Deputy Cutler is visiting the carwashes. Maybe the Subaru owner is washing it so it doesn't stick out when they go to town for supplies."

"If they are living off-grid, they might not be going to town for anything," Ava suggested.

"You ever live off-grid, missy?" Levi snapped at her.

"I told you, it's *agent* or Ava, Mr. Kemper."

"Yeah, yeah, I seem to remember something like that," he said with his back to her. He let the dogs out of the bed again. "Harry, there's a barn about half a mile up the road. I ain't taking my truck on this road, but me and the dogs are going to check that barn before we go anywhere else." He turned to the team. "I hope you city folk are ready for some real boots to the ground. We walk everywhere from here unless you want to load the dogs in one of your government-funded SUVs and navigate this road."

Ava motioned for him to go and they would follow.

Metford laughed. "I really like him."

"Then why don't you stay when we head back home?" Santos asked.

Metford chuckled and looked at Ava. "Out here women are known as 'missy,' 'honey,' 'sugar-tits,' and 'mama,'" he said, imitating Levi's gruff voice and accent.

"Stuff it, Metford. I'm really not in the mood," Ava grumbled. She had been in a good mood until starting to deal with Levi. She was starting to think of him as Levi the Caveman, and she could only hope that his tracking skills were better than his people skills.

It was no wonder Loretta had brought Lumen to the Wyoming wilds. A person could hide out in a place like this indefinitely, and if she did have access to a property with shelter, the team might never find them. Taylor wasn't like the town, or even like most of the county they had seen so far. It was a true mountain, with a mixture of new-growth and old-growth trees, a river, and endless streams. But it was already July, and the weather got cold quicker in Wyoming than it did in Maryland. Loretta would have to find somewhere to hole up for the winter. That would limit her choices if she truly was off-grid. If she decided to hit the road, though, they could have an even harder time catching up to her and the little girl. She could move from motel to motel for months without ever being recognized. If she paid with cash, she could even move around for years without being recognized.

Maxie didn't go on a lead, and Levi turned the other four loose once they were around a steep curve and headed up an incline in the road.

"You just turn them loose?" Metford asked, jogging to catch up to Levi and the sheriff.

"They're bloodhounds, boy, not Greyhounds. If they run off, you can't lose 'em, they're too loud." He cupped a hand around his ear and made his eyes wide. "Hear that?"

Metford nodded. "Got it," he said, and immediately fell behind to join Ava and Santos again.

"Still really like him, *boy*?" Ava asked, laughing.

"Let's just concentrate on looking for clues," he said, moving to the side of the path to inspect practically non-existent tire tracks.

Santos laughed. "Andy saw a Subaru, and we know Loretta Schmidt owns one. I bet it was her."

Ava didn't bet on anything. She'd been in the Bureau long enough to know better, but her gut told her it was very likely that Loretta and Lumen were close.

"You know why Loretta brought that baby out here, right?" Santos asked.

Ava nodded. "I do, but it was still against the law."

"So, it's our job to take that baby and her grandmother back and hand them over? Even if it means that little girl has to be around her abusive prick of a father?"

Ava huffed. "I know it sucks, but it's our job. Besides, how well can an old woman take care of a four-year-old? The kid could be in just as much danger out here. They're likely staying somewhere without running water or electricity. What kind of life is that for a little girl and her grandmother?"

"Pioneers did it just fine," Santos commented hotly.

"And had a life expectancy of about thirty-five or forty if they were lucky."

"It's not right." Santos took to the other side of the road, leaving Ava to scan the big picture.

The dogs took off running to the right into the woods. Levi gave a short, sharp whistle, and the dogs stopped barking and put their noses to the ground, going in five different directions, but still heading to the right of the road. Ava squinted into the woods as Levi and the sheriff walked into the shadows.

Five minutes later, the dogs converged into a tight group and moved straight ahead, barking with their noses in the air.

"Got a hit at the barn!" Levi yelled back to the team.

"Barn?" Metford asked.

"I don't see a barn," Santos added as the three of them caught up to the tracker.

They pressed on through the dense woods for a couple of minutes until Ava made out the straight edge of a large doorway. She pointed. "There. I see the door. It's open."

Metford and Santos finally spotted it, too. The trees had camouflaged the structure so well that Ava thought they would have walked right past it without ever seeing it if not for the dogs and their owner.

Loretta might have been there at some point, but she wasn't there any longer. In fact, the tumble-down barn hadn't been used for anything in decades. The bags of livestock feed had turned to almost complete powder, and the hay had decomposed until there was hardly anything left.

"Whose barn is this?" Ava wondered. "It wasn't on Ashton's list, which means it wasn't on the satellite maps he searched."

"Belonged to the Werners until about ten years ago. The youngest son inherited it, but I heard he's living in Argentina or somewhere like that," Sheriff Monroe told him. "And as for the fancy satellite maps… you'll find a lot of buildings out here that the satellites just don't pick up on account of the thick trees, and a lot of them are old, covered with vines and weeds."

"Is there a home that goes with it?" Ava asked.

"About two miles on up the mountain," Levi said. "Used to have horses and a stable up there, too. Don't know about now, though."

"Horses?" Metford pointed to the hay and feed.

"Yeah. They rented out the horses to tourists and let them ride through some of the trails on the other side of the mountain. This was just where they had the feed and hay delivered to. They took it on up to the stables from here," Monroe said.

Metford rolled his eyes and grumbled. "Goody, looks like we get to keep hiking."

"Hey, it's not all bad," Ava chided him. "You finally get to spend some time enjoying nature."

"Ha ha," he replied.

Ava wasn't exactly looking forward to spending more time with Levi but felt good about their current direction. If Loretta was on the run, Taylor Mountain would be a prime spot.

CHAPTER EIGHT

Nova joined the laughter even though she was worried. Akira and Cai had snuck into her room and opened the window as a joke. Fine. She could live with that. It was the part about them thinking she had done the same to them earlier that bothered her. She hadn't. Trevon hadn't either. They'd both been sleeping like logs all night, and neither had left the bed.

"Come on, Nova, just admit it. We're not going to be mad about it," Akira needled her. "We thought it was funny. Good try at scaring us, though."

Nova shook her head. "But I didn't open your window. I promise you that I was asleep all night. I didn't even get up to go pee."

"Now I know you're lying," Trevon said, clapping a hand over her thigh. "You can pass up anything. Beats any woman I've ever been around. You can pass up food, purses, shoes, everything but a bathroom." He turned to the others laughing. "I swear she gets up two or three times a night to go. Always snapping that light on in the middle of the night."

"Ain't my fault you don't stay hydrated," she clapped back, which set the laughter even higher. "But I swear, I didn't open that window."

She went into the kitchen with Jonathan and Desiree. Jonathan had a bottle of aspirin and a cold bottle of water. He offered the aspirin to Nova. She shook her head and opened the fridge for a water.

"You really didn't open their window?" Desiree asked before putting three aspirin in her mouth.

"No," Nova said, sitting heavily in a chair across from Desiree. "I know everybody thinks I'm lying, but I didn't do it. And if I didn't do it..." She let the words trail off and shrugged.

"Don't look at us," Jonathan said. "I took my meds. I was down for the count." He pulled out a chair and sat.

"I didn't do it," Desiree echoed.

"No, I didn't really think either of you did it, but if I didn't, who did?" Nova glanced back to the living room.

"Probably that ass, Banks," Jonathan muttered angrily. "That's all we need is to have to worry about him sneaking into bedrooms while people are sleeping."

Desiree turned her attention to her water, but the way she pursed her lips, Nova knew there was some definite tension between the two, and BB was the cause of it. She wished everyone could just get along for the summer. It was probably the last they would have together as a group.

Jonathan shot a look at Desiree. "He has a habit of creeping around other men's women."

"Jonathan, stop it. Why can't you drop it?" Desiree snapped, her eyes flaring in anger.

"It's the truth, and you know it. Nova wondered who the culprit could be; I'm just letting her know." He pushed away from the table and stalked toward the bedroom again.

"Great, he's going into pout mode, looks like," Desiree said barely above a whisper.

"Don't worry about it. He'll be okay. They're just being guys."

"Yeah, well, I'm not a piece of property that he owns, and I'm not into BB at all. I told him so yesterday, too."

Not knowing what to do, Nova was silent for a moment, and then smiled. "Hey, what does everybody say we go to town and grab some pizza and beer for lunch? Let's get out of the house and off the property for a while." She stood and reached for Desiree, taking her hand in hers with a sympathetic squeeze.

It took some effort, but the women finally corralled everyone and got them out the door. They piled into three separate cars and found an

Italian joint that looked like it had been unchanged since the fifties. They ordered three large pizzas with an assortment of toppings and multiple pitchers for the table, and for a little while, all the tension and drama faded away. None of the couples got into any snits, BB remained on his best behavior, and even Kalen made some jokes that made everyone laugh. For two hours, it was perfect.

It was early afternoon by the time they came back to the lake house, and most of them hadn't been out of bed longer than three or four hours, but Desiree wanted a shower and a nap. She supposed it was partly because of the emotional stress Jonathan was putting on her over BB—as if she had any interest in him. It had been impossible to convince Jonathan of that, though, and the more she tried, the more he insisted she had a thing for Banks.

Trevon and Cai headed to the black box of smoke. Desiree's stomach turned just thinking about more booze or weed.

Jonathan followed her into the room. "So, you're going to be antisocial all of a sudden? Not much point in it now, is there?"

"I'm not arguing with you for the entire month. Get off my ass about him. Whatever beef you have with Banks, take it up with him. I have nothing to do with it. I'm going to take a shower and a nap." She opened her top dresser drawer and stopped, staring down into her panty drawer. "Did you do this?" She pointed at the drawer.

"What? No. Don't change the subject." He strode over and looked down.

"Then who did it? We've all been gone. And don't even think about saying it was BB because he was with us and the doors were all locked."

"Defend him first thing. I should have expected that." Jonathan yanked open his drawer and stopped short.

Desiree looked over to see that his things had been tossed as well. "I guess BB did that, too." She opened the other drawers and saw that the clothes were still in order but obviously had been pushed around as if someone had been searching for something hidden underneath them.

Nova came to the door. "You guys want a beer?"

Desiree shook her head. "I just want to know who was in our things."

Jonathan couldn't even deny that someone had gone through their clothes, and for once, he was at a loss.

Nova turned back to the living room. "Hey, which one of you assholes got in their dresser?"

Everyone denied it, but they all came to have a look.

"Maybe we have a poltergeist," Kalen offered.

Desiree leaned close to Jonathan. "Your theory is starting to sound more plausible by the second," she whispered.

"No kidding," he whispered back. "Kalen, are you smoking something stronger than the rest of us?"

"No, dude. Just listen. This is what poltergeists do—they mess things up and make noise. Things go missing only to turn up somewhere you already looked. Strange noises wake you up at night. Things get broken."

"Kalen, we know what a poltergeist is and what it supposedly does," Nova said.

"And it's just kids' stories anyways," Trevon added as he headed back to the living room.

"A ghost? Seriously, Kalen?" Banks scoffed.

"Well, did *you* get in their stuff?" Kalen pressed.

"Hell no. I was with the rest of you, eating pizza and drinking beer."

"That's my point," Kalen said smugly. "I challenge any of you to explain what's been going on, then. We lock up every time we leave or go to bed, but windows are being opened, noises are waking people up in the middle of the night—mind you, three in the morning is also known as the witching hour, when spirits are most active. Especially the bad ones."

"Well, we opened Nova's window last night," Akira said, pointing to herself and Cai. He nodded in agreement.

"But did Nova really open yours? She swears she didn't," Kalen said.

"And I didn't. I would admit it if I had. And who opened Desiree and Jonathan's the night before? You know, the one all of you made fun of me over because I got spooked. I'm telling you there was *something* here. Or someone." She crossed her arms over her midsection and looked around defiantly at them.

"We've gone on several ghost-hunting adventures," Cai said proudly. "I think Kalen might be onto something here."

"You've *what*?" Banks asked incredulously. "You've really gone *ghost hunting*?"

Cai and Akira smiled and nodded in unison.

"God, you two are some kind of messed up," Banks muttered, chuckling dryly. "Did you ever see a ghost on these adventures?"

"Mostly just glimpses of figures from the corner of the eye sort of thing," Akira said.

"Dark figures," Cai added. "But we've seen inanimate objects move when there was no logical reason for it."

"And we've caught audio proof that *something* was there with us and trying to communicate. I think Cai's right and Kalen is onto something here. Who knows what might have happened at this house in the past?"

"Or on this property before there was a house," Kalen added, getting excited that his theory was gaining traction.

Akira faced Cai. "Let's start some research. This might not be a wasted summer after all."

Cai smiled broadly and nodded. "We should totally message the owner and ask if anyone else has ever mentioned experiencing these sorts of disturbances."

"Wait, what did you mean it might not be a wasted summer?" Jonathan asked, propping himself against the dresser and crossing his arms.

"Oh, no, here we go. Good going, Akira," Nova groaned, dropping her arms to her sides and walking past Kalen and Banks to get out the door.

"I just meant it might be fun… more fun… doing this. havHaving an adventure, you know…" she stammered before finally giving up. She pulled out her phone and started typing and swiping.

"Oh, so a summer spent with your best friends would be a waste if not for the possible poltergeist," Banks piped in. "I got it."

"Don't be like that, BB. You know that's not what I meant. Of course it's not a waste." She held up a hand. "Wait, here's the website. Cai, you're better at talking to people over messages than I am. You write to the owner. It says her name is Harper Kelshaw. Is that right, Jonathan?"

He nodded. "You're seriously going to ask the owner if the place is haunted?" He laughed and rubbed his forehead.

"You don't know if you don't ask," Cai pointed out, taking the phone from Akira and typing out a message. "There. Done. Now all we have to do is wait for a reply." He grinned and headed toward the living room.

"Just to be honest, I hope it's a poltergeist," Desiree said. "The alternative is way scarier."

"I know, right?" Akira said. "Some creep breaking in and doing this stuff." She shuddered.

Desiree felt eyes on her, and it wasn't the eyes of any of her friends. It was a foreboding feeling, as if the person, or thing, watching her held some sort of malice toward her.

She hoped like hell it was a poltergeist.

CHAPTER NINE

At nine-thirty that night, Akira's phone trilled a notification. She jumped, grabbed the phone, and pulled it close to her face. She'd been drinking pretty heavily and her vision was blurry.

She pumped one fist in the air and motioned for Trevon to turn the music down. It took him a lot longer than she liked, but at least he did it without putting up too much of an argument. The man definitely liked his music, and he didn't care too much if anyone else did or not.

"What's going on?" he asked, still holding the remote pointed at the stereo. If what she had to say didn't catch his interest, he would just turn the volume back up.

"The owner got back to us," she told him, smiling and feeling loopy.

Cai leaned over and snagged the phone from her. "Miss Coleslaw? You sure?"

"Kelshaw," Jonathan corrected as he took a sip of his vodka drink.

"Whatever her name is." He read the message and nodded. "It's her."

Akira grabbed her phone back. "I want to read it to them."

"Knock yourself out," Cai said.

"That wouldn't take much, she's hammered," Banks remarked.

Everyone laughed, including Jonathan. Akira let it slide because it had been two days since she'd seen him even give a genuine smile. If a little humor at her expense made Desiree's life a little more bearable, she'd take it gladly.

"She says: 'I don't know about any ghostly activity at the house, and just to be honest, I don't believe in that sort of thing. To each his own, though, right? The couple who rented the house last year said that some of their personal items had been moved on more than one occasion, and that their food would randomly go missing from the fridge. They also said they heard footsteps in the house in the middle of the night, but never saw anyone when they checked. Also, windows would be open the morning after that they swore they didn't leave open. I don't think there was a ghost, though. It was likely a flesh-and-blood person wandering in because the doors and/or windows were left open. Probably some teenagers doing stuff on dares. At least that's my guess. Harmless, but annoying. Be sure you lock all windows and doors. Use the deadbolts and chain locks, too. I just had them installed before your group rented the place. If the activity escalates, feel free to contact the local PD and have them look into it. I'm in New Zealand on personal business." She looked around. All eyes were on her, and they all looked a little shocked. "Well?"

"Well, what?" Banks asked. "I tend to think she's right. Probably some stupid teenagers. We're getting blasted every night… who's to say we didn't slip up and leave a door unlocked, or a window open?"

Nova shook her head. "Nope. The first night, I checked everything when I got up. Everything was shut tight except their window—which has no screen, by the way." She pointed to Desiree and Jonathan.

Akira was on the fence about what had happened. She'd known Nova long enough to know she wouldn't lie to them—not even for a little while for a prank. "Maybe Jonathan opened it before he laid down and Desiree didn't notice because the curtains were shut."

Jonathan shook his head. "I didn't. Why would I? We have central air in this place and it's hot as hell outside during the day and humid enough to suffocate at night."

Desiree nodded. "I would've noticed the heat and humidity in there if it had been open even for a little while."

"Unless you were too messed up when you went in there," Trevon added with a grin. "And we were all pretty much wasted that night when we called it quits. We even cracked open the nice whiskey."

"The whole thing with the screen missing, though," Cai said, his brows wrinkling, "that does bother me. Ours is missing, too. With the window open like that, who knows what or who could come inside."

"And I think I would've noticed that there was no screen if I had opened the window," Jonathan corroborated. "I want to have a good summer, not end up getting robbed or eaten by a bear because of my own stupidity."

"I don't think a screen would stop a robber or a bear if they really wanted in," Trevon pointed out. Laughter spread through the room, but it was noticeably more uneasy than before.

"Do bears eat people?" Banks asked, draining his beer. "I don't think they do. Unless provoked, that is."

"Wow, this sure went off the rails quick," Kalen said. "I still say poltergeist."

"And you say it like you mean it," Nova nodded.

"Because I do. I like that idea a lot better than the ones y'all are throwing around."

The next morning, Nova was the first one up. She went to the kitchen to make coffee and wait for the others to get up. Nothing woke her up in the middle of the night, and her window was still closed when she got out of bed.

Desiree was the first one to join her. "Coffee… mmm…" She inhaled and walked toward the coffeemaker with a dreamy smile and half-open eyes.

"Did you hear anything last night?" Nova asked.

Desiree shook her head. "You?"

"Nope. Did you check your window?"

"Closed," Desiree said.

Akira stretched and yawned loudly as she walked into the kitchen and straight toward the coffeemaker. "I slept the whole night. Not a sound other than Trevon snoring like a bear, and our window was still closed. Nothing was out of place at all."

"And you two don't find that strange?" Nova asked.

"Why should we?" Desiree asked.

"Because whatever's going on, it stopped on the same night that Cai sent that message to the owner."

"Who is in New Zealand," Akira said.

Nova nodded, but it didn't feel right. Something felt off about the whole thing. Maybe she was just being a chicken. Maybe the others were right and she'd just been citified. The isolation of the lake house was just getting to her and she was being paranoid.

Kalen confirmed that nothing was amiss in his room, and he hadn't been awakened either. BB's story was the same as the others. Nova had no choice but to let the subject go. At least for now.

CHAPTER TEN

After a day of hiking up a dusty, hot mountain, Ava was glad when they headed back to the hotel. Dinner and bed sounded like an awesome plan to her. And it would mean an end to the barrage of grumpy and snide comments from Levi. She wasn't sure how much more she could take from him without losing her cool, but surely if Metford could hold his temper around the man, she could, too. Maybe.

Her room had a definite western theme, and she had a definite distaste for it. There was nothing wrong with a decorating theme, but buffalos, burnt-orange and sienna bed linens and curtains, elk head table lamps, and a framed print of what looked like the Marlboro man were not her idea of a *good* theme. If it was any more masculine, she feared she might sprout chest hair just from entering the room.

"You coming down to the saloon to have dinner with us?" Metford asked, hooking his thumbs in the waistband of his pants and striking what was supposed to be a cowboy pose.

Ava laughed and shook her head. "Maybe I'll stop in for a beer, but I'm going to eat in my room tonight. I just need a while to unwind from today."

Santos nodded. "I feel you. If that man called you 'honey' or 'little miss' one more time, I was tempted to clock him with a tree branch."

"He was only doing that because he saw it riled her up," Metford offered. "If he knew her better, he would have been calling her something like—"

"Argh, don't you start, too," Ava interrupted, walking between the two and nodding at Sal and Ashton as they made their way up the sidewalk toward them.

"A few miles back that way, there's a real town with fine dining and all sorts of nightlife and bright lights," Ashton said. "Well, for Wyoming, anyway."

Metford clapped his hands once. "My man, Ashton. You up for a little excitement?"

Ashton shook his head. "No, no. I'm going to the bar with everybody else. I've had all the excitement I can stand for one day."

"You and me both," Santos said.

"Any luck?" Ava asked Sal as they stepped to the side.

"Not really. Just the same stuff we've already heard. A few people have noticed that Subaru around. The Maryland tag gives it away as being out of place, but it's not unheard of for tourists to come out here, too, so no one paid a whole lot of attention to the driver. One woman said she saw a man driving with a ball cap on, another woman was certain it was a younger woman with her hair in a ponytail and big sunglasses. A twelve-year-old kid said she saw an older woman with short, straight, grey hair driving it, but that was at least two weeks ago."

"So the kid is the only one who possibly saw Loretta driving the car?"

Sal nodded. "Unless there are other Subarus driving around out here with Maryland tags, I'm having to wonder if she has accomplices. Maybe she didn't come out here to be alone with the granddaughter. Maybe she had a whole support group out here."

Ava inhaled deeply and then blew the air out slowly. "That wouldn't make it any easier to find them."

Sal shook her head. "Nope. If there's a group of them working together to keep them hidden..." she shrugged. "They could keep them moving around one step ahead of us indefinitely." Sal glanced at her watch. "You eating at the bar?"

Ava shook her head. "My room. I need to decompress. Levi's hard to deal with and he's an energy vampire."

"So I noticed. And the good sheriff kind of warned me about Levi beforehand." She chuckled and walked toward the hotel. "I'm eating in my room, too. I have a headache that feels like it should register at least a solid six on the Richter scale."

"I hope you get rid of it," Ava said.

"Before morning, anyway. I plan on more canvassing tomorrow, and I am going to speak with PD over in the city to find out if they have traffic cams that might have picked up anything."

"I'm sure they do."

"I'll see you in the morning for the briefing in the conference room. Seven."

Ava nodded. "See you then."

Ashton called to Ava, and she waited for him by the front door. "They want to go into the city and find what they call a real bar or a real restaurant." He shook his head. "I told them I was going to eat with you and the boss."

"We're both taking dinner in our rooms tonight, Ashton. I'm sorry," Ava said, wishing she felt like being more social.

Metford and Santos had moved close enough to hear the exchange. "Guess you're going with us, then, Ashton," Metford said.

"Unless you're going to eat alone," Santos added.

Ashton looked at them and let his shoulders droop slightly. "See you in the morning, Ava. Looks like I'm going with them."

"Have fun," she said, turning away before they could delay her longer.

After dinner, she laid back on the bed. The day played over in her head, but she couldn't focus on any of the actual progress they'd made because all that kept running through her mind was Levi being a jerk to her. She couldn't get around his purposeful rudeness to concentrate on the details of the search or even the case.

Her phone rang. She seriously debated not even looking at it, but her sense of duty forbade such actions. What if they had a lead on Loretta? Rolling to her side, groaning the entire way, she plucked the phone from the bedside table to thankfully discover it wasn't a work call. It was Uncle Ray.

Instantly happy, she sat and put the phone to her ear. "Uncle Ray, hi," she started. It had been a while since she'd heard from him or Aunt Kay. She was starting to feel the effects of loneliness, she supposed.

"Someone's in a good mood even though they're all the way across the country."

"Not all the way. Besides, it's kind of nice out here. Seriously different than Maryland, but that's not a terrible thing," she said, shocked that she really felt that way.

"Sometimes a change of scenery is good for you," he said. "They haven't talked you into being a bronco buster or cow puncher yet, have they?"

She laughed. "What the heck is a cow puncher? Is that the next level above a cowpoke?"

"Something like that," Ray replied.

"Well, thankfully, I haven't been put in charge of any livestock. Yet," she said, thinking about how rude and crass Levi would be if he even heard her discussing it.

"I called because I have some good news on your mother's case. Molly's, too."

Ava's heart skipped a beat and she held her breath for a moment. "Good news? How good?" She was afraid to let her hope get too far out of hand.

"I think it could be really good. Do you remember Ash Patterson?"

"Yes. He was in jail when I met him, but he worked for the Cornbread Mafia. It was him and another man," she said, trying to remember the other man's name. He'd been as rude, if not more so, than Levi Kemper.

"Kearns," Ray supplied.

Ava snapped her fingers. "That's him. They worked together sometimes in the trafficking business, right?"

"That's what we know, and it gets better. Ash has been jailed on murder charges. I didn't bust him, but I did go talk to him. He's going up the river for the rest of his life on this murder charge."

Ava turned that over and over in her head. "How is that good news for Mom's case? Or Molly's?"

"Because I said I went to talk to him. He's agreed to help us with Molly's case if we can get him a deal on the murder charge. I told him that wasn't good enough, and offered him a position of slightly more protection if he would pass along some information."

"And did he take that offer? Not many people in his profession would want to be a confidential informant even if it meant getting a reduced sentence on a murder charge."

"Nope. Not many. But I told him that I would get him completely cleared of the murder charge and released right after I put the word out on the street that he snitched about a shipment of drugs that I recently seized from the Cornbread Mafia."

"You didn't, did you, really?" Ava couldn't help but grin at the clever tactic.

"I did. And it worked. Good ol' Ash said it was better to be my CI and help with Molly's case and alive than labeled a snitch and made into an example by the Cornbread Mafia."

Ava laughed and covered her mouth. Ash was right. The Cornbread Mafia was nothing if not brutal. Like all trafficking rings, they hated snitches and weak links. Anyone in their midst deemed a traitor ended up dead in a horrible way. Not that Ava had any sympathy for them, but she'd seen some of the crime scene pictures before, and they were some of the worst.

"So, he'll help with locating Molly, right?" Ava's heart thrilled at just hearing the words.

"He will, or I'll put word out about Ash the snitch just like I promised. He didn't kill that man, anyway, and we knew it. Wrong place, wrong time sort of thing, but it worked out for the best. The man he keeps saying did the killing is pretty high on our priority list, and he'll be in custody soon enough for other murders committed in Arizona and Florida. But of course, he doesn't know that, and what he doesn't know won't hurt him."

"Smart."

"In any case, Ash is sure he can get us the location where Molly and other girls are being kept. The only thing is, they apparently move them around often, and it might take some time before we can pinpoint a location and actually get to her before she's moved again. He called it..." he paused and she could hear the disgust in his voice as he said it, "...moving out the old stock and bringing in the new."

"Disgusting. I can't even imagine what she's been through. I can't imagine what any of the victims have been through." Ava's heart sank as she wondered whether there was really any coming back from something like that.

"With Ash's help, maybe we can disrupt the ring enough to save a lot of them. I know we can't save them all, but we'll give it our best shot, Ava. That's all we can do."

She closed her eyes. "I know, Uncle Ray. I know. That's helping us with Molly, but how is he going to help find Mom? Has there been a development?"

"No, I still think she's trying to locate Molly. If that's true, when we find Molly, Elizabeth is sure to be close by."

"Unless she's not tracking Molly," Ava reminded him. "Unless she has been taken because she was alone out there with no backup, an easy target for people like them. I'm sorry, for *animals* like them." Her eyes burned when the tears welled, and she pressed her fingers to the center of her forehead.

"Listen, Ava, I've known Elizabeth for a very long time and the one thing I can tell you is that she is no easy target for anyone or anything. Man or beast would have their hands full with her. You knew her as a loving, caring, doting mother figure. I knew her as an agent from years past. She didn't want you knowing much about her past, and I understand why, but just know that she is *not* an easy target. She's one of the toughest and smartest women I've ever met."

"Why wouldn't she want me to know much about her past?" Ava's tears stopped, her curiosity now piqued.

"That is totally her choice, and everyone around her respects her wishes."

"Did she do something bad? I knew she was an agent for a while, but she decided it wasn't right for her. So, what else is there?"

"Then you know enough, kiddo. It wasn't right for her. She wanted to be safely home every night with her family so she could make sure you were safe and always knew a mother's love."

"Okay, now you're just getting all weird and stuff. That just makes me more curious. You act like she was an infiltrator or a merc or something."

He laughed. "Okay, I think that's a sign that it's time for me to get off here. It's getting late, and I promised your Aunt Kay that we would go out to this swank new seafood place tonight. She'd kill me if I was late. Love you, kiddo. Talk later."

"Uncle Ray—" The phone line went silent and she looked at the screen with shock. He had practically just hung up on her.

"He can't just give me tantalizing, juicy little tidbits about Mom's past like that and then hang up on me," she groaned. She called back right away but it went straight to voicemail.

At first, she fumed, angry that he had teased her imagination awake and then refused to fulfill any of her desires to know the truth—any little truth about her mother's past would have sufficed, but he couldn't even give her that satisfaction.

After the fifth call went straight to voicemail, Ava tossed her phone aside and flopped back on the bed. What use would it be to keep being upset? If Uncle Ray was determined to keep a secret, he would. At any cost.

But her father might not.

It was too late to call him, but this case wouldn't keep her in Wyoming forever, and when she returned to Maryland, she could corner him and finagle something out of him. She was sure of it.

CHAPTER ELEVEN

Kalen was flipping burgers on the grill next to the dock. He had a broad white streak of goop down the center of his nose, but the red underneath showed through at the very tip and along the sides. Desiree felt sorry for him when the wind blew his unbuttoned shirt back and off his shoulder. It glowed red, and the blisters were visible from yards away. They'd only been at the lake house for five days, and he was going to be miserable for at least the next week. More if he didn't get a base tan or stay out of the sun a little more.

Banks dipped into the cooler near Kalen to grab another beer. Desiree wondered how he was even still on his feet. He'd made a career out of smoking and drinking since they'd arrived, and she couldn't remember seeing him drink anything other than booze the whole time.

"Banks!" Nova screamed angrily as she stalked through the yard toward the dock, still in her shorts and wearing her favorite bikini top. It was the one with the bright flowers printed all over it. "Banks, you perv, where's it at?"

Banks stood and looked at her half-amused. "What are you screaming about?"

She stomped straight up to him and held out her hand. "Give it back. Give it back and mark me off your friend list because this is some kind of messed-up bullshit. I knew you were a little twisted, but this is unbelievable."

"You're even prettier when you're angry, and usually I'm inclined to do anything a beautiful woman asks of me, but I have no idea what I have that you want. Unless..." he trailed off, with a suggestive look down at his crotch.

Before he could chuckle and look back up, Nova slapped him hard. "Nasty little bastard!" she screamed. "You'll regret this shit."

Desiree and Akira ran for Nova as she headed back toward the house still muttering and cursing.

"What the heck was that about, Nova?" Akira asked, trying to get in front of her.

Nova held up both hands and shook her head. "His nasty ass needs to go home, girls. I don't think I can stay here if he's staying."

"Nova, what happened?" Desiree asked, jumping in front of her and putting her hands on Nova's shoulders.

"He took my bikini bottom, Des. That shit ain't right, I don't care who you are. He's a pervert and I'll kick his ass if he comes near me again. Ever." She stepped to the side and continued into the house.

Akira's eyes nearly ate her forehead. "What?" she asked Desiree.

Desiree shrugged. "I don't know, but if he did that..."

"No way. He's a creep, but that crosses all boundaries," Akira said.

They went inside. Nova had gone into BB's room and was tossing his things around and cursing him for every kind of pervert she could think of.

Desiree tried to stop her, but it wasn't happening.

"Come on, Des. Help us. If the bikini is in here, we'll find it and that will put an end to this."

"What if it's not in here?"

"Well, who the hell else would have taken it?" Nova asked. She scoffed when Desiree didn't have an answer. "That's what I thought. Y'all think he's just rowdy, but this is sick. He needs professional help."

After five minutes, there was nothing left to toss. "It's not in here," Desiree said, eyeing the mess with a pit in her stomach.

"Huh-uh. Has to be." Nova flipped the mattress up and off the side of the bed, grabbed the pillow and yanked off the slip, then went for the bedspring.

Desiree grabbed her arm. "Nova, no. It's not in here. Stop before something gets broken and we get kicked out."

"Kicked out? Might have to pay for it, but it'd be worth it to prove to you two he's a creep."

"We'll go look through the rest of the house. Come on," Akira said. "Maybe it got picked up by accident and dropped somewhere else."

"Not unless someone was accidentally in my room and picked it up."

They searched the rest of the house except Kalen's room and found no bikini.

Nova began dumping contents of the trashcans on the floor and rummaging through the refuse. Desiree was horrified, but she could also understand the obsession with finding the missing bikini bottom.

The living room door banged open and Kalen came in. "Sorry, my bad." He grabbed the door and shut it. "Did you find the bikini?" he asked Desiree.

"No, not yet and we've searched everywhere except your room. The door's locked."

"Not a problem. I don't have it. You can search there, too." He leaned closer and whispered, "I don't want her slapping me like she did Banks. That was fierce. He'll have a handprint on his face 'til the end of summer."

"If he did what she says, he deserves it," Desiree muttered, taking the key to Kalen's room. "Kalen gave us his key," she called to Nova.

"It's not here." Nova stood and walked toward Kalen. "For your sake, I hope I don't find it in your room."

"You won't," Kalen replied, taking a step back.

They searched while Kalen stood in the hallway propped against the wall. There was no bikini in his room, either. Nova exited the room with her arms crossed and her brow wrinkled.

"I don't understand. Do you know if Banks took it?" she asked Kalen.

"No, I swear, I don't know. If he did it, that would be a first. He acts like a horndog, and it's embarrassing most of the time, but it's just an act. Makes him feel special in a weird way."

Nova nodded. "If no one here took it, then who did?"

Kalen shrugged. "I swear I don't know."

Akira tugged at Desiree's shirt. "Who did take it, you think?"

"Not a clue, but like she said, if BB didn't do it, who did? It had to be some outsider, right?"

"Maybe the poltergeist did it. If it did, the bikini will show up somewhere we've already searched." Akira grinned sheepishly. "It's the only explanation I have."

"It's not much of one." Desiree sighed and took one last look back at the bedroom before exiting and dropping Kalen's key back in his hand. "Sorry about that."

He shook his head. "No problem. I just hope Akira's right and it's the ghost. We keep everything locked, so how could someone be getting in here?" He leaned close again. "Maybe it's just misplaced, you know?" he asked in a whisper.

"That would be awesome, but I don't think that's the case." Desiree caught up to Nova and the women went into the kitchen. "So, what now?"

Nova shook her head. "I don't know what now." She pointed out the window toward the dock. "Banks looks upset still. I don't see no laughter or joking. Maybe he really didn't take it."

"That would be a good thing, right?" Akira asked.

"Not really because it means I'm an ass and I have to apologize to him," Nova said.

"That's not so bad. It means we're all still friends at the end of our vacation." Desiree grabbed three bottles of water from the fridge and offered one to Akira and Nova. They took them.

"I came to let you know the burgers and dogs are done." Kalen ran a hand through his hair and nodded toward the dock. "Nobody's got much of an appetite, it seems."

Huffing out a sigh, Nova went to the door. "God, I hate this."

"What?" Akira asked. "Burgers?"

"No, Akira, *apologizing*."

Desiree smiled at Kalen and nodded as they followed the women outside. Maybe everything would be alright after all. She hoped the bikini never showed up. If it did, it would just raise suspicions again. She, for one, would rather not know who had taken it. She didn't want her opinions and feelings about any of her best friends to be changed forever.

But the more time they spent in this house, the more she thought that it was inevitable.

CHAPTER TWELVE

As the twelfth day at the lake house came to an end, Desiree was happy. Nova never found her lost bikini bottom, but she and Banks had made up. Or, they were at least getting along as well as they had before the incident.

Jonathan had some sort of illuminated moment about Banks and held a bit of sympathy for him following the whole bikini scandal. They weren't, and never would be, fast friends, but Jonathan had stopped accusing Desiree of flirting with Banks and egging on his advances.

There had been only one other time when a window was mysteriously opened while everyone slept, and it was the one in Desiree's room again. It freaked her out, but since all the drama and tension had eased in the house, she didn't make a big deal out of it even though it worried her. She had locked the bedroom door on their ninth night when she went to bed. The next morning, the window had been open halfway. With everyone talking about ghosts, she was partially inclined to believe them. It would just be easier to go along, and much more fun, too.

But now, two full days later, nothing more had happened, and she was content. Their vacation was almost half over, and it was starting to hit her that she and her friends would most likely never be together as a whole group ever again. They were all moving to different parts of the country to start their own lives. She swung between being sad at the thought and being elated at the prospect of the future.

She and Jonathan had been in couple's therapy for a couple of months, and it had taken hold finally just before the vacation. Desiree thought that was part of the reason she had been so keen on making all the arrangements, and he had happily gone along, feeling as if they were mending their relationship.

Jonathan went to bed before Desiree, and so did everyone else, giving her time to go through the house and check that all the entry doors and windows were closed and locked. He had told her that she was paranoid and that it was a waste of time to go behind the others to check everything, but she didn't care. It made her sleep a bit easier knowing that she had double-checked.

Flipping off the overhead kitchen light, Desiree made her way to the bedroom where Jonathan was already snoring softly. She watched him sleeping peacefully for a few minutes letting it sink in that she was really about to commit to spending the rest of her life with him.

Was she too young to make such a decision? Were they both too young for it? She was twenty-two. He was twenty-three. By those ages, her parents had already been married for four years, and Desiree was almost three. By comparison, she thought she was more mature and ready to handle the commitment.

But she still wondered.

Akira and Cai had been living together for over a year, and they seemed to get along better than Trevon and Nova and especially better than Jonathan and Desiree. Was that the way to go? Maybe live together for a while and see if things got better? She wouldn't mind living with Jonathan for a while unmarried, but he wasn't crazy about the idea. He had wanted to get married almost since they'd started dating, but Desiree had balked at the idea of being a married college student. She'd seen too many relationships fail, and far too many women drop out of college and give up on their dreams because of their marriages.

Jonathan was beautiful as he lay there in peaceful slumber. She wanted to run her fingers down his cheek, through his hair, and lay her head on his shoulder, but she didn't. He was grumpy if she woke him when he'd taken his sleeping pills—and that was every night. That's just how it had been for the last eight months since the doctor had prescribed them.

Smiling, Desiree blew him a kiss from her side of the bed and pulled off her overshirt. Slipping between the cool sheets, she resisted the urge to snuggle into his side. Instead, she settled for laying her hand gently on his chest so she could feel him breathing, and she slipped into a light but restful sleep, content that she was making the right choice.

The sound of a window scraping in the frame woke Desiree a few minutes before three in the morning. She sat bolt upright in bed, heart pounding, with the smell of stale cigarette smoke in the air. Her hand shot out to Jonathan as she scanned the shadowy corners of the room for movement. She saw nothing but a ripple through one panel of the curtains. Her heart lurched up into her throat and her hands clenched.

Jonathan yelped and knocked her hand away. "What the hell, Des?" He sat up, bleary-eyed, and turned to her.

"The curtain. Someone was in here."

"Bullshit, Des. You're crazy. This is getting ridiculous," he grumbled as he threw the covers back so hard they hit her and crumpled to the bed in a pile.

"I made sure the windows were down and the doors were locked. Everybody went to bed and I was the last one up. It's not bullshit, Jonathan." She eased her feet over the edge of the bed. "Do you not smell that cigarette smoke?" It was fading, but the scent was definitely still there.

"No, I don't. Besides, there has been a tiny little bit of pot smoking going on since we got here. That's probably what you're smelling." He grabbed the knob of the door and turned it roughly, and then looked at it, confused. He turned it again.

"It's locked, isn't it?" she asked from the other side of the room. She felt exposed and vulnerable as her eyes went back to the curtains. The window was open, and there was no screen in it. No barrier at all. The window was so low she could easily step inside and then back out again.

"Yeah, it is, but that means nothing." He turned and looked out the window. He saw how focused on it she was and he walked over, yanked the curtains back, and stuck his head outside.

Desiree covered her mouth and gasped. She wanted to make him stop. What if someone really was standing out there? They could hit him, shoot him, stab him, *kill* him.

He turned his head right and then left. "Hello!" he called out loudly into the night. The only reply was the sound of crickets.

Desiree rushed toward him and tried to pull him back inside. "Stop it, Jonathan. You've made your point, just stop and get back in here."

"Whoever's messing around out here, you're screwing around with the wrong person. I catch you and I'll kick your ass. Leave us the hell alone before you get hurt, mother—"

"Jonathan," Desiree hissed, yanking his arm hard enough that his head banged the window.

He jerked his arm away from her, rubbed the back of his head, and slammed the window down. The glass rattled. "That was my fucking head, Des!" he yelled into her face.

"Well, I'm sorry, but you were being *stupid*!" she roared back. "What if someone was standing out there with a gun?" Tears slipped down her face. She hated arguing with him, but she was really scared. Instead of putting her mind at ease, he'd made her fear worse with his show of bravado.

"Obviously, there was no one out there. If there was, it was one of the jerks we came up here with just playing around again. How stupid can you be?"

"I'm stupid now?" Was she really thinking of marrying him? They were already in couple's therapy and they didn't even live together. He thought she was stupid, and she was seriously considering marriage?

"What would you call it? Do you really believe in ghosts?" He tossed up his hands and turned his back to her.

"No, but someone was *in here*," she insisted. "I smelled the stale cigarette smoke and none of us smoke cigarettes. The sound of the window moving in the frame is what woke me, probably when whoever it was went back outside and tried to shut it."

Jonathan chuckled, looked toward the ceiling, and ran both hands through his hair. "God, Des, this is a *rental* house. How many people have stayed here before us? How many people must have smoked in the house even though it's against the rules and agreement? Hell, we all did. If we smoked pot in the house, do you really think others would think twice about smoking cigarettes in here? Smoke sticks in fabrics, carpets, on furniture, on *everything*. My grandpa's house smelled like stale cigarette and pipe smoke fifteen years after he was gone. Fifteen *years*, Des. You're driving me crazy with all these stalker theories. I'm sleeping in the living room," he said, snatching his pillow from the bed.

"Jonathan, please," Desiree said, rushing to try to stop him.

He unlocked the door and yanked it open. "No, you know I've already taken my meds, I can't stay up and argue with you over this, or I'll feel like hammered shit in the morning. Go to bed." He tossed his pillow onto the couch and flopped down with his face to the back of it.

"Jonathan, please don't make me sleep alone. I'm scared. I'm sorry, but I am." She swiped away the tears and looked around. Akira peeked out of her room and motioned to ask if she should come out. Desiree shook her head and motioned her back into her room.

"Grow up, Des. Go to bed, we'll talk about this in the morning." He pulled the throw cover from the back of the couch and let it drape over his bare arm and back.

There was no way she could go and stay in that room by herself, and even less of a chance that she could sleep at all. She went to the kitchen and sat at the table in the dark, ears perked for any sound that didn't belong.

The best day of the vacation had taken a quick, hard left, and now it was the worst.

CHAPTER THIRTEEN

Ava looked around the relatively well-maintained property of the homestead. The house was quite large, made of split logs, and had large windows and a wraparound porch. Some of the paint had faded a bit and there were hints of cobwebs up in the corners where a broom couldn't reach, but it looked pretty nice. There were no rotten boards, no ivy or weeds overtaking the structure, just the natural patina on the wood from years of being exposed to the elements. It was a nice place. The small plot of land on which the house—well, small barn—and shed sat was mostly flat, which surprised her seeing as how it was on a mountain. There was patchy grass, but the flat was mostly rocks poking up through the dirt which made it difficult to walk over without stumbling.

A dead pig lay in its stall inside the small barn. Its soft parts were missing—something had eaten its belly, part of the rump, and the insects had taken the eyes. A swarm of green flies wafted lazily around the carcass. Ava covered her nose and turned away. The cow was still alive but obviously terrified, and surely hungry and thirsty. Levi, for all his faults, was the only one to help the animal. Ava reassessed her feelings about him. How bad could he be if he helped an animal in distress?

Back outside, Ava looked around the perimeter. The mountain was higher all around, making it seem as if the house and other structures sat in a bowl-like depression. To the left of the barn, she saw several cords of firewood stacked between trees. The yellow police tape across the path fluttered in the wind. The bloodhounds bayed from the other side of the property where Levi had tied them. The sound was mournful and fitting for the situation.

Sal motioned from the other side of the police tape.

Ava took a deep breath and ducked under the tape to join Sal and Ashton.

"You okay?" Sal asked.

Ava nodded and then shrugged, her eyes sliding to the bloody mess behind one of the cords of wood. "Such a waste. So… I don't know… *unnecessary*," she muttered as she looked at the mangled corpse of Loretta Schmidt. "Have they determined the likely cause of death?"

Ashton blew air between his lips and turned his attention to his iPad. Sal nodded.

"They're not making an official determination yet, but they think it was a mountain lion attack."

The very faint cry of a child drifted to Ava and she turned toward the house.

"Come on," Sal said. "Let's go see what the determination is about Lumen."

"Poor baby. Do we even have a clue as to how long she's been in there alone?" Ava asked as they entered the house.

"Not yet, but they think Loretta came out to get firewood at least three days ago, maybe longer."

Like the outside, the interior of the house was surprisingly neat, but the telltale signs of neglect were evident around the edges. Trash hadn't quite made it into trash cans, the beds in the bedrooms were a mess, and the pantry had been ransacked only as far as a preschooler could reach.

Her gut twisted as the girl came into view. Her curly blonde hair was lank, oily, and stuck to her emaciated, dirty face in clumps. The arm Ava could see was far too thin and was dirty or bruised, it was impossible to tell which.

One of the EMTs had her wrapped in a blanket and was doing her best to calm and reassure the child, but she kept crying weakly, one little hand grasping at the air as she called for her nana.

"Dear God, how did that child survive? She didn't have access to food or anything, did she?" Ava had seen nothing but a box of Cheerios within the little girl's reach. There was an empty bottle of water on the floor, but they had no way of knowing if the little girl had drunk it or if it had been empty and she'd just knocked it off the table.

Sal shook her head. "I'm sure she'll be in the hospital for a good while. We'll be done here and heading out in the morning. I'm sending someone to the mother's house back in Maryland to inform her of the situation."

"What about the father?" Ava asked.

"There's another guy on the way to his work as we speak. Nasty situation all the way around."

"No winners in this case, for sure," Ashton muttered.

"Well, not quite," Sal groaned. "The mother will most likely spend some jail time for her part in sending the little girl with Grandma to keep the father from having visitation with her. If she goes to jail, who do you think will get custody of Lumen? The maternal grandparents are now both dead, and the mother will likely be charged with negligence and child endangerment on top of everything else."

"So, you mean the *abusive* father will have custody of her when she gets out of the hospital?" Ava asked, pointing to the little girl who was too weak to even cry properly.

Sal nodded. "Afraid so. It was never proven that he was abusive. We only have the mother's word to go on now that he threatened Lumen in the first place."

Ava felt sick. "Do you really think the mother would have sent away her mother and her daughter if he was a *good* father? She said he threatened to kill Lumen if he didn't get his way, for God's sake."

Sal held up her hands and her eyebrows rose. "Hey, you're preaching to the choir, but there's nothing we can do about it. This could've turned out a lot worse for everybody. At least Lumen is alive. We'll be leaving in the morning. I'm going to talk to Lumen in the hospital this evening, and we'll have a ton of paperwork to do once we're back in the office." Sal walked off with her shoulders drooping and a defeated look on her face that mirrored Ava's own feelings.

Ava couldn't decide if she was angrier or more depressed about the situation. Yes, it could've turned out much worse, but what was that little girl going to endure after she left that hospital? Her rich, persuasive father had been getting out of domestic abuse charges for two years. What else might he get away with if the mother and the grandmother were out of the picture?

"Hey," Ashton said. "He might have just been threatening, you know. He might not lay a hand on her to hurt her. A lot of times, these kinds of men are simply wanting the upper hand in a marriage, power freaks, control freaks, but they mean none of the threats."

Ava appreciated his efforts to put her mind at ease, but she wasn't buying it. "Or, he could be a real narcissistic, sociopath who will either make her life a living hell, or maybe even kill her like he threatened." Ava patted Ashton's shoulder with a sweetly sarcastic smile and turned to walk away.

Before getting into her vehicle, she looked over the scene again. It was another place that was beautiful, serene, should have been pleasant and a place to make lovely memories for the people who visited. But, as she had seen so many times before, it had been permanently tainted by death, destruction, and needless suffering.

And now who knew what was going to happen to that poor girl.

∽

Two evenings later, Ava walked down the familiar streets of Fairhaven to Doyle's Irish Pub. She was thankful to be back home. She opened the door and walked into the bar to join the rest of the team. They had closed another case successfully, and it was time for their ritual: burgers, beers, a few baskets of fries and onion rings, and a night of laughter. Why did they always celebrate closing cases? What was the human need for certain rituals? This had been a case that should have never happened, and she had a hard time feeling as if they should be celebrating.

"There you are," Santos called from their usual table.

Ava raised a hand and nodded. She was unable to force a smile.

"Nice to be back home where there's a real bar, eh?" Metford asked, raising his beer to her.

She nodded. "Yeah. Nice to be back home." The server set a beer in front of her and she thanked him.

"They've already ordered. Do you know what you want, or do you need a minute?" he asked.

Ava looked at him. Thirty-ish, handsome in a boyish way, jeans, tennies, and a polo shirt. He was clean-shaven, and his black hair just brushed the collar of his shirt in the back. His smile was quick and bright, but there was a look in his eyes. A masked sadness, as if he'd lost hope a long time ago but was still putting on the mask every day just to fit in, or, perhaps, just so people didn't question that sadness. What had he seen in his life to make those brown eyes so soulfully cheerless?

"Ma'am?" he asked, his smile faltering a bit.

"I'm sorry," she said, looking sharply down to collect herself. "I was, uh... *thinking*." She shrugged and grinned up at him. "I'll just have the jalapeno nachos with sour cream and extra cheese."

He nodded and left, still holding onto that smile that didn't fool Ava. Had the justice system failed him? Had he lost someone close to him to violence? Or, had he simply seen enough ugliness in the world that it made him hopeless and sad?

Metford raised his beer again. "To another case being successfully closed." He didn't smile, and no one else did as they raised their glasses.

"Just seems *wrong*," Santos remarked, setting her beer aside.

Ava wordlessly grunted in agreement.

"Wrong?" Ashton asked, looking around at each of them.

"The father will likely get custody of the little girl; the mother will most likely spend some time in jail on top of the fact that she lost her mother in a terrible way. Not only that, but she will have to know every single day that she nearly also lost her little girl, and the man she was trying to protect her from now has custody of her."

"Lily might be able to raise enough of a stink to get Barrett investigated. Maybe," Sal offered.

"That's about the best hope she has from what I've gathered about the legal side of it," Ava added.

"Cooper said the father acted excited when he was given the news," Metford said. "I spoke to him this morning, and he says the dad is a nasty piece of work."

"And he has a bank account that's fat enough to afford him a team of lawyers who will likely get him off the charges and ensure that he's seen as the victim here, because of the broken visitation from the divorce settlement," Sal told him. "His little girl disappeared, was *kidnapped*, by Loretta with Lily's help. He was distraught, heartbroken, and scared to death that he'd never see his precious little Lumen ever again. Loretta and Lily will be painted as troublemakers who ganged up on him and ran off with his daughter just to hurt him." She took a swig of her beer.

"Sounds like you've seen this more than a few times," Ashton commented.

"More times than I'd like to think about, Ash."

"Makes me sick to see a little kid get used like that. She's just a pawn for him." Santos turned up her beer and drained half of it. "This case left a bad taste in my mouth that the beer isn't even washing away."

Everyone raised their glasses to that.

Ava couldn't have said it better herself.

CHAPTER FOURTEEN

TREVON SAT UP, HIS EYES HEAVY WITH SLEEP, AND LOOKED AROUND at Nova before flopping back on the bed and crossing his arms over his face.

Nova shook him again. "Get up, Trevon," she yelled. "Jonathan says Des is gone. Get up and help us look for her, dammit." She swatted his bare arm hard and the sound it made under her hand was sharp.

Trevon jerked his arm down. His eyes were wide. "What the hell, woman?" He tossed back the cover and sat up on the edge of the bed glaring at her.

"Des is missing. We need to find her," Nova said again with less patience. "Everyone is already looking for her and Jonathan is getting frantic."

"Missing? You sure she didn't just drive to town?" He stood and pulled on his clothes from the day before.

"The cars are still here. Come on." She wasn't going to stand around and wait on him to get his head clear. She had tried to get him to avoid getting totally wasted the night before. As usual, he hadn't listened to her and had stumbled into the bedroom in the wee hours of the morning. She decided to let him deal with his hangover and hurried back outside to join the others.

Banks and Kalen were at the dock. Everyone was yelling Desiree's name, and Nova had the sudden feeling as if she were dreaming. None of it could be real. One of her best friends wasn't missing. Stuff like that happened to other people. Stuff like that happened in *movies*.

Akira and Cai motioned to her from the edge of the woods, and she ran to them.

"Since we're used to being in the woods and all, we're going to go walk through and see if maybe she went walking and just…" Akira shrugged.

"Got lost, or had an accident," Cai finished for her.

Nova nodded. "Trevon is getting his shit together. We'll check on the other side of the property line as soon as he's out here."

They nodded and Akira suddenly shot forward and embraced her briefly. Shocked, Nova barely had time to react before Akira let go and grabbed Cai's hand to head into the woods.

Trevon came out and yelled for her. "I'm here. Sorry it took so long. What do I need to do?"

"Come with me. We're searching over there." She pointed to the tree line on the near side of the house.

"She'd hear everybody yelling at her if she was over there, Nova. There's hardly even any trees there."

She led him toward the area anyway. "I know you're trying to be logical, but what if she fell in one of those craggy little ditches or got snake bit or attacked by some animal?" The words twisted her insides as they came out. Thinking them was one thing, hearing them aloud was totally another thing. It made it more *real* that her friend was missing and possibly in danger. Or worse.

"We heard her and Jonathan arguing last night. She just got mad and stomped off toward town probably. You heard them, too."

Nova nodded and pulled him into the wooded area. "She wouldn't head to town on foot, Trevon. Use your big ol' head for something other than holding your hair. She would've taken a car, don't you think? Especially if she was that upset and determined to get away. Besides, she would have told me or Akira if she was planning on leaving because of Jonathan."

The subdued look on his face let her know that she had finally broken through the cloud of last night's partying and gotten him to understand the seriousness of the situation. Desiree wasn't a brawny mountain girl. She wasn't even tomboyish. If she was in the woods, someone or something had forced her in there. She was missing, and Nova knew in her gut that it wasn't something Desiree would do of her own free will.

After searching the entire length of the property on that side, and looking down into the craggy ravines and ditches, Trevon and Nova emerged and stood in the side yard looking over the place.

"Where can we look now?" he asked.

Nova shook her head. "I don't know. I guess we should go down and make sure the guys checked under the dock and in the sheds."

"Dang, you don't think she drowned, do you?"

Nova's breath hitched in her chest. "No. No." She shook her head. "Des can swim like a fish. But we have to make sure, right?"

He nodded. "She could've slipped on the edge of the dock and hit her head, maybe. If the argument was really bad, she might have gone as far as the dock to cool off."

Nova nodded, a wave of nausea gripping her midsection as they walked toward the water.

"Desiree!" they called out, the edges of their voices increasingly ragged and tinged with fear. "Desiree!"

But there was no sign of her. No sign that she had even been outside. Jonathan came out of the woods. His face was drawn and pale, and his eyes flitted everywhere. He shook his head.

Akira and Cai were close behind him. They had stopped calling out for Desiree. Kalen and Banks came from the far side of the lake looking lost and worried. They shook their heads as they neared the group behind the dock.

"Nothing? Anybody?" Jonathan asked, his eyes shining with tears.

"Man, where'd you see her last?" Trevon asked.

"In the bedroom last night. She woke me up again and we got into an argument over it. I hope if any of you were screwing around with the windows and doors you're happy with yourself right now. I don't know why you assholes couldn't just *quit* with all that shit."

"Didn't you go back to bed with her?" Akira asked.

"No, I didn't. I went to the damn living room again. I've slept in there as many nights as I have in my bed, I think. She was driving me crazy with all that stalker shit and I couldn't sleep undisturbed."

"Our window was cracked open again a few nights ago," Nova told him, taking Trevon's hand.

"Is that your way of saying it wasn't you, Nova?" Jonathan asked, glaring and putting his hands on his hips. "What about you, Banks? Was it you screwing around and keeping her scared just so she'd drive me up a wall? Did you do it hoping we'd break up and you could slide in?" Jonathan advanced on Banks.

Banks took a step back and held up his hands as he shook his head. "Whoa, you're stumbling, dude. I thought we worked out our differences."

"Stumbling? No, Banks, that would be you." Jonathan took a swing.

Banks leaned back and the punch went wide, spinning Jonathan to the side. Banks rebounded and grabbed Jonathan to keep him from falling. Jonathan caught his balance and shoved roughly away from Banks.

"Don't touch me!" he snapped, spinning on his heel. He dug into his pocket and got his phone. "I'm calling the cops. They can sort you all out."

Cai put a hand on Banks' shoulder. "You didn't do any of that, did you? I mean, it wasn't you doing that stuff to keep the poltergeist theory alive, was it?"

Banks shrugged Cai's hand off his shoulder and scoffed. "Screw you, too, Cai." He stomped toward the house. "And any of the rest of you who think that."

Akira and Nova exchanged a worried look.

"They were arguing like mothers last night," Trevon murmured to Nova.

"And? That's nothing new with them," she replied, keeping her voice low so the others wouldn't hear.

Trevon drew up his shoulders and made his eyes big. "And..." he drew the word out long. "What if it got out of hand?"

Nova couldn't even answer him. The thought was too far outside her comfort zone to even consider, but when he said it out loud, she had no choice but to consider it. Still, the lump in her throat, the sudden tightness in her chest, and the pit in her stomach wouldn't let her speak. She shook her head and only barely achieved that as she watched Jonathan walk into the house with the phone pressed to his ear.

"Just saying," Trevon continued. "What if? She's not anywhere any of us looked, and who knows how long he's been up. Definitely didn't look puffy around the face like the rest of us did when we came out, did he?"

Nova shook her head again as tears and fears welled up. Could Jonathan have done something to Desiree? He did look wide awake, but panic had a way of jolting one from drowsiness, she supposed. But was he panicked because he couldn't find her, or was he afraid she *would* be found?

"If he did anything, she could be literally anywhere. He had access to the cars."

Nova put her hand on Trevon's arm and shook her head. "Stop. Please. I can't think like that. I just can't."

"Think like what?" Kalen asked, coming up beside them.

Nova turned and shook her head. "Nothing, Kalen. Nothing. We just need to go over everything out here again. Did you look in the sheds? In that little building there?" She pointed to the little building that was still closed and locked with a padlock, and her heart sank.

"Yeah, but we didn't go in the building. It's locked from the outside."

"Where's the key?" Trevon asked, his grip tightening on Nova's hand.

Kalen shrugged. "I thought we didn't have one and that's why we'd never opened it."

She shook her head. "We're supposed to have access to the canoe and paddleboat that are supposed to be in there."

He shrugged. "But we had innertubes. Who needs that stuff?"

"Kalen, she is missing. You do understand that, right? She could be *anywhere*. We need that key," Nova said, leaning toward him, not understanding his nonchalant attitude.

"She couldn't be in there if the door is padlocked from the outside, Nova," he retorted, showing that he was flustered for the first time.

"She could be if someone *put* her in there!" Nova fired back, the fear rising to a fever pitch.

Kalen took a step back and looked as if someone had slapped him. Trevon pulled Nova back and into an embrace.

"Maybe we should just wait for the cops to get here," he said.

She nodded and felt sick all over.

"You don't think someone did something to Desiree," Kalen said in a voice that sounded thin.

Nova turned to him. "I don't want to, but if she's okay then where is she?"

Kalen's face blanched as he looked around. "Shit."

Cai and Akira joined them. "You okay, Nova?" Akira asked.

"I don't know. This all feels like a nightmare. Like none of it's real."

Cai nodded and looked to the ground. "We didn't see any sign of her on the trail, either."

"It's like she was never even here," Akira added, swiping at her eyes.

"Let's go in the house with Jonathan and wait for the cops," Trevon said, turning Nova in that direction and not waiting for the others.

Nova let him lead her. There was nothing more they could do except open the storage shed, and she wasn't sure she wanted to. What if Desiree was in there? What if she was dead? Could it even be possible that something terrible had happened so close to the end of their vacation? They only had eight days left at the cabin. Eight days until they parted ways and began their own lives in different cities. Eight days until they entered what they had all come to think of as true adulthood.

No. Nova refused to believe it. It wasn't possible. That was not what they had meant when they said they would likely never be together as a group again. Not what they had meant at all.

CHAPTER FIFTEEN

Almost an hour after Jonathan made the call, and as the morning sun crept higher in the sky, a sheriff's car idled up the long driveway. Akira shot to her feet and pointed out the window. "Finally," she said and rushed to the front door, swinging it wide.

Jonathan and Cai were on her heels. Trevon and Nova were next.

Akira waved her arms in the air.

"It's not like he's going to pass us up," Cai said as he came up alongside her.

"I can't help it, Cai, I'm just scared, I guess." She dropped her arms, realizing he was right. There was nowhere else for the cop car to go.

The man driving looked to be in his mid-fifties. He had thick white hair and looked like he'd been around the block a few times in that little town. He stepped out of the car and took his sweet time adjusting his belt below his somewhat sizable paunch. Sliding his sunglasses on, he walked toward the group slowly.

"Our friend is missing," Akira nearly yelled. What was wrong with him? Why was he being so slow?

"I got that from the call-in, miss," he replied, looking everywhere but at her.

Jonathan stepped forward. "I'm her fiancé. I called it in," he said.

The sheriff nodded. He consulted his pad briefly. "Jonathan Williams, right?"

"Yes. Her name is Desiree Smith. She's twenty-three. Well, she'll be twenty-four in a couple of months. We've been here twenty-three days..." Jonathan's face went blank and his breath hitched. "I didn't even realize we'd been here as many days as she was years old." He looked to the sheriff with wide eyes.

"You think that has some significance, son?"

Jonathan shrugged and shook his head. "I don't know what's significant anymore. All I know is that she's gone and we can't find her."

Akira stepped forward again. "Excuse me, sir, we've looked everywhere. Shouldn't you call in like, a search team or more officers or something?"

The sheriff smiled paternalistically at her. "Well, that would be a little premature, don't you think? How old are all of you? Early twenties all around?" He pointed to each of them in turn and they told him their ages. "That's what I thought." He walked to the trash bins beside the house and lifted the lid on the first one. He whistled low and let it drop. He opened the second one, pulled the top of the bag open, and chuckled. "How long you say you've been up here?"

"Twenty-three days. We have the house for eight more days," Kalen said as he joined the group.

The sheriff pulled down his sunglasses and eyed Kalen. "Late to the party, aren't you, son?"

"I was in the bathroom when you came, sir," Kalen said, shoving his hands into the pockets of his shorts.

The sheriff nodded and hooked his thumbs on his belt. "Looks like you've been drinking pretty heavy and pretty steady. Way I calculate, that's all accumulated over the last six days. Tomorrow's trash pickup, right?"

"Yes, sir," Cai answered.

"How many of you are here in total?"

"Eight, counting Desiree," Nova said.

"Uh-huh," he said, turning toward the house. He pointed toward the front door. "Let's go in and have a conversation."

Everyone followed him inside. Akira was nearly coming out of her skin with anxiety. How was the cop being so calm about the situation?

"Okay, so when was the last time anybody saw…" he stopped and consulted his notes again, "Miss Smith?" He pointed to Akira.

"Before I went to bed last night. We were all in the living room watching TV and listening to music."

He nodded and wrote something in his notebook. "Name."

"Akira Lin," she told him.

"It smells a little bit like there was more going on in here than just watching TV and listening to music, Miss Lin."

Heat rushed to her cheeks and she looked at Cai.

"You're not really going to bust our balls over smoking a little pot, are you? Not when my fiancée is missing," Jonathan said.

The sheriff looked around at him. "Young man, I will, as you put it, bust your balls on whatever the damn hell I please. Now, when did you see Miss Smith last?"

"After we'd gone to bed, she woke me up because she thought someone was messing around with our window again."

"Then you went back to bed?"

"Yes, but not in the bed," Jonathan said, his voice losing volume.

"Then where?"

"Living room. The couch."

"So, what happened? Get into an argument or something?"

"I guess." Jonathan looked down and ran a hand through his hair.

The sheriff sighed. "You *guess*. You don't know if you argued? Were you smoking marijuana?"

"No, I take sleeping pills, and I don't mix the booze or the pot with the sleeping medicine."

The sheriff nodded. "Yeah, I hear bad things can happen if you do."

Jonathan stared at him without speaking.

"We searched everywhere," Akira said again. "We were all in bed, and then we got up and she was just gone."

"You know for a fact that everybody else was in bed?"

Akira nodded. "Well, yeah. We all went to our rooms to go to sleep."

"Just like that? Nobody heard anything, saw anything?"

They all shook their heads.

"So, what did you say you argued about?" He looked at Jonathan.

"She woke me up because she thought someone was messing around with our window from the outside. There was no one there. She was just being paranoid for some reason. Every time she wakes me up, there's no one around. I don't know what had her so worried about every little noise."

"Maybe the marijuana. You know, one of the top side effects is feelings of paranoia? Sometimes, they're severe, and sometimes there are even auditory hallucinations to go along with the paranoia. If she was drinking, too…" He tilted his head to one side and scribbled notes.

After several seconds, he shut the notepad and sighed. "I'll take a look around and call in the troops if there's a need, but my bet is that Miss Smith and Mr. Williams here got into an argument, and she left mad. Probably high-tailed it toward town. She'll likely call an Uber or whatever those ride shares are you kids use, and she'll head back to wherever home is. By the way, where is home?"

"Fairhaven, Maryland," Jonathan said quickly. "We all just graduated college and we're here for the last group vacation before we all start our lives in different places."

"Ah, the last hurrah sort of thing." He walked into the living room, eyeing everything for longer than necessary.

Akira wanted to scream at him. More than once, she had the urge to call 911 and tell them to send someone else, anyone else, and more than one old man to help them find Desiree.

Jonathan guided the sheriff toward the bedroom. "This is our room," he said.

"Where you saw her for the last time?"

"Yes," Jonathan said tightly, his face reddening.

The sheriff gave the room a brief once-over, a lot less thorough than Akira and her friends had done. He gave the other rooms even less attention and walked outside. He slid his sunglasses back on and breathed deeply as he looked around.

"Anyone check the vehicles?" he asked, walking toward them.

"Yes, all of them," Jonathan said. "But feel free to look."

"Oh, I will. I need you to pop the trunks."

Akira tossed her hands up. "We already checked. This would go faster if you just called in some help, sir."

"It's Sheriff Alexander for future reference, Miss Lin, and I told you that I would call in help if it seemed necessary," he grumbled. "At the moment, there's no evidence of foul play. Just a lot of evidence to point toward partying gone wrong and someone got her feelings hurt. She's probably on her way back down to Fairhaven by now."

"She wouldn't have left without telling me or Akira first," Nova said.

"And your name is?"

"Nova Taylor."

"Did you see Miss Williams before or after she argued with her fiancé?" He moved from the cars and pointed to the shed.

"Before," Nova said.

"Uh-huh. Did anyone check the shed?"

"We don't know where the key is," Kalen said. "I'm Kalen Hamilton."

"We didn't need the canoe or paddleboat that's supposed to be in there. We have innertubes, so we didn't see any problem with not having the key to it," Banks added. "I'm Banks Becker. BB to my friends."

"Banks. That's an odd first name. Did she swim?"

"Like a fish," Nova said.

"What about if she was high and drunk?"

"She wouldn't have come out to take a swim in the middle of the night if she was afraid someone was messing around outside her window," Akira pointed out.

The sheriff made a finger gun at her and clicked his tongue. "Good point, but I have to cover all the bases in a case like this."

"Well, she could swim better than anyone except Jonathan, and that's only because he's been on school swim teams since he was in junior high," Nova said, crossing her arms.

The sheriff walked the perimeter of the entire lake and then the property, but he didn't step foot into the woods. Akira was furious.

"You aren't going to look in the woods at all? And what about that shed? Why are you not taking us seriously?"

The sheriff's withering look at her could have fit perfectly in the dictionary under 'exasperation.' "Young lady, I'm taking this seriously. You were all up here boozing and smoking pot and doing God-knows-what other kinds of drugs, and your girlfriend got upset and decided to leave you to it. And I'm going to bust that lock off the shed just to have a peek inside. It'll prove that there's nothing more to this situation. If I were you, I would be calling her cellphone. She had one, I'm assuming? When she's over her mad spell, she'll answer or she'll call you back. Seen it a hundred times before."

He took a screwdriver from the trunk of his car and went to the shed to take the hasp off and open the door.

"I'm absolutely, one-hundred-percent sure she did *not* walk out of here," Akira pressed as he worked. "She had access to the cars. Why would she *walk out in the middle of the night*? And after thinking someone was outside her window?"

"Miss Lin, you need to calm down. Hysterics never helped a situation at all. Your friend is fine. And who knows why you young people do half the stuff you do? Trust me, when you're my age, you'll think the exact same way, like it or not."

"With all due respect, sir, we know our friend very well, and we didn't call 911 for them to send someone out to give us little life lessons," Banks said.

The sheriff got the hasp undone and flipped it back. He pulled the door open and glanced at Banks. "Uh-huh. Seems to me that you need more than *little* life lessons, son." He turned and stepped inside the shed.

Akira and the others crowded around the doorway to peer inside. Her stomach was knotted with frustration at the sheriff, but she kept her mouth shut. She didn't want him to call the search off completely because he considered them young *and* rude. It seemed that the young part was enough of an obstacle for him.

The inside of the shed was practically empty. There was a canoe hanging on the back wall, the paddleboat sitting to one side on a platform, and a toolbox on the other. There was a window screen propped behind it that looked like it had either been torn or cut.

Akira nudged Cai and pointed to the window screen. He nodded.

"See something, Miss Lin?" the sheriff asked.

"The screen. There's only one there, but we're missing two," she replied.

"The one in Desiree's room and the one in our room," Trevon added.

The sheriff inspected the screen without touching it. "Looks like it needed to be repaired. Frame's bent a little on the side, the springs are broken, and the screen has a hole in it. Nothing suspicious about that."

"Where's the other screen?" Akira asked.

The sheriff stood and motioned them all to back up. He closed the door and replaced the hasp. "That's something you'll have to ask the landlord. Probably got messed up and is being repaired just like this one."

"Why isn't it in there with that one, though? What if someone really was messing around outside and that person took the other screen?"

Did the sheriff really not see anything suspicious about any of it? Akira looked from him to Cai and then Jonathan. She couldn't keep the heat from her gaze. She was mad. Mad at Jonathan for not believing Desiree and arguing with her all the time over everything. She was mad at the sheriff for being so purposefully dense. And she was mad at herself and Cai for lending credence to the poltergeist theory. Maybe if Desiree hadn't had that possibility clanking around in her head, she would have done something differently and she wouldn't be missing.

"And why would someone *take* the screen? If they were trying to break in, they would have simply tossed it aside, or better yet, cut it, crawled through, and it would still be in the window. But if it needed repairing, it would be taken out." The sheriff hitched his belt and headed for his car again twirling the screwdriver in his hand. "Unless you have a screen thief and someone took it because they needed it for their house."

Akira's blood boiled. He was just being a jerk for no reason. Cai put a restraining hand on her arm and shook his head at her. He was right, but it was physically painful for her not to blow up on the man.

"I'll go back to the station and make a preliminary report. If your friend doesn't surface in a day or so, come in and file a missing persons report on her, and we'll go all out to find her. You gotta remember, she is an adult, and painful as it can be for the ones left behind, sometimes adults just walk away from everything and everyone they know. That's your right as an adult. You can disappear if you want to. I'll tell my people to keep their eyes open. I'll let you know if they see anything."

"So, that's it?" Jonathan asked incredulously.

The sheriff nodded. "For now, Mr. Williams, yes."

"I'm sorry, we didn't get your name," Akira said, trying to keep her tone level.

He grinned and took off the sunglasses. "Sheriff Alexander, Miss Lin. Sheriff Michael Alexander." He slid under the steering wheel and put the shades back on. "Now, if you find anything, don't hesitate to call again, but your friend will turn up. Most likely back home." He nodded and smiled as he pulled his door shut.

The group watched as he turned around in the grass and drove back out faster than he'd driven in.

"What a fucking asshole," Nova said.

Akira glared at her.

"Don't give me that Mom-eye, Akira, I'm not in the *damn* mood for it," Nova said, turning her head.

"Sorry, I didn't mean to. It's just habit, I guess. I can't believe that's all he's going to do about Desiree."

"You can't believe it; you should be in my shoes," Jonathan muttered, walking toward the house and looking about as miserable as a person could.

Akira's heart clenched. As bad as it was for all of them, she had to think it was worse for Jonathan. He had argued with his girlfriend a lot since they'd arrived at the lake house, and a few of the arguments had been intense. If Cai had spoken to her the way Jonathan had spoken to Desiree, they wouldn't be a couple, and she might have left. But she would have definitely let her other friends know beforehand. And so would've Desiree.

CHAPTER SIXTEEN

For the second time in three days, Sheriff Alexander drove up to the lake house at Bumbee Ridge. One of the kids up there had finally drowned. He knew he should have searched the house and busted them all for the marijuana. He should have at least made them all show their IDs to prove they were of drinking age. That Akira Lin didn't look a day over eighteen.

Now there was a death, and his ass would probably be in the sling for it when everything came out.

Pushing on the gas pedal harder, he led the way to the lake house with his siren and lights on.

The two girls were crying inconsolably when he arrived on the scene. Cai met him and pointed toward the missing girl's bedroom.

"He's in there. In the tub," Cai said, and promptly broke down.

The sheriff headed in that direction, steeling his gut against what he might find in the bathroom. It was never easy to find a body, but the younger the person was, the harder it was to deal with. Every passing year, it seemed to get more difficult for him.

The door frame was broken inward at the striker plate. A large piece of the wood had splintered off and lay across the threshold. The door had a large indentation in the middle where someone had kicked it. Whoever had done it had a large foot. Trevon was the tallest one there, so it was likely that he did it. Which meant the door had been locked.

Jonathan Williams looked as if he had dozed off in the bathtub. Except that his head was submerged in the water. His eyes were closed, his head was slightly tilted to the right, and his cheek rested against the tub. There were a few splashes of water on the floor, but not enough to indicate a struggle. A bottle of prescription sleeping pills sat open on the back corner of the tub beside a bottle of Head & Shoulders for men. It was the Old Spice Swagger scent.

The sheriff stood and looked around the bathroom. The towels were folded neatly on the shelf above the toilet. He looked back to the tub. There were no suds from the shampoo in the water. The bar of soap still rested on the built-in shelf high above Jonathan, and there was no wash cloth in or near the tub. Like the towels, they were neatly folded on the shelf on the other side of the room.

Something wasn't right about the scene. Most people would have a washcloth in the tub with them and a towel close at hand for when they stepped out. There should have been clean clothes nearby, but the bedroom was attached to the bathroom, so it wouldn't be a stretch of the imagination that he would simply walk in there to put on clean clothes. But it just *felt* wrong. The soap wasn't even wet.

He pulled on gloves as Officers Beau and Fulton stepped inside. He took the pill bottle off the tub and read the label. It had been filled ten days earlier at the pharmacy in town. "Thirty-day supply," he mentioned to Officer Fulton. Tipping the bottle to the side, they could both see there were only three pills left. "There should be about twenty of those left." He turned the bottle so Fulton could see the label, and the officer nodded.

"Maybe he was taking them recreationally and took one too many this time," Fulton offered.

"Kinda what it looks like," he replied, setting the bottle back where it had been. "Be sure you don't contaminate anything, the both of you," he ordered, peeling his gloves off and stuffing them into his pocket. "I'm going to go talk to the rest of them."

"Good luck," Beau said. "They're pretty upset, and the girls can't stop crying long enough to talk straight."

Michael nodded toward Jonathan's body. "Probably the first death they've ever seen up close and personal. Totally understandable. At that age, they think they're invincible and they're going to live forever. If you've already forgotten, just ask Fulton there. He's still just a pup, too. It was a mortality check for them." He shook his head and walked out.

The group was in the living room, and there was only one set of dry eyes. Michael couldn't recall the young man's name, just his nickname—BB. He motioned for BB to join him in the kitchen away from the others. Divide and conquer was a motto that worked on more levels and in more situations than battles.

"Yes, sir?" BB asked as he pulled out a chair and sat.

"Give me your full name and tell me what happened here."

"Banks Becker. I don't know what happened. I just know the girls wanted to check on Jonathan this morning because he wasn't out here when we all agreed to be. At seven. We were going to go out looking for Desiree again because she never answered her phone for any of us. Not even a text. We think maybe she's hurt or lost in the woods. We don't know where else to look. Anyway, Nova and Akira knocked on his door and he didn't answer. Not even when they started yelling. Me and Trevon and Cai joined in, all of us yelling and pounding on the door and wall. Kalen said we needed to get in there somehow before we panicked because we weren't even sure Jonathan was here. Kalen thought maybe he went out early. He was really messed up about Des."

"How did you get in there?"

"Trevon kicked the door open. I tried to shoulder it open, but I just bounced off it. Kalen and Cai are smaller than me, so they didn't even attempt it." Banks' grin was small and fleeting.

"Who found Jonathan?"

"Akira and Nova were the first two in there, but I don't know which saw him first. Then the rest of us sort of filtered in there. Kalen reached in the water to pull him out, but he jerked his hands back and said the water was cold and Jonathan's lips were grey-blue."

That explained the splashes of water on the floor. "So no one attempted to revive him?"

Banks shook his head and his brows knitted together. "Man, anybody who saw him would know he was dead, like for a while. Too long to be brought back by a little CPR. The water was cold." He made his eyes big and flipped his hands palm-up. "You know, he'd been in there probably since last night."

Michael nodded. That was his guess, too. "Did he take his sleeping medication recreationally?"

"Hell no. He was so anal about those pills. Took them very seriously. That was the only thing wrong with him, and he milked it for all the attention it was worth." He scoffed and shook his head.

"Mr. Becker, how did you and Mr. Williams get along?"

Banks looked up at him sharply. "Oh, hey, I didn't mean anything bad by saying that. I was just telling it how it is… or, how it was, I guess." He looked down at his hands on the table.

"So, he wouldn't have taken too many?"

"No way. Not Jonathan. He even took them at exactly the same time every night. Ten sharp. Never eleven. Never nine. Never an exception. Ten o'clock every night, and he was ready for bed by ten-thirty. Eleven at the latest."

Michael nodded and put it in his notes.

"He was really upset when you left the other day without taking us seriously about Desiree, you know. Have you heard or seen anything?"

Michael looked at him steadily for a moment. Was it strange that he was asking about the missing girl when there was a dead man in the tub in the next room? "No, we haven't. Was Mr. Williams… Jonathan… was he suicidal?"

Banks shrugged. "I just know he was more upset than any of us have ever seen him."

"About his missing girlfriend, right?"

"Fiancée, sheriff. She is his fiancée. As in they were going to get *married* and start a life together in a few months."

"I'm aware of what the term fiancée means, young man. Now, back to the deceased. Was anyone in there with him last night?"

Banks shook his head. "We were all in here at ten forty-five when he said he was going to bed and would see us in the morning. We all went to our rooms after that."

After talking to the others, the story seemed the same from person to person.

The removal of the body was completed two hours later after the scene was thoroughly photographed and processed. The group of friends had moved outside to a picnic table under a shade tree, muttering glumly amongst themselves.

"I'm sorry for your loss," the sheriff told them. "Nothing is for sure, yet, but it looks like your friend took too many sleeping pills, fell asleep in the tub, and drowned. It's being ruled accidental drowning for now, but after the ME finishes, it could be changed to suicide. I've gotten all your statements, but if you think of anything else that might be relevant, call me." He handed Banks a card with his number on it and then handed one to Akira.

"Isn't it relevant that you brushed him off when he called about Desiree?" Nova Taylor asked.

"I didn't brush off anyone about anything, Miss Taylor. We're still looking for Miss Smith."

"But it's not very high on your priority list, right?" Banks pressed.

"I'm sorry to inform you that your recently deceased friend takes priority over a missing person. And Miss Smith isn't the only missing person we're looking for. There are other cases we're investigating, believe it or not."

"And that's our problem how?" Banks asked.

"It's not, son, but you need to understand that this looks bad. One friend missing, her fiancé dead by possible suicide... He said they argued, and I could tell by the looks on your faces that day that all of you *knew* they argued. It was probably a volatile relationship. Would any of you blame her if she did just up and leave of her own free will? And if anything bad happened to her, my money is on Mr. Williams."

"You think he felt guilty and took too many pills on purpose?" Cai asked.

"Doesn't matter what I think. We look for facts in my line of work, and we know nothing for sure yet."

"If you think it's possible that he hurt her and then killed himself, why isn't this a top priority?" Nova asked.

"Have any of you notified Mr. Williams' next of kin?" he asked, changing the subject completely to remind them that one of their friends was *dead*. Not missing, but dead. And when there's a death, certain things need to be done.

They shook their heads.

"I'll have to call them, but if one of you would rather give them the news, I'll give you time enough before I call them."

None of them volunteered. It didn't surprise Michael. He'd been a cop his entire adult life, and not even cops wanted to tell a parent that their child was dead.

"All right. I'll take care of it." He got in his car and drove back to the station, trying not to look too closely at the pained looks on the faces of the kids in his rearview mirror.

They'd come to town as eight. Now there were only six.

His receptionist Kathy brought him a slip of paper and put it on his desk. "Property owner is in New Zealand taking care of a family matter that will have her out of the country for an extended amount of time," she said.

Michael read over the note. "New Zealand." He sighed.

"Yep. I tried the number, but she didn't answer. Couldn't leave a voicemail, either."

He nodded. "I'll call her later. Did you try to contact her through the rental website?"

She shook her head. "Didn't know there was a website for it."

"Hell, there's a website for everything nowadays. Message her on there and see what comes of it."

She nodded and went back to her office.

The more Michael thought about the happenings at the lake house, the less he liked it. It was a sticky situation at best. For all he knew, Jonathan Williams had killed his girlfriend and disposed of the body, and then killed himself in a fit of guilt.

He just wanted the cases to be closed. Done. Over. The sooner, the better. He wanted that raucous, rowdy group of pot-smoking, partying twenty-somethings out of his town before they messed it up any more than they already had. If there hadn't been drugs and booze involved, none of this would have happened, and he wouldn't have two more open cases on his board.

CHAPTER SEVENTEEN

Sal walked into the bullpen for the morning briefing and case update. She held a paper up. "We're going out of town again." She nodded at Ava to hand out the casefile.

"Already?" Metford asked.

"Already. Bad guys don't take a break just because you're tired, Metford," she said.

"I know, boss, but we've only been back a few days." He took the file and opened it. "Bumbee Ridge, Maine. Where is that even at?"

"In Maine," Santos deadpanned, not even glancing at him as she looked into the file.

Ashton took his file and turned to his computer, clacking away at the keyboard. "It's right here," he said, pointing to a small spot on the zoomed satellite image of the state in question.

All eyes turned to his screen.

"Put it up on the big screen, please," Sal told him.

"County Crider," he continued. "Bumbee Ridge is a tiny lake community at the northwestern edge of the county. Mostly it's a wide spot in the road where a few homegrown businesses sprang up over the years. There are three lakes in the area with very few houses near them, and the one central town." He scanned another page on his computer screen. "Looks like it's mostly a tourist spot. People rent out the houses to tourists through the warmer months."

"We're only focused on the lake in the center of Bumbee Ridge. Locals call it Crater Lake," Sal said. "Eight friends, fresh out of college, rented the house there for a month-long hurrah before starting their lives as adults. That's a direct quote from the report, by the way. Sheriff Michael Alexander's words, not mine."

"One missing, two dead in a span of four days," Ava added. "Desiree Smith went missing first. The next morning, her fiancé was found dead and it was ruled an accidental drowning."

"The evidence photo shows he's in a bathtub," Metford said, flipping the picture so she could see it.

Ava nodded. "Took too many sleeping pills and drowned in the tub."

Metford grinned but stifled his chuckle. "On vacation at a lake and he drowns in his bathtub." He shook his head.

"Why are we going to Maine for this?" Santos asked.

"Because all eight of the friends were residents of Fairhaven," Sal told him.

Metford sighed and shook his head again. "Why do so many people leave home just to find trouble in other states?"

"Just so you have something to wonder about, Metford," Santos said.

"We're leaving in two hours. Get your stuff together and let's get going." Sal turned to her office and disappeared.

"We flying this time or driving?" Metford asked Ava.

"There's a rush on us getting started with this case, so we're flying," she replied.

"I guess that's a plus."

Ava didn't think there were any plusses to the case. None at all. "Just this morning at five, the other man was found dead in his room. They think it was an accidental overdose, but the sheriff up there needs our help. He doesn't think it's a coincidence that all this has happened in just four days."

"Well, someone's got their thinking cap on," Metford said sarcastically.

"Nevertheless, we have a Fairhaven woman missing, and two Fairhaven men dead in Bumbee Ridge, Maine. Let's just get up there and see if we can prevent any more of them from disappearing or dying."

"Do they think the girl is just missing, or do they suspect some sort of foul play?" Ashton asked.

Ava shrugged. "As of right now, they're just listing her as missing. She's an adult and there were no signs of foul play."

Ava couldn't help but think about Prague. She and Molly could've been listed the exact same way. They were eighteen—legally considered adults. It wasn't likely that Desiree Smith had been snatched out of a house full of people by one of the trafficking rings, but the possibility was still there in her mind no matter how small.

The team met with Sheriff Alexander at the Bumbee Ridge lake house.

"Why are the others still here, sheriff?" Sal asked, pointing to the group of friends at the picnic table near the dock.

"I didn't know what to do with them since I knew you were coming up today. I just told them to stay close. There's only the two little hotels in town, and that's not very close."

"Metford, Ava, go talk to them. Get their statements, and then sequester them in one of the hotels. Preferably in rooms in the same hallway. Sheriff, I need you to post a round-the-clock guard in said hallway to make sure no one goes in or out of the rooms until we figure something out here." She turned back to Ava and Metford. "Don't freak them out any worse than necessary. From the looks of it, they're already upset and scared enough."

Ava and Metford went to the table by the dock. They all looked as if they'd been crying recently, and Ava noted the tension and high emotion in all their faces and in their body language. Lots of self-soothing motions were happening. Hand-wringing, hair-twirling, leg-bouncing, and even rocking.

It wasn't lost on her that they were only a few years younger than her. Ava must have looked more like one of their peers than an authority figure. But she gathered herself and stood as tall as she could and tried to project an air of confidence.

"Special Agent Aviva James and Wayne Metford," she introduced, badging them but also offering a hand to shake. The five friends replied with their names one by one.

"We need to get everyone's statements, and then we're going to board you in one of the hotels in town until this is cleared up. We're sorry for the losses you've suffered, and we're here to help," Ava said.

"That's great, now could you tell us why the sheriff thinks BB killed himself?" Nova asked.

Ava and Metford looked at each other and then both flipped through their files.

"It says here accidental overdose," Ava said.

"Accidental or suicide, it's all the same because it's bullshit. Banks didn't do drugs," Trevon said.

"Just the booze and marijuana going on up here all month, then?" Metford asked.

"Yeah, that's it. None of us ever did anything stronger. Jonathan had a script for sleeping pills and the rest of us smoked weed and had some drinks. Now, tell me how Banks died of a heroin overdose," Trevon challenged.

"With the needle still in his arm," Cai added.

"Someone needs to be checking for fingerprints and DNA all over that room. Banks was an ass, not a junkie. Just check his arms. No needle tracks, I promise you," Kalen said.

"We'll be conducting a thorough investigation into all three incidents," Ava told them.

"Incidents. That's what all this has been reduced to… fucking *incidents*," Trevon fumed.

"Trevon, please," Akira said.

"Screw you and your little dislike of cussing, Akira. This is shit. We don't mean anything to them. All this is just *incidents* in their stupid little files. Something to make them feel important," he said and turned to storm off toward the covered pavilion.

Nova followed him.

Ava and Metford took their statements. Everyone agreed that Banks might have been rowdy, but he was not a drug user. With his college record, Ava tended to agree, but who was to say he wasn't experimenting just that one time? Just that once could be fatal.

It took an hour to get their statements and another hour to get them into the hotel. Thankfully, the ride was mostly silent.

"How long do we have to stay here? We're not criminals," Cai griped as he stepped into his and Akira's room.

"No one is saying you're a criminal, Mr. Huang. We just need you to stay close to help us out until we get this cleared up," Ava said.

"We were supposed to head back to Fairhaven in a few days," Nova added from across the hallway.

"I understand, and your cooperation is greatly appreciated. We'll work as fast as we can and still be thorough. Don't leave the hotel, and don't talk to anyone about the case. There will be a guard posted in the hallway around the clock. We can't have any of these cases being compromised."

"We know the rules," Trevon said. "You made them real clear before we even got here."

Ava nodded. "You all have our numbers if you need anything, and Maven from the hotel will see that you get three meals a day. If you need anything more, you'll have a chance to let her know."

Trevon scoffed and Nova pushed him into their room.

"Kids," Metford muttered.

"They've been through a lot, Wayne. This was supposed to be their last summer vacation as a group, and look what's happened to them. Nearly half the group is dead or missing, and to hear them tell it, the locals weren't much help. We can't just dismiss them."

He grunted but didn't argue.

Ava nodded to Metford. It was time to leave so the friends could get settled in their rooms and calm down.

Ava's phone rang as they were walking to the car. She tossed the keys to Metford and answered the phone. It was Sal.

"We need to find out who is running the website for the lake house rental. The name of the site is Three Lakes at County Crider Vacation Rentals. The property owner is in New Zealand and isn't answering calls or replying to texts from the sheriff's office, but someone is running the website because it was updated just a few days ago, and the sheriff says Akira was in touch with someone via the website at the beginning of their stay here."

"What about Ashton? He's the computer whiz."

"He's working on the online end of it to see what he can come up with. I need you to try to find the number or some way we can get ahold of the owner in New Zealand. Her name is Harper Kelshaw. We aren't sure if she has any idea what's happened here. If you can get hold of her, find out who's running her website while she's away."

"Got it." Ava hung up and filled Metford in on the situation.

It wasn't going to be easy by any stretch of the imagination, but they would do their best. Ava hoped the missing woman was okay. She knew what it was like to be afraid because someone had kidnapped her from what was supposed to be a vacation. She knew exactly what it was like, in fact. And she remembered every inch of terror that slithered down her spine to this day whenever she remembered it.

Desiree Smith was out there somewhere, not even knowing that two of her friends were dead. Or she was dead herself. Either possibility was too grim to think about.

It hit her hard that it could've been her and her friends in that situation if she'd not chosen to go into the Bureau. If she'd had time for a summer hurrah before going off to her adult life… She shook her head. The group seemed like it was comprised of upstanding young adults, more or less. They'd graduated college, and they all had future jobs and lives planned out. They had it together, and still, they found themselves in the middle of something that would leave its mark on their lives forever.

Ava didn't envy them at all. She had her own darkness to deal with.

CHAPTER EIGHTEEN

Sal called in the FBI forensic team to scour the lake house for evidence. She and Ava stayed at the house with them while the others worked on finding out all they could about Harper Kelshaw and her rental business.

"Got something," the agent in the living room said. He was on a ladder, pulling something off the high shelf above the entertainment center that had been decorated with fake vines and real potted cactus gardens and terrariums, which had been checked and cleared at the beginning of the search.

Ava and Sal moved closer. "What is it?" Sal asked.

"A small piece of industrial strength tape. The double-sided kind. Super strong. It was used here recently. I'd say in the past couple of weeks. When it was removed, it took up paint and wood." He finished removing the piece of tape and put it in a clear evidence bag.

Sal reached for it and he handed it over. She held it so Ava could see. It was a small, triangular-shaped piece of black tape, about a half-inch wide.

"What do you think?" Sal asked.

"Looks like something you'd use to secure one of the glass terrariums maybe. Or something else you didn't want broken. Something important."

Sal nodded. "It might be nothing, or it might be something." She moved back to the agent. "How sure are you about when it was used?"

He shrugged. "Pretty sure. Adhesives behave in a certain way when exposed to the air, and that is still sticky on both sides. The top side shows signs that something was attached to it but has been removed, but it has retained some of its adhesive ability. If it had been left out for more than a couple of weeks, we'd expect to find a layer of dust and other debris that would eliminate its effectiveness."

"How long before we'll have a confirmed timeline on it?" Ava asked.

"Depends on how much the lab has to do when we're finished collecting everything, but I'm guessing no more than a few days at most."

"Could we get a rush put on this?" Sal asked.

"Sure thing."

"Thanks," she said. She turned to Ava. "Let's go make sure the others look for any of this in the other rooms."

They walked into the room where Jonathan and Desiree had stayed. Ava looked at the mussed bed, the neatly folded men's clothes on the dresser, and the basket with dirty clothes in it behind the bedroom door. A man's wallet lay on the bedside table with his glasses on top of it. A cellphone rested in its dock in front of the lamp. Her stomach tightened. They were just regular people going about their normal lives, and now one was dead and the other was missing.

"Be on the lookout for any signs that double-sided, industrial-strength tape was used in this room," Sal announced.

The agent in this room turned to her and held up a finger. She climbed up a step ladder and pulled down a thin shelf. She turned it and climbed down to show it to the women. "Like this?" She pointed to a spot where there was residue from the tape.

Sal pulled a glove on and tapped the spot. The glove stuck to it as she pulled her finger back. She nodded. "Yes, just like that. What was on that shelf?"

The woman pointed to the dresser. "All that fake vine, and three glass terrariums. The shelf was so high that I doubt any of that stuff was moved very often. If you look at the shelf in the light, you can see the clean spots where the terrariums sat and zigzag line where the vine was laying."

"Was the vine attached to the shelf?" Ava asked.

"Nope. It was behind a terrarium on each end and in front of the one in the middle of the shelf. Just laying up there."

Sal nodded. "Be sure to take the shelf. I want that adhesive residue tested to make sure it's the same kind as what we found in the living room."

"Yes, ma'am," the woman said, placing the shelf across the end of the bed.

"Has everything in the bathroom already been processed?" Sal asked.

The woman nodded. "Yes, ma'am. That's where we started."

"Good. Thank you," she replied, stepping into the other room.

Ava looked around. The theme color was pale teal green and white. The bathroom looked like a bathroom she might have had in her house, or one in her parents' house. It was typical, average, nothing special, just like ninety-nine percent of the bathrooms in the US.

"To look at it now, you'd never know someone died right there," Ava remarked as she moved toward the tub. She stood over it for a moment, hands on hips as she examined the space. She shook her head.

"What is it?"

"Could a man over six-feet tall really fall asleep and drown in this tub?"

"Well, one did, so, yeah. What are you getting at, Ava?"

"It's a short tub, is all."

"Yeah, and his legs were bent, laying to the side here," Sal said, pointing to a place on the side of the tub nearest them.

Ava nodded, but it bothered her that such a tall man had drowned in that short tub. She shook her head again. "I could see a kid drowning in it by accident, or even a shorter person, but maybe that's right."

"Come on. Let's go through all the clothes and other belongings to see if we can find any more tape," Sal said, turning on her heel and leaving the rooms.

An hour later, they had come up with no tape at all.

"I want to get a list together of situations in which that tape would be used in a residential setting. They say it's industrial tape, right?" Ava asked.

Sal nodded. "That's right."

"Then why would it have been used recently in a residence? And who put it on those shelves if the property owner is in New Zealand and the group of friends were the only ones up here?"

Sal's brow wrinkled and she shook her head. "See what you can find out about that tape. Who carries it, who buys it, what is its main use whether industrial or residential?"

Ava smiled. It was something to do. Something that would feel useful and as if she was making progress.

CHAPTER NINETEEN

Ava and Sal headed the next morning's briefing in the conference room on the first floor of the hotel only a few blocks from the one in which the friends had been sequestered. That had been Santos' idea, so the group wouldn't bother the team with the investigation at all hours of the night. There had been many developments, and Ava was excited as she passed around the new files.

"There was trace DNA found on the band around Banks Becker's arm just above the injection site," Sal started.

"What's that mean for the accidental death by overdose theory?" Santos asked.

"It means that it might not have been an accidental overdose or a suicide at all," she said.

Metford looked up from the papers. "You mean, the friends were right?"

"Maybe. A match for the DNA hasn't been identified in the system. It's being run through another system now. If the owner of that DNA is in the system for anything, we'll know by tomorrow or the next day."

"That changes the dynamics of all three cases, though, doesn't it?" Ashton asked.

Ava nodded. "It does. Sheriff Alexander was working off the theory that Desiree Smith left of her own free will and headed back home, but her belongings were all still at the house as far as we could tell. Everything except her cellphone was in the house."

Metford whistled low. "That means that someone in the group might be responsible for all of this."

"All five remaining guests are suspects as of this moment," Sal nodded. "There is more, though. See the pictures of the shoeprint?"

Everyone nodded.

"That is actually three separate shoeprints. Someone was stepping in roughly the same spot each time they were there. This print was found outside the bedroom where Desiree Smith and Jonathan Williams stayed."

"Did the same person leave all three prints?" Santos asked.

"We're not sure," Ava said. "The lab is working on that. It looks like it could be the same person wearing different types of shoes. They think it's a work boot, a smooth-soled shoe, and a tennis shoe. In that order. The work boot print was on the bottom. Each print was skewed off to the right just enough to let a bit of the print below show through."

"So, we're going to have to go through every pair of shoes at the house and in their possession," Metford said.

"We will," Ava said. "The prints aren't whole, either. If you notice, they are partly on soft, black dirt and partly on the decorative white gravel."

"What size are the shoes?" Ashton asked.

"We're not certain, but it could be size nine and up in women's, or size eight and up in men's," Sal said. "The foot size seems to be within the average range."

"Guess that probably rules out the Asian girl," Santos mused.

"Her name is Akira Lin," Sal pressed hotly. "Be sure you remember that from now on, Agent Santos. Or would you rather someone refer to you by your race?"

Santos held up her hands in surrender. "Sorry. I guess that rules out Akira Lin. Didn't you see her feet? Like size five at most."

Metford nodded. "Yeah, I saw that. She doesn't look twenty-three, either. I pegged her for sixteen."

"Okay, enough speculating about Miss Lin. She's not automatically off the suspect list because she is small and looks young," Sal said. "She's a suspect, and we will treat her as such until we find a definite reason not to anymore. Understood?" She looked around at each team member.

Each agent nodded and answered her in the affirmative as she looked at them.

"Good. Now, keep your eyes and ears open. Pay attention to details with this one. If it's one of this group who did all this, I want to make sure they are caught. It has to be clean and by the book. No shortcuts. Is that understood?"

"Yes," they all said in unison.

"Ava, do we have pings on Miss Smith's cellphone?"

"No, but I will be requesting them after the briefing. Had to wait on paperwork to go through before they would do it."

Sal nodded. "Good. Let's catch some bad guys, team."

Ava had a bad feeling about Desiree Smith. She didn't know any woman who would have an argument with her lover and leave all her things behind, only taking her cellphone. All her cash and cards were in the small purse hanging on her side of the headboard. Her suitcase and carry-bags were still in the closet, and all of them were empty. She had three sets of dirty clothes in the basket, and her four drawers in the dresser were full.

Ava couldn't imagine that she left in the middle of the night, in pitch darkness, passed up all the cars, and walked back toward town with no money or anything. It just wasn't believable.

"Hey," Ava said from Sal's doorway.

"Yeah, come on in," she replied, smiling. "What's on your mind?"

"Desiree Smith. I really don't think she just walked out of there with the clothes on her back and the phone in her hand, Sal."

"But there were no signs of foul play. Hell, nothing was even out of place after she went missing."

"But that stuff could've been straightened up afterward," Ava pointed out. "Her *purse* was hanging right there on her side of the bed, on the corner of the headboard. And she left all the cars? That doesn't make sense. It must be darker than a nun's robes out there in the middle of the night."

Sal grinned. "I agree. It doesn't make a lot of sense, but these friends were admittedly smoking a ton of weed, and you saw the pictures of all those beer and liquor bottles in the bins outside. They already drank enough to float the Titanic. She might not have been thinking rationally when she walked out. Stranger things have happened, and you know it."

Ava nodded. "I don't have a good feeling about her situation, though. Just saying. It *feels* wrong, but I hope I'm wrong. I hope we find her alive and well."

"I think we will. I've seen this happen time and time again. She'll eventually be found safe and she'll be oblivious to the deaths of her friends."

"She will probably feel guilty over Jonathan's death. She'll always wonder if he committed suicide on purpose because she left."

Sal nodded. "That's probably the truth, but we can't do more than go where the evidence leads us. Follow the facts. Follow the evidence. And so far, the evidence says she left of her own accord."

"You're right, of course," Ava said, tapping the casefile against her hand. "Thanks, Sal. I'm going to call again about the paperwork for the cellphone pings. If we can see where it was the last time it pinged, it might lead us to her, or at least get us in the general area. She needs to know what happened at the lake house after she left."

Sal nodded. "You do realize that if she is still in the area, we have to consider her a suspect in the suspicious death, right?"

"No, I didn't realize. Why?"

"Because she had argued with her lover, and from what the friends said, including Banks Becker, some of the arguments were *because* of Mr. Becker. She had motive."

Ava sighed and nodded. "Thanks again," she said with a tight grin.

"Any time, Ava. Any time."

Ava went back to the conference room. The hotel had set out the continental breakfast, but Ava ignored the food and went straight for the coffee. On a day like today, she would need all the caffeine she could get.

CHAPTER TWENTY

Ava and Sal sat in the car in front of the lake house that afternoon. The forensic team had just finished processing the house and the property, and Sal had wanted to go back to what she called a clean look around while nobody was there.

Ava looked at it and wondered how such a charming little place had turned so sinister in the short span of a week.

"I've called Harper Kelshaw's phone twice today, no luck. Try her from your phone," Sal said as she began flipping through the casefiles they'd brought along.

Ava dialed the number and put it on speaker. There was no answer. She hung up. "Should I leave her a message?"

"Tell her she needs to call back immediately and that there has been a death at her Bumbee Ridge rental property. No more details, though. Not until we speak to her."

Ava nodded and dialed the number again. She left the message as Sal had instructed and then hung up again. "You think she'll call back?"

"She should." She opened her door and motioned for Ava to follow. "Let's go have a walk around and see what might turn up."

"You don't really think anything was missed, do you?" Ava pointed out skeptically.

"Not really, but you know how I am… just can't leave anything to chance."

"Is it really leaving it to chance if our own forensic team went over everything with a fine-toothed comb?"

"No, I just need to see for myself. A whole lot like someone else I know." She grinned at Ava.

"Better be careful. People will say you are obsessed and a control freak," Ava said, holding the front door open for Sal.

"Oh, is that what they say about me when I'm not around?"

"No, sometimes it's much nicer."

"Not often, though, is it?" Sal laughed and went to the kitchen. Ava followed and stood by the table in the center of the room and looked around, examining everything within sight. Even though the forensic team was done here, the place was still untouched and would remain so until the case was definitively closed—or at very least until they got in touch with Harper Kelshaw.

The various empty cans and bottles piled up in the trash can and the dirty dishes in the sink were starting to reek, but they couldn't do anything about it. Even if it was extremely unlikely that something in the kitchen could help them find Desiree, they couldn't take the risk of contaminating the scene by cleaning the kitchen.

"What exactly are we looking for? Anything in particular?"

Sal shook her head. "Not really. This is just a prime location where I can see most of the house from. You have the back yard out this window, front yard out that window, side door to the outside right next to the fridge, living room, and another door leading to the backyard, left hallway where Desiree and Jonathan's bedroom door is very visible, and the right hallway where you can plainly see the other three bedrooms on the right side and the bathroom Kalen and Banks used on the left."

Ava nodded. "Yeah, you can see almost the entire property, inside and out from here."

Sal walked into the living room and sat on the couch where Jonathan stated he'd slept the night Desiree went missing. "If Jonathan slept here, with his head here," she began and pointed to the arm of the sofa, "he would not have had a view of his bedroom at all. He would have been facing the other hallway, which means he could see anyone coming or going there."

"But if he was sleeping, he wouldn't have seen anyone or anything."

Sal nodded. "If he was awakened and had an argument, it's likely that he would've been sleeping lightly, if at all."

Ava looked toward the bedroom. "Wouldn't he have been able to hear a struggle in the bedroom from there? Even if he was asleep, a struggle in there would have been loud enough to rouse him."

"Unless he smoked and/or drank before taking the sleeping meds."

"Everyone agreed that he was strict with his medication, though. That was the one consistent thing everyone said. Every single night he refused because of his meds. I guess it's a possibility, but that really doesn't strike me as likely," Ava reminded her.

"Then I surmise that there was no struggle to get Desiree out of the house. You said it yourself, how could he have slept through it? The room is twelve, fifteen feet away at most. Even with the door closed, he would've heard her scream, heard the sounds of a struggle." Sal got up from the couch with an expectant smile.

Ava sighed. "Which means, maybe she did just leave." She squinted one eye at Sal. "That was your whole intention when you sat down there, wasn't it? To let me disprove my own theory of what happened to Desiree."

Sal patted her shoulder. "That's why I like to visit scenes after the crews have all left. It gives me time to really consider different scenarios and see how they might have turned out."

Ava added the technique to her mental rolodex as her phone trilled a notification. She pulled it from her pocket. "It's from an unknown number." She opened the message and showed it to Sal.

"She's in New Zealand helping family and will be there two more months unless we *need* her to return?" Ava asked incredulously. "If that was me, I would already have been on my way back."

"Well, she says she is horrified that there has been a death," Sal said, shaking her head. "Okay, just let me think for a minute." After a few minutes of pacing, Sal held out her hand for the phone. "May I?"

Ava handed her the phone and waited for her to finish typing. "What did you tell her?"

"I told her that there had been two deaths and a missing person at the lake house, and that it all happened within four days. And I asked who was overseeing the website for the rentals."

"Ashton never found out?"

"No. Whoever is running the site has a VPN that randomly changes the location of the IP, which makes it nearly impossible to track its location. Or something like that. He's the techie and I'm not—for a reason."

Several minutes passed before a reply came. Sal shook her head and typed again.

"What did she say this time?"

"Her boyfriend is overseeing the website for her while she's away. It's apparently a family emergency that is keeping her there. Elderly parents she's having to help out because she's the only child. I asked why he was being unresponsive to us and how we could get in touch with him."

The phone trilled again. "Okay, the boyfriend's name is Antonio Rutherford. He lives on Munroe Street, the Sumner Building, apartment 405. She says he's probably unresponsive because he's been busy with his job. He's a freelance web developer."

"When did she leave for New Zealand?" Ava asked.

"She said she left a week before the college kids paid for the place. This Antonio messaged to let her know they had paid in full online and things were set and ready for them, and then she hadn't heard from him but a couple of times since then."

"Is that normal? I mean, for them to go so long without communication."

Sal shrugged. "Who knows? For me? No. For them? Maybe yes."

Ava took back her phone and added the number to the list of contacts as Harper Kelshaw.

"What now?" she asked after putting the phone back in her pocket.

"I want you to verify the owner's story and the timeline. It's probably right, but I want everything scrutinized. We can't be too thorough seeing as how one death is now looking suspicious."

Ava nodded. If Banks Becker had been killed, it changed the entire case. They would have to re-evaluate everything. All the evidence, all the statements from the friends, and even the reports from the sheriff's department.

Sal's attempt to disprove Ava's theory about Desiree not leaving on her own did nothing to assuage the feeling that the woman had indeed been taken by force, though. Whether it might have been Jonathan in a fit of jealous rage, or one of the others, she didn't know.

All she knew was that for every answer they got, about ten more questions opened up.

CHAPTER TWENTY-ONE

THE THIRD DAY'S BRIEFING WAS SHORT AND THERE WAS REALLY nothing new to report to the team. Sal had told Ava to take the lead with the meeting while she saw to some paperwork at a nearby table.

"There's nothing really new or good to report on any of the cases this morning," Ava started. "Have any of you come across anything relevant?"

They each shook their heads.

"The trace DNA wasn't enough to get a complete profile, but the lab did confirm that it was *not* Banks Becker's DNA. It does belong to someone else. That means we need to go to the hotel and ask for voluntary samples from each of them today. Remember, don't threaten them, and keep your tempers in check. I know they can be hard to deal with when they get riled up, but just keep your cool and get the samples. If someone refuses, we'll handle it back here."

Metford looked dejected. "What about the print from outside the bedroom window?"

Ava nodded. "We need to see all their shoes so we can take pictures to put in the system and check them against the layered prints found at the house."

"What if someone refuses that request?" Santos asked.

"Again, if someone refuses, try to convince them, but if they still refuse, just move on to the next person. We'll handle all refusals here. Any other questions?"

"Is the property owner coming in to give a statement or anything?" Ashton asked.

"No, she's in New Zealand with a family emergency. We have her boyfriend's address, and we will need to go see him at some point soon. He's overseeing the site for the rental business she runs while she is away."

"And Ava is going to verify Miss Kelshaw's story and the timeline she gave us, just to make sure she is where she says and that she's been gone since before any of this happened," Sal added.

"I can help with that," Ashton offered. "I can find out which flight she left on and when she departed. I can even find out when she arrived in New Zealand."

"How long will that take?" Ava asked, thankful that he had volunteered to help.

"I can run it through the system as soon as you want me to. Should have an answer within a day, I would think. Unless there's something weird about her trip that we don't know about. But usually, I can get that information within a day."

"That's great," Ava said.

"It will take a while on the computer to get the search started. You want me to do that now?"

"No. I need all of you to go with me down to the hotel. We need to get those DNA samples and shoe pics as soon as possible."

"Got it."

"Anything else?" Ava asked the group.

She looked to Sal when no one spoke up.

Sal nodded and stood. "Alright, team. Let's get this day started. I'll see you all back here this afternoon."

They all stood and headed for breakfast again. Only Metford took any food, though. Ashton, Ava, and Santos went straight to the coffee pot.

"Metford, you're with me. Santos, you and Ashton take the other car," Ava said.

Santos nodded and dropped her sunglasses from her head to her nose, pushed them up with one finger, and went outside with Ashton following.

It was nice to not have the tension that the group had experienced before. The trust-building classes had worked as far as Ava could tell. She went to the car and waited for Metford. He got in the car a few minutes later with a cup of coffee in one hand and his portfolio in the other. He had made himself a scrambled egg and bacon sandwich, which stuck out of his mouth. She chuckled and looked out her window.

"This breakfast is pretty good. You should try it." He buckled his seatbelt and kept eating.

She shook her head. "I'm just not hungry. And you're cleaning the crumbs out of the car when we get back."

"Fine by me," he shrugged through a mouthful of it. "But don't come crying when your stomach starts rumbling in an hour."

"You wish."

They first went to Trevon and Nova's room.

"DNA samples? Are you serious?" Nova asked.

"Yes, ma'am. We just need to eliminate everyone who was staying at the house," Ava told her.

"Eliminate us from what? The suspect list?" Trevon asked, shaking his head.

"Yes."

"You mean to tell me that *we* are on the suspect list for a missing woman, an accidental overdose, and an accidental drowning?" Nova asked.

Ava stalled for a moment. How should she tell them that they no longer thought Banks Becker's death was accidental? Sal hadn't given her guidance on that matter, and she hadn't thought to ask about it.

"I'm not giving anything until we know what the hell is going on," Trevon said.

"No, you come up in here asking for DNA samples and shit like we're on trial or something…" Nova shook her head and sat back on the chair, crossing her legs and her arms. "No, me neither. You make it sound like we need a lawyer."

"Do you think you need a lawyer, Miss Taylor?" Ava asked pointedly.

Metford shot her a look. She glanced at him and then looked back at Nova.

"I didn't do anything illegal other than smoke a little if that's what you're asking. Which is legal in Maine, by the way. None of us did. The sheriff said Desiree left on her own. Jonathan took too many sleeping pills and they thought it was an accidental drowning, or maybe a suicide. They said Banks overdosed on heroin, but he didn't do hard drugs, and we tried to tell the good sheriff that, but he wouldn't listen. So, what's really going on? Why do you need DNA samples from us?"

"It's not just you, Miss Taylor," Metford said in a shockingly calm and pleasant tone. "We need them from everybody who was staying at the lake house, as Agent James said before."

Nova regarded them skeptically. "Level with me, and I'll do my best to help you out. Don't level with me, and you can turn yourselves right back around and get out."

Ava sighed. Nova was right. She almost didn't blame the young woman for being so suspicious. The truth was the last card she had left, and it would have to work. "Okay. Here's the deal. Banks died of an overdose. That much is obvious and true. Did he take the drugs, or were they given to him by someone else? That is what we don't know. There was trace DNA found on the band around his arm, and it wasn't his. There's not enough for a complete profile, but we can probably eliminate all of you by comparing the samples to the trace."

Nova looked at Trevon, and they seemed to have some sort of silent communication going on. Was that what a relationship was like? That *connection* with someone else.

"What if the samples don't eliminate us? What if it's just enough to leave a question, not because we did anything, but because your *trace* DNA can't give you a full profile. What then?" Nova pressed.

"It just means we'll have to find another way to eliminate you as a suspect, Miss Taylor. No one is accusing you, or anyone else, of doing anything. We don't think you had anything to do with the deaths or the disappearance. We just really can't afford to skip any steps, and I assure you that this is just procedure." Ava was already doing what she had warned the rest of the team not to do—losing her patience.

"Cheek swabs, you said?" Nova asked. Trevon put a hand on her arm across the dinky little table and shook his head slightly. She pulled her hand away and looked back to Ava.

"That's it. Doesn't hurt or anything," Metford nodded.

Nova scrutinized him for a moment and then looked at Trevon. "We need to do it, Trevon. We need to help get this cleared up." She turned to Ava and nodded. "I'll do it."

Ava collected the swab from her. Trevon wasn't happy about it, but he allowed Metford to swab him.

After securing the swabs, Ava turned to Nova again and smiled. "I have one more thing to do and then we can get out of here and leave you two alone."

"Dear baby Jesus," Nova groaned. "Wasn't that enough?"

"We need to see all your shoes. All of them," Metford said. He pulled out his phone. "Just need to take pictures of the soles, and we're done. Even less invasive than the swabs." He smiled first at Nova and then at Trevon.

Nova stood and went to the side of the bed where she hauled a gym bag onto the bed. She unzipped it and threw the flap back. "Knock yourselves out."

Ava worked quickly, as did Metford. They were finished in less than five minutes. Ava zipped the bag closed and put it back on the floor under the bedside table where it had been earlier.

"Thank you," she said to Nova. "We'll keep you posted with any updates on the cases."

"Yeah. We've heard that before, but you go on and have a nice day, agents," Nova said.

Metford stopped abruptly in front of Ava and she nearly ran into his back. He pointed to Nova and Trevon's feet.

"We need pictures of those, too," he said.

Nova kicked up both feet and shook her head as if disgusted by the whole situation.

Trevon lifted his feet one at a time and scowled as Metford positioned the camera and adjusted the flash to get the best pictures of the tennis shoes.

"Thanks. You two have a good day. Remember, if you need anything," Ava said as she pointed to her phone.

The couple didn't speak, only watched Ava and Metford as they left. Ava couldn't figure out if their reactions had been totally normal, or not. Under the circumstances, they had a right to ask questions, and at this point, everything was voluntary. They were under no court order to give DNA samples.

She hoped the others would be more inclined to help with the investigation, or it was going to be a very long and tedious day.

CHAPTER TWENTY-TWO

AFTER LEAVING THE HOTEL, AVA AND METFORD HEADED TO THE address for Antonio Rutherford. It would be a blessing to get out of the hotel where the friends were all in varying states of high emotion. There had been arguments, mild combative attitudes, and even some tears as Ava and Metford tried to do their jobs.

"Nobody tells you how hard this job can be sometimes, do they?" he grumbled as she drove them toward Munroe Street.

"I had a clue beforehand. My uncle is an agent," she said simply.

"You knew and you still signed up for it? Dang," he remarked, shaking his head and drinking from his cold coffee. "You must be a glutton for punishment or something."

"You mean that you wouldn't have joined the Bureau if you'd known it wasn't going to be a sexy job like they make it out to be in the movies?"

He laughed. "You know, when I first joined, I kind of thought it was going to be like that, but it didn't take long to learn better. The sexy washed off this career as fast as the new shine wears off a fake gold ring."

It was her turn to laugh. "Yeah. Usually, the first case or two does the trick."

"You ain't kidding."

At one point, Ava would never have thought she and Metford would ever get to a place as coworkers where they could simply chat with one another. To have laughs added to it was a definite bonus.

"We're almost there," he said. "Munroe should be a right-turn at the next red light." He looked at the GPS on his phone and nodded. "That's what it says, anyway."

"This looks like a nicer part of town," she commented after glancing into storefront windows and seeing pedestrians dressed to the nines. Women walked up and down the sidewalks with perfect makeup and clothes, beautifully coiffed hair, and the overall vibes that the elite always seemed to emanate. As if their importance should be obvious to all who see them.

Ava preferred the more laid-back coastal town vibe of Fairhaven, personally. There were nicer places in town where one could dress up if they preferred, but there wasn't a huge societal pressure to constantly preen away at your garden or make sure your roots were touched up every week just to keep up appearances. Fairhaven was a town where people actually lived and worked and did things, not just sauntered in during the summer to flaunt their wealth.

She took a right at the light and delved into a gorgeous green neighborhood.

"Sumner should be about halfway up the street on the left," Metford told her, putting away the phone. "This isn't a street that just anyone could afford to live on," he added, leaning forward and looking up at the buildings on either side of the road.

The street was tree-lined, it even accomplished looking quaint but high-end at the same time. There were benches under trees, lots of meticulously manicured grass, and flowers hanging from lantern-shaped street lamps. The sidewalks looked brand-new, but it was only because there was no trash blowing around them, no blobs of gum melted into them, and no cracks or holes.

"Even the dirt is afraid to sully the place. This might be one of the cleanest places we've ever visited on a case," she joked.

"Yeah, but you know what they say about places like this," he replied, still craning to see everything. "It's only clean because they sweep it under the rug. Sumner building coming up." He pointed to the entrance on the left side of the road.

An Audi slipped past them followed by a 1956 Chevy Bel-Air that was in pristine condition.

"That car would cost more than I make in a year," Metford commented with a whistle, turning in his seat as the Bel-Air rumbled by them. "I would have painted it Cherry and Vanilla instead of baby blue and white, though."

"I'm more of a modern electric car type of girl," she said. "But I'll admit, that does look nice." She made the turn into the parking lot of the Sumner building. "Which apartment was it again?"

"405," he said and looked up. "There's only six floors."

She nodded and stepped out of the car.

They went up to the fourth floor and found the apartment. It was a corner unit. She wouldn't have called the apartments in that building *units*, though. The carpet in one of the hallways probably cost more than the flooring in her entire house. Everything was done in shades of tan and gold, and for accents, the decorator had used a red color that didn't contrast very starkly with the other colors.

She knocked on the door and a man opened. He was smiling. He was tall and very fit. His well-defined muscles rippled as he put one hand high on the door and the other on his hip. Ava was taken by his unusual eyes. They were gray—the color of storm clouds over the ocean—and seemed to stare straight into her soul when he looked at her.

"Mr. Rutherford?" she asked. "Antonio Rutherford?" She and Metford showed their badges.

His smile faltered but he nodded. "Um, that's me. How may I help you, agents?"

"We need to speak to you briefly. Your girlfriend gave us your name and address," Ava told him.

He moved aside and motioned them in. "Is everything alright with Harper? Has something happened to her?"

"No, Mr. Rutherford," Ava said. "She's fine. It's the Bumbee Ridge rental property. The lake house rented to a group of eight recent college grads."

He nodded. "Yes. They rented the house at Crater Lake for a month. They should be gone by now, though."

"No, Mr. Rutherford. The house is a crime scene," Metford said.

Antonio blanched and looked from one to the other. "A crime scene? What happened?"

Ava waited for the hint of a second to see his reaction as she spoke. "One of the women went missing while she was staying there, and now two of the men are dead."

He put a hand over his mouth and sat at the long, oval, oak dining table. "I need to call Harper," he said, reaching for his cellphone.

"There's no need," she told him. "We've already been in touch with her and she gave us all we need from her right now. It's you we need to speak to. Are you overseeing Ms. Kelshaw's website for the rentals?"

He nodded. "Yes. I usually do when she goes out of town. Is there a problem with the site? It's my job to keep it running smoothly. She'd kill me if it went down and I didn't fix it right away." His grin was quick as a lightning flash and then it was gone, as if he suddenly realized that given the situation, joking that his girlfriend was a murderer was the least appropriate thing to do.

"The site seems fine. We couldn't get a response from it, though," Metford said.

"Oh. I'm sorry. Honestly, I've been busy with work, and since we had tenants in the house already I figured it was fine for a while. I knew the house would need a deep clean after the college kids left and before I could list it as open again, so I just didn't get back on that section of the site. I was planning on having the cleaners go up there next week."

"No, don't do that. We'll let you know when it's okay to do all that," Ava said. "Was it you who messaged Akira Lin shortly after they arrived at the lake house?"

"Yes. They were asking if anyone had ever said anything about the place being haunted."

"Haunted?" she frowned.

He shrugged. "That's what they asked. I don't really believe in that kind of stuff, but I told them no one had said anything of the sort except the last tenants before them. That wasn't a haunting, though. I think they left a door unlocked and some local teens were having fun at their expense."

"And that's what you told Akira, right?" Metford asked.

"Yes, exactly." He picked up his phone. "I can pull up the site and the messages if you would like to see them."

"No, that's fine, Mr. Rutherford," Ava said. They had already seen the messages from Akira's phone. "Have you been to the lake house since the grad group arrived on July 1st?"

"No. I have no reason to go there. We try to run everything remotely, and never intrude on vacationers' time there. We don't go on site unless there's a pressing maintenance concern, and they never messaged me for that."

She nodded. "So you were… where on the evening of July 23, morning of July 24?"

"I was probably here. I can consult my calendar and tell you." He once again fiddled with his phone. After a few seconds, he nodded. "I was here that evening and the next morning. I don't leave the apartment a lot because I work online."

"Can anyone vouch that you were here that whole time?" Metford asked.

He shrugged. "I was alone. Harper is in New Zealand. I've just been kind of around, taking extra work while she's gone."

Ava nodded. "You haven't been to the house at all?"

He shook his head. "I've no reason, as I said before."

She asked a few questions more just as a matter of procedure and formality, and then stood. "Thank you, Mr. Rutherford." She handed him a contact card. "If you think of anything," she said, pointing to the card in his hand.

"Certainly. Anything to help out."

Metford stopped as they walked by the kitchen. He pointed to the counter and Ava moved closer to see what it was. There was a Big Mama Pickled Sausage wrapper and an empty Haribo Goldbears Sour bag lying on the end of the counter.

"Mr. Rutherford, you have a killer diet going on," Metford commented.

Antonio laughed, but it sounded thin and a bit forced. "Some things you just never outgrow no matter how old you get. My mother used to buy those for me when I was a kid, and I've taken them up again since she died earlier this year. It's not easy losing your anchor, your rock in life." His chin quivered and tears welled in his eyes. He inhaled deeply and kept smiling at Metford.

Ava thought Metford was going to evaporate. He turned and headed quickly to the door without a word, leaving Ava to do something with the emotional man. "Mr. Rutherford—"

He raised a hand. "Please, call me Antonio or Tony. My father was Mr. Rutherford." His hand stole up to the corner of one eye to swipe away a tear before it ran down his cheek.

Ava averted her gaze to give him a minute bit of privacy. "Tony," she said. "I'm sorry for your loss. It must be terrible to lose someone you're so close to. We'll leave you alone now." She beat a hasty retreat toward the exit, and the man followed closely.

As she joined Metford in the hallway, she glanced back to see that Mr. Rutherford had already closed the door. She was glad.

"Damn, what was *that*?" Metford asked.

"I think it's called emotion," Ava said.

"Ha-ha. Never mind. Do you think he's a suspect?"

She shook her head. "No. He had a good reason for slacking on the website. He admitted freely that he had been the one to text Akira, and he said he just didn't think to tell her that he wasn't really the owner, because he would've had to explain about her going away and leaving him in charge. He had work to do and didn't have time to get involved with a long conversation. We can both totally understand that."

Metford nodded. "Seemed like an upstanding guy with nothing to hide."

She nodded. "That was so much more pleasant than going to the hotel earlier."

He scoffed and nodded. "Ain't that the truth? Trying to get a simple swab was like trying to convince someone to have open heart surgery without anesthesia."

She laughed as they got back into the car. It was a bit dramatic, but the sentiment was true enough. "Why'd you run away when he started talking about his mother's death?"

"Nope. I don't do the touchy-feely icky things you call emotions. Don't understand them, don't know how to deal with them, not sticking around for it. Sorry."

"You totally left me flapping in the wind back there," she scolded him.

"You're a woman. You know how to handle tears and snot, right?" He tried to look defensive, but he just looked like a scared kid.

She gave him an irritated look. "Jesus Christ, dude, do you have any idea how sexist that is?"

He shook his head again. "Uh-uh. It might not be what you want to hear, but it's true, isn't it? Women are just better equipped to deal with that sort of thing."

"Would you have run off and left Santos to deal with it?"

"Maybe, but she might have botched it worse than I would have," he cracked. "I can just see her looking at him like he was a little green bug from Jupiter and telling him to get a grip and grow some balls." He giggled at the thought, and despite herself, Ava had to stifle her own. She could see Santos reacting that way, too.

Ava blinked it away and returned to her serious voice. "So, you just admitted that you don't think all women are suited to handle those icky things called emotions, just certain ones, and I'm not so sure how I should take that."

"Are you seriously mad over me running out like that?"

"No. But just so we're clear, don't leave your partner hanging like that again. I don't handle that crap any better than you do. I'm just as uncomfortable around tears and grief as the next person, and I could've used some moral support back there." She grinned at him. She had given him almost a direct quote from the teacher of the trust-building classes.

He chuckled. "I see what you did there. The teacher told us almost that very thing in the classes we took. You just wanted to see if I had paid attention in class. Just so we're clear," he said, leaning forward to look directly at her and grin. "I did, and I'll try not to leave you hanging if another person starts getting emotional."

"And?" she pressed.

"And I'm sorry for the sexist comment."

"Oh, thanks, but I was expecting, 'and I'll buy you a beer.'"

Metford barked out a laugh. "All right, all right. And I'll buy you a beer."

She finally relented. "Thank you. It's nice to know someone has your back."

He held out his fist and she bumped it with hers. "That's what I'm here for."

They went back to the hotel and waited for Sal. She would be pleased to know that Antonio had answered all the questions they'd had.

Ava was ready for the day to be over. When Antonio had talked about his mother, and Ava had seen the genuine hurt in his face, and heard it in his words, it had upset her more than she could ever tell Metford.

All she could think was how she would feel if the situation with her own mother turned out badly. She didn't know what she would do if she lost her anchor, her rock in life.

CHAPTER TWENTY-THREE

A va knocked on Trevon Marcus and Nova Taylor's door at the hotel.

Santos had teamed up with Ashton to do some minor field work, and Ava was convinced it was only to keep from going along with her to the hotel. She still held some bit of animosity toward Ava for some reason, and Ava wasn't sure how to turn that around. Even Metford had come around after a while, but Santos wasn't following his lead at all. Maybe she had eyes on becoming a leader one day, or maybe she thought Ava had some special treatment because she had family in high positions and in the FBI. Ava wouldn't go out of her way to explain her situation to Santos, but if the opportunity arose, she wouldn't shy away from it either. She wanted the team strong, whole, and united. They were stronger that way, and everyone was safer.

After what seemed an inordinately long time, Ava cut a glance at Metford and raised her hand to knock again. The door opened before she could, though.

Nova stood there, glaring out at her for a second. "Oh, it's you," she said.

Metford scoffed. "Were you expecting Doordash or Uber Eats or something?"

Ava shot him a look and he bobbed his shoulders as if he hadn't done anything wrong.

"Yes, we've come to ask you some questions about your time at the lake house," Ava said, cutting off any further remarks that might upset Nova and make her less than cooperative.

"Mm. We already talked about all that." She turned and let the door drift toward the wall as she walked away without inviting them inside. "More than once, and to several officers, actually, but if you *must* hear it all again." She turned and flopped onto a chair by the window.

Trevon wasn't in the main room. Ava looked around, saw the bathroom door was closed, and nodded toward it. "Trevon in there?"

Nova nodded. "He'll be out in a minute. Just finishing his shower."

Metford shut the door and propped against it with his arms crossed. Ava had to give him an A for effort because he was trying to look casual and not uptight. He hadn't quite mastered it, but she was sure he would get better at it eventually. She took a seat across from Nova at the little round table.

"We could go ahead and start while we're waiting on him if you want," Ava suggested. "I just need to hear about your time there from each of you."

Nova nodded but shrugged at the same time. "I mean, we did normal stuff for a bunch of recent grads looking to celebrate together for the last time. It was a lake house out in the boonies. We partied. A lot. We floated around the lake in the tubes; we smoked, drank, cooked on the grills, had a good time. I'm not sure what you want to hear, lady."

Ava tried not to bristle because she didn't think Nova was being scathing by calling her lady. "Agent, actually, but you can just call me Ava. Nova, what I'd like to know are some details about the trip. Who suggested the vacation? Who actually went on the website and set up the whole thing? That kind of information to start with."

The bathroom door opened, and the heavy scent of Irish Spring wafted out in the cloud of condensation that followed Trevon. "Well, I'm here now. Man, when's this gonna be over with?" he asked as he flopped into a chair.

"We have no idea, sir. We're working as fast as we can to find out what went on. I was just asking Nova—"

"Yeah, yeah. I heard you. I was listening from in there. Like she said, though, I don't know what you really wanna hear. It was Jonathan and Desiree's idea. She's the one who set the whole thing up. At least, that's what we were told. They called us to join them."

"Begged us, really," Nova added.

"Okay, that's good," Ava nodded. "Did everyone in your group get along with each other? Was there any animosity between friends?"

Nova and Trevon glanced quickly at each other and then shook their heads.

"What was that?" Metford asked, pointing between the two of them. "That look says you're not being completely truthful."

Nova glared outright at him. "You're calling me a liar?"

He shrugged. "I'm just saying that I caught that look, and it says there's something you're not saying. What is it?"

The couple shared another look, and Trevon nodded as he looked down and ran a hand over his hair.

Nova shifted in her seat. "It was Jonathan and Desiree."

Ava nodded. "Okay. What about them?"

"They argued, like, most of the time," Trevon explained. "It was uncomfortable."

"The arguments were pretty damn bad, too," Nova said. "I don't know how she didn't knock his block off a few times."

"The arguments ever escalate to physical violence?" Ava asked.

Nova and Trevon looked at each other and then at Ava before shaking their heads.

"Not that I ever saw, anyway, but it was pretty damn close a few times," Trevon finally admitted.

"I think if they had been alone instead of right in front of all of us..." Nova shook her head and shrugged again. "You know, I think it would have been bad. Maybe."

"We don't know that, though, but they screamed and sometimes threw stuff at each other," Trevon told them. "The rest of us just tried to look the other way because they were never throwing punches."

"Might not have been such a good idea, huh?" Metford asked, a hard look invading his eyes.

"Hey, man, we don't know where she's at, and he's dead," Trevon defended himself. "He didn't kill her; he didn't do anything of the sort to her."

"Then where is she?" Metford asked.

"Well, if we knew that, we wouldn't be sitting here like prisoners, would we?" Nova asked.

"Would you?" Metford asked hotly.

Ava turned to him and shook her head, warning him that he was about to cross a line. She turned back to Nova and Trevon. "We're trying to figure this out. Any help you could offer would go a long way. That's all we're saying. Nobody is accusing anybody of anything. Tell us more about Desiree and Jonathan's arguments, please."

And they did. They took turns describing arguments that took place inside the cabin, and it seemed that no space was off-limits. They told about some dramatic arguments that happened outside, by the lake, on the lake, and even in town when the group would go out to eat together.

For some reason, it struck Ava that they seemed hyper-focused on describing the fights between Desiree and Jonathan. It was almost like they were trying to get the spotlight off themselves. Did they have something to hide?

Ava took notes and sat back in her seat. Nova uncrossed her left leg and crossed the right one. She bounced her foot in the air and her shoe made a rhythmic popping sound as the back slapped lightly against her heel. The sound and movement caused Ava to glance down. Trevon was barefoot, but Nova wore leather sandals.

"Nova, why do you have sandals on instead of the knock-off crocs we supplied when we collected everyone's shoes?" Ava asked, looking pointedly at the sandals.

She held out her foot. "These? They're mine. The ones you gave us made my feet sweat. It was gross. Besides, they're just sandals that I forgot were stuffed between a couple of beach towels. What's the big deal, anyway?"

Ava sighed, trying unsuccessfully to stop her frustration from showing. "The big deal is that they were supposed to be turned in with all the other shoes. That's the big deal. They are possible evidence. Take them off and hand them over, please." She scooted her chair back and away from the table.

Nova scoffed. "What the hell ever. They're just sandals. I don't even think they were ever out of the suitcase at the lake house." She snatched them off her feet and dangled them in front of Ava with two fingers.

Metford brought a plastic evidence bag over and Nova dropped them inside.

"Wow, y'all act like I got some kind of cooties. Trust me, my feet are probably cleaner than most people's faces," she said, shaking her head and curling her toes into the short pile of the carpet.

"It has nothing to do with cleanliness," Ava said. "We have to preserve any evidence as best we can, and we can't contaminate any possible evidence by improper handling. It could affect any case and court proceedings later."

Standing, she moved toward the door. "Are there any more shoes here?" she asked, turning to eye them both.

"No, that's all of them, but you can go check if you want," Nova said in a hateful tone.

"Thank you both for your time, and for the shoes. If we need anything else—"

Nova flapped a hand in the air at her. "Yeah, you know where to find us."

Ava stared at her for a moment, unsure how exactly to handle the situation. She had done nothing wrong, but Nova was acting as if she had. In the end, she figured the best course of action was to let it go.

"All right. Have a nice evening." She opened the door and stepped into the hallway.

Metford stepped out behind her and shut the door. "Ready to go talk to the other couple now?" he asked, raising his hand to knock on the door across the hall.

"No, I'm not. Give me a minute," she said.

It took her a few minutes to let all she'd heard sink in properly. She didn't want to talk to the next couple and have their stories mingling with the details of the last couple's stories. She liked being able to keep things straight and orderly even in her own head.

CHAPTER TWENTY-FOUR

Cai and Akira were eager to invite Ava and Metford into their room. They ushered them in, offered them water, and then showed them to their seats. It was quite a different experience from the way Nova had welcomed them in.

"Are you sure you don't want a glass of water? The officers got us a bunch of these paper cups. I know they aren't very fancy, but…" Akira turned, holding up one of the cups she'd taken from the plastic sleeve.

Metford nodded. "Since you're so insistent, I guess I could take a cup. Thank you," he said, smiling.

Ava shook her head. "No, thank you. I'm fine." She turned to Cai. "We just need to ask you both about your time at the lake house."

He smiled. "Of course. Anything to help. What do you specifically want to know about?"

"What were your days like? Did everybody get along? Was everyone having a good time? Detail a normal day, you know, what you would do from the time you got up until you went back to bed."

He nodded but looked a bit confused.

Akira handed Metford the cup of water. "Oh, that's easy. We were all having a blast. Of course, there was lots of alcohol to kind of grease the cogs, I guess." She chuckled and Cai nodded, laughing, too.

Ava nodded. "A lot of drinking went on, eh?"

They both averted their gazes and nodded again.

"We'd get up sometimes before noon, most days not, but that was because we stayed up until the break of dawn most of the time," Akira said.

"We were just having a great time," Cai interjected. "Sometimes, we all fell asleep in the living room."

Akira nodded. "Except for Jonathan. He didn't drink or anything else most of the time. He was the straightest one of us because he took medication."

"Yeah, he was real anal about his meds. Wouldn't mix them with anything. If he did drink, it was very early in the day. Wouldn't touch anything after about six in the evening, though," Cai added.

"The sleeping pills?" Ava asked.

Akira and Cai nodded in unison again.

"Was that all he was taking?" she asked.

"If he was taking anything else, he never mentioned it," Akira said.

"Okay, what did a normal night at the lake house involve?" Ava asked.

The couple looked at each other and grinned. Ava wondered if the same stories about Desiree and Jonathan were getting ready to be told.

"Well, there was some weird stuff happening from the very first night there. Of course, we didn't believe Nova to start with. We all just sort of thought she was being a scaredy-cat-city-dweller," Akira said and then looked up sharply. "That's what BB called her when she told us about the window being open that first night."

"A window was open?" Ava was puzzled.

"People don't open windows at night when they're on vacation?" Metford asked. For once, he wasn't being sarcastic.

Cai shook his head. "It's not that. Some strange sound woke her up and she found Desiree and Jonathan's window open while they were sleeping in the bed."

Ava furrowed her brow and shook her head. "And that was strange?"

"Yes," Akira said. "And we didn't know how much stranger things would get after that. We had the central air on. There was no need for the windows to be opened. No one ever said they opened it, either."

Cai shook his head. "Everybody denied it, but still, we passed it off." He leaned forward and made his eyes big. "Until it happened again."

"And a third time," Akira added. "That's not all that happened, either. The activity escalated and there were things being messed up. Like we would find our clothes and personal items moved around the house, or they'd disappear completely only to reappear in their proper places days later." She shook her head and rubbed her upper arms as if warding off a chill.

"Poltergeist is what we had. It was obvious from the first few days we were there. None of us was safe from it, either," Cai said.

"Wait, wait," Ava said, holding up a hand. "I'm sorry. You think you were being haunted by a ghost of some sort?"

Metford nearly choked on his water. "No shit?"

Ava glared at him, and he coughed, turning his head away.

"Yes. A poltergeist," Cai said. "It got really bad for a while."

"See, Cai and I are… amateur ghost hunters. That's kind of our hobby, I guess you'd call it," Akira explained. "So, we know how these things work. How they escalate. It was a poltergeist; I'm almost a hundred percent sure."

"Ghost hunting is your job?" Metford asked incredulously.

"No, man," Cai said, shaking his head and looking as if he were about to try explaining an advanced calculus problem to a five-year-old. "It's a hobby. A side gig. We do YouTube for a living. We couldn't make much money just ghost hunting."

"We tried," Akira said, shrugging. "But it'll be a while before we can spin it off into a full-fledged content stream. It's hard to get it with the way the algorithm promotes personality-based content these days."

Ava blinked. She knew most of those words individually, but the combination of them whooshed right over her head. "Okay."

"She's right about the activity at the lake house. It was a poltergeist for sure," Cai said.

"Did you ever get a picture of it? Was it ever seen by anyone?" Metford asked. The grin on his face said he was being partially sarcastic and was getting ready to go full-blown Metford smartass on the couple at any moment.

"That's just not how it works with the paranormal world," Cai explained. "It's a slow progression of activity, and if the spirit manifests, it won't be right away, and it will probably only look like fog, vapor, or a dust cloud. They need massive amounts of energy to actually manifest in human form. It takes lots of time for them to draw that kind of energy from the people and electronic equipment interacting with them."

"Yeah, we're talking months or even years of draining energy from this realm. That's why cameras, cellphones, and anything else that runs on batteries just kind of goes kaput in a haunted locat—"

Ava shook her head and held up a hand to stop Akira and Cai. "No, I don't want to hear about the ghost stories you told each other. I need to know what really took place during your stay."

"But that did really happen," Akira insisted. "There was no other explanation for the stuff that went on. How do you explain that our toothbrushes and every pair of socks in the sock drawer ended up in the living room and kitchen while we were all in town together?"

Ava shook her head and scribbled notes. "I don't know… maybe someone broke in."

"Just to mess things up? Not even stealing anything?" Cai pressed. "I messaged the property owner and asked her if anyone else had ever said anything about the lake house property possibly being haunted. You know what she said?"

Metford sat forward and laced his fingers. "Please tell me that she gave you a story about some long-ago murder victim that still walks the property seeking vengeance for her untimely death." He grinned ear to ear.

Cai gave him a befuddled look and shook his head. "No, man. Most of the stuff you see like that is just for the movies and stuff. It's not real." He shook his head and took a deep breath. "She said that there was some activity there last summer, but she and the renters thought it was just someone coming in and messing with them by moving stuff around and taking some of their food. The owner convinced them that they must have left a door unlocked more than once and that the local teenagers probably just wandered inside and helped themselves to food and drinks." Cai shook his head. "We started making sure everything was locked before we all left the house to go to town or anywhere else, but the weirdness just kept happening."

"And the random footsteps in the hallway and kitchen at night," Akira said. "We'd check but there was never anyone there."

Ava sighed. "Right. Okay, but I don't need to know about ghosts. I need to know about tangible things. Did you cook out a lot? Stay in the house? Did everyone get along?"

"Yeah, we all got along," Cai said.

Akira shot him a look. "Well, BB could…" she trailed off and looked up at Ava.

"Go on. It's okay. Just tell us. What about BB?" Ava asked.

"Well, he could be…" she said, pausing again, "*intense* to deal with, but we all loved him anyway. He was a good guy."

Cai nodded. "He really was a good guy. Most of his mischievousness was just juvenile pranks and a foul mouth. We all knew he was harmless. And he really had a thing for Des."

"I wished that he wouldn't flirt with her so much, but he wouldn't quit. That was one of the problems with BB. He just never knew when enough was enough, you know?" Akira asked. "There was some… friction between him and Jonathan about it at first. But for the most part, things were good."

"You still think he never took drugs?" Metford asked.

Cai and Akira looked horrified by the suggestion. "No. None of us did that. Weed and alcohol. That's as hardcore as we ever got." Cai licked his lips. "I think the poltergeist had it out for all of us. It was picking us off—"

Tapping the table loudly with the end of her pen, Ava shook her head. "Okay, let me ask you about Desiree and Jonathan," Ava said, getting fed up with the crazy ghost talk. She was beginning to wonder if the two didn't need some professional help. "Did you ever hear or see them argue?"

The couple looked at each other, silent, unmoving for several seconds. Cai looked to the floor.

Akira looked at Ava. "They had bad arguments. Scary arguments, but I don't think he did anything to Desiree. For all their fighting and threats, they really loved each other. They just had a volatile relationship, is all."

"Earlier you said that BB had a thing for Desiree. Was that why they argued?"

"Part of it, I guess," Cai admitted. "I don't know, I tried not to listen. I didn't want to be disrespectful, you know? But it wasn't just that."

"It was a lot of little things," Akira said. "They'd get mildly irritated or something and it would spiral out of control. The whole thing with Banks was part of it, but like I said, it got better the longer we were here."

"Do you think Jonathan would have done anything to him, if it was that much of an issue?"

Akira sighed. "It's hard to say. But all of them are gone now. So who knows?"

Tears welled up in her eyes and Cai wrapped her up in his arms.

The rest of the story seemed to basically confirm what they'd already been told by Trevon and Nova. Ava flipped her notepad closed, apologized for their loss, thanked them for their time, and excused herself and

Metford. The day was still young, and they still had a lot of work ahead of them.

In the hallway, Metford stepped in front of Ava as she headed for Kalen Hamilton's door. He held his hands over his head and wiggled his fingers like a kid doing the ghost at Halloween.

"Woo-oo," he said, snorting laughter. "Couple of real kooks in there."

Ava wanted very badly to agree with him, but clung to her professionalism with desperation. "Metford, please. They're young. Just out of college—"

"Oh," he said, dropping the smiles and playful attitude immediately. "They're *so* much younger than you. You've got a whole two or three years on them at most. I guess that makes you so wizened in comparison."

Ava stopped and looked at him, amazed and offended. Just hours ago, they'd been getting along great. Was this the moment when all his true feelings would come out about Ava? Was this going to be when and where he opened up about the reasons behind his previous dislike of her? She couldn't let it happen there, in the hallway of a small hotel, in the middle of investigating a case.

"Metford," she said.

He ran a hand through his hair and looked at her. "What?"

"Not the time or the place for airing grievances. If you have a problem with me, my age, my job performance, or anything like that, we can handle it outside, or in Sal's office. Not here."

He nodded, his cheeks flaming. "I don't have a grievance. It's just…" He let the words fade and shook his head. "You know what? It's nothing. I'm just being a jerk. You know how I am."

Ava stood in the hallway with him for a while longer, letting the situation cool down.

He finally turned and pointed to a door across the hall. "So, we going to talk to this Kalen dude or just stand here watching the dust kitties float around our heads?"

Ava nodded. "Whenever you're ready."

He gave her one more look, but she couldn't quite decipher it. Was he pissed at her? Did he just outright despise her and had been acting otherwise all this time? What happened to the progress she thought they'd made toward getting along and bonding?

CHAPTER TWENTY-FIVE

A YOUNG MAN WITH WILD, CURLY HAIR OPENED THE DOOR THE instant Metford knocked. It was super-fast. Almost as if he had been standing on the other side watching for them through the peephole. Ava supposed that was possible, given the fact that she and Metford had been talking loudly in the hallway only moments before.

"Kalen Hamilton," Ava started, plastering on her best professional manner.

"Was that a question?" Kalen asked.

Metford scoffed and shook his head. "No. We know who you are. She's simply addressing you. You know, like a semi-professional way of greeting you."

Kalen gave him a blank look and nodded twice. "Coming in?" he asked, stepping aside and motioning to the room.

"Yes, thank you," Ava said, wondering if Metford had just defended her or if he was just being his usual sarcastic self with Kalen. Ava stepped into the doorway and smiled at Kalen. He didn't move. "After you," she said.

"Oh, right," he said, chuckling as he walked ahead of them. "It's like standard, what do you call it? Protocol? Something like that. Don't let the bad guys get behind you. Always keep them in front of you, or some shit, right?" He flopped on one of the sofa chairs, and it seemed to swallow him.

"Are you a bad guy, Mr. Hamilton?" Metford asked pointedly, walking to the open bathroom door and peering inside.

"What?" Kalen asked, his eyebrows shooting up toward his hairline. "No. I was just saying…" He flipped his hand over as if asking what the hell was going on.

Ava shook her head. "Mr. Hamilton, we just need you to tell us about your time at the lake house."

"And before we get off on some weird side route here…" Metford shook his head and held out his hand in a *stop* gesture. "We're not interested in ghost stories."

Kalen nodded and grinned. "You talked to Cai and Akira already."

"You heard us?" Ava asked.

Kalen shook his head. "Have you found out anything about Desiree? What happened to her?"

"We are investigating her disappearance. That's why we need to know about your time at the lake house, Mr. Hamilton," Ava said.

"It's just Kalen. I don't like Mr. Hamilton."

Ava nodded. Did he mean that he didn't like being called Mr. Hamilton, or did he mean he literally didn't like Mr. Hamilton, as in his father?

Metford finished looking over the place and took a seat at the little round table with Ava. "So, tell us about your time here, Kalen."

Kalen shrugged and shook his head. "It was a vacation. What is there really to tell about it? We cooked out at the dock. A lot. All of us enjoyed it. We drank a boatload of beer and listened to Trevon's horrible music way too loud for far too long every evening. We sat on the dock and talked. Jumped off it into the water to swim. Paddled around in those stupid little boats." He shrugged again and shook his head. "Now, have you found out *anything* about Desiree? Has anyone seen her in, like, another town or anything? Has any of her stuff turned up?"

Ava shook her head. "We're not at liberty to discuss the details of an ongoing investigation, Kalen."

"Bullshit. Des isn't just some ongoing investigation. She's a friend. We all loved Des." He dropped his gaze to his hands and bounced his left leg. "What about BB and Jonathan?"

Ava shook her head. "I'm sorry, Kalen. We can't—"

He scoffed and threw a hand into the air, palm in her direction. "Whatever. You're so full of it, you know that?"

Metford shifted in his chair. "Listen, we understand that you're real upset about your friends here, but there's no reason to be disrespectful to the people who are trying to help you."

Kalen held Metford's gaze rather easily to be so nervous.

In a deadpan tone, he said, "Sorry. I just wanted to know if you have any suspects yet. In any of the cases. Any leads? Or, if you have any fucking idea what the motive might have been. You know, the totally normal things one would wonder about in these types of cases."

Metford's jaw muscles clenched and relaxed repeatedly. He shook his head.

"I'm going to go against what my partner said earlier and I'm going to ask you to tell me about some of the weird stuff that happened at the lake house," Ava said, giving Metford a slight nod as he looked at her with surprise.

"What weird stuff? You mean, like the ghost stuff?" Kalen shifted in his seat, tugged at the knee of his pants, and cleared his throat as he glanced out the window.

Metford gave Ava a questioning look after seeing the way Kalen reacted to the question.

"Yes, the ghost stuff," Ava said.

"You ever witness anything like that?" Metford asked.

Kalen's face reddened and he cleared his throat again. His hands were in constant motion, fingers lacing and unlacing, and his knee was bouncing fast enough that it was mostly just a blur of movement. "Kind of, yeah."

"Kind of?" Ava asked.

Kalen nodded and huffed out a stuttering sigh as he planted his elbows on his knees. "Listen, we all got pranked by someone or something in the beginning, but some of the later stuff wasn't a ghost."

"And you know this because..." Metford left the end of the sentence unsaid, dangling in the air for Kalen to fill in.

The young man looked from Ava to Metford several times and then nodded, looking to the patch of worn brown carpet between his feet. "Because the later things were mostly me. I was doing it because the vacation was boring as hell for me." He held out his arms and then lifted the bottom of his shirt to reveal his stomach. "I mean, look at me. I can't be out in the sun without blistering. Doesn't matter that I slather on pounds of sunscreen; I still burn if I'm out too long. Which means more than an hour or so. There were mosquitoes the size of helicopters, snakes, slugs, lizards, gnats, rodents running around the lake and in and out of the woods. Some of the rats looked big as terriers, swear to God. The humidity was suffocating, the heat was like hell's furnace blowing in my face all the time, and I was pretty much miserable for most of the day. Even when I was smoking or drinking, there were still reminders of how much I didn't like the outdoor stuff. Everything my friends were doing, I didn't like. When the activity in the house started, I just thought it would add some excitement to the vacation, you know?"

"So, you were just pulling pranks on your friends to entertain yourself?" Ava asked.

"And them. They loved it. You should see how excited Cai and Akira get when they suspect paranormal activity of any kind."

"Did Desiree or Jonathan find the pranks entertaining?" Ava asked.

Kalen cleared his throat and shrugged. "Yeah. As far as I could tell. I honestly think they all knew it was someone playing pranks. I mean, deep down, even Cai and Akira had to have known."

Ava nodded and took notes. "Did any of your pranks ever get out of hand or cause anyone to act in a way you didn't expect?"

"You mean, like did anyone ever get hurt because of the pranks?"

She nodded.

He shook his head. "No. I never did anything that would hurt anyone. Swear to God on that."

Ava continued to write.

"Hey, why did you all want our shoes? What was that all about? Was there a print or multiple prints found somewhere near the house?"

Metford cocked an eyebrow at him. "What makes you think that?"

Kalen chuckled nervously and flopped back against his seat shaking his head. "I don't *think* that. I was *asking* about it. I mean, why did you need the shoes? Did you get Nova and Trevon's shoes, too?"

"We collected everybody's shoes," Metford said.

Kalen sat up straighter. "And?"

"And what?" Ava asked, wondering why he was so interested in what they'd found at the crime scene.

"Did you find a print at the house or something? Is that why you took the shoes and left us with these prison slides?" He held up a foot and dangled the black slip-on from his toes.

"Like I said, we can't discuss details about an ongoing investigation," she reminded him.

He nodded and bit his lower lip as he sat back in the chair. His eyes took on a glazed look as if he was daydreaming. "You know, Desiree wears leather sandals most of the time. I hardly ever see her in any other shoes. She loves those things. I still don't know how she can stand walking in sand and dirt, though. It has to get under her feet and between her toes." He wrinkled his nose and bobbed his shoulders. "Must not bother her, though."

Ava and Metford exchanged a look. Kalen's questions and his actions moved him onto the list of possible suspects. Actually, she reckoned it moved him up pretty close to the top of the list for the time being.

In a way, she understood the pranks and the insistence that there was some sort of paranormal activity at the house, and Kalen owned up to that much easily. But murder? What possible motive could he have for that?

CHAPTER TWENTY-SIX

AVA WAS GETTING READY FOR BED AT ELEVEN-THIRTY THAT NIGHT. After work, she had spent the evening going over everything she had written down for the case of the missing woman. There was still a chance that Desiree might be alive, and Ava didn't want to miss any shred or sliver of evidence that might lead them to her in time to save her life.

The two dead men were a different story. There was nothing to do for them except make sure their deaths weren't foul play, and for some reason, her gut kept telling her that was unlikely. The whole situation just felt wrong. Something was off about it, but she couldn't find any evidence that pointed in a different direction.

"But if I can find Desiree, maybe I can figure out what really happened in that lake house," she muttered as she grabbed her clothes and headed for the shower. "Where would I go if I was running away from a boyfriend because of a fight?"

She stopped just outside the bathroom door and consulted the map she had pinned to the wall there. There was a whole lot of not much at all around Bumbee Ridge. Crider was the sort of place where an outsider—especially a young, pretty college grad who was upset—would draw people's attention. Someone would have noticed her. If she had gone there.

Officers were still trying to find anyone Desiree knew. If she had contacted anyone, there was no record of it.

A chilling thought occurred to Ava, and she let her finger drop from the map. Walking into the bathroom, she exhaled as she tossed her clothes to the vanity. What if Desiree had made it to Crider and then something terrible had happened to her there? What if someone had taken notice of the pretty college grad, offered help, and then kidnapped her from town? There was no telling what had been done to her or where she was after so long.

She ripped back the curtain and grimaced at the metal on metal as the curtain rings slid over the bar. Just as she flipped on the water, her phone rang in the other room. She bolted for it and answered without looking at the caller ID.

"James," she said in a demanding tone.

"Agent James?" a man's voice asked.

"Yes, this is Agent Aviva James. To whom am I speaking?" The voice sounded familiar, but she couldn't readily put a face to it.

"It's Kalen. Kalen Hamilton."

She nodded as she turned off the water and wrapped herself in a robe. "Oh. Kalen. What's going on?" Why was he calling her a few minutes before midnight? He didn't sound panicked, so it wasn't an emergency. At least, she didn't think it was.

"I have been thinking a lot. Especially after you and Agent Metford were here earlier."

She waited, but he remained silent. "Okay, and...?" she asked in an attempt to get him to finish his thought.

"And, I just wanted to tell you some things. About the lake house."

Ava rushed to get her notepad. She yanked a chair away from the window and thumped it down near the little table, then plopped into the chair and flipped the notepad open. "I'm listening, Kalen."

He took a deep, ragged breath. "You already know about Des and Jonathan arguing."

"I do. Do you have something to add to that?"

"Kind of, yeah. I know what a lot of their worst arguments were about."

Ava bit her tongue. She hated having to drag information out of people, but it was part of her job, and a step in the investigation that she was unwilling to skip. She wanted to tell him to just spit it out, but she didn't. "Kalen, what were some of their worst arguments about?"

He chuckled dryly. "BB, of course. Banks was an ass, and he was *obsessed* with Des. That drove Jonathan crazy. He was psycho jealous over Des, anyway, and when Banks would do or say inappropriate things to her in front of Jonathan, it pushed him over the edge and he'd start in on Des about it. Act like it was her fault or something. It wasn't, though. She only had feelings for Jonathan."

This echoed the story that Akira and Cai had told her, but she was thankful for the clarification. Those two had seemed like they didn't want to speak ill of their friends, especially since all three parties in question were now dead or missing. Ava understood the impulse, but wished these people would just own up to the truth instead of trying to pretend like everything was nice and dandy.

"So, why did Banks pursue her like that?"

"Because he thought she deserved better than Jonathan. Which she does, in my opinion, but my opinion doesn't matter. That's between Des and Jonathan."

"I'm confused. Banks thought Desiree deserved better than Jonathan, and so he caused trouble between them to do what?"

"He thought she would eventually come to see he was right if Jonathan kept treating her badly. He thought she would eventually just break up with him. Banks was sure that all his compliments and flirts would convince her of what a good guy he was and that she would go running to him when she broke up with Jonathan."

Ava shook her head. It made no sense to her at all, but she knew she didn't think about things the way others did. Especially not relationships. "Instead of wooing her, Banks caused her trouble to try and win her heart?"

"Basically. It's a little more complicated maybe, but that's the gist of it, yeah. And, bad as I hate to even think the way I have been thinking lately, I have a theory. I don't like it at all, but it's all I can come up with."

Ava closed her eyes and cleared her head for a moment. Did she really want to hear his theory? It was possible to learn more about Kalen by listening to his theory than it was to learn about the others. Always and forever, a theory was a direct insight into the way that person's mind worked.

"Okay. I'm ready, Kalen. Give me your theory," she finally said.

"I really don't want to think like this because Banks was my friend. He was a jerk sometimes, but he was my only close friend. Best friend, really. I think that maybe he got really drunk and came onto Des. She would have rejected him no matter what. She just wasn't into him at all. But if he was drunk, maybe he got, I don't know, *carried away* and hurt her somehow." He blew air between his lips and Ava could practically hear his wince through the phone. "I'm really afraid Des might not be… alive anymore. Like I said, I hate to think this way, but maybe Banks tried to force himself on her and she started freaking out. He could have hurt her or even killed her trying to calm her down. He was aggressive sometimes—especially when he was drunk."

"Okay," Ava said, trying to keep her tone even and neutral as she scribbled away frantically. "Is there anything else you think *might* have happened?"

"Yeah. That's the damnable part of it. My mind won't quit spinning the possibilities. Banks hated Jonathan, but there was no love lost. Jonathan despised Banks, too. So, if Banks accidentally hurt or killed Des, he would have blamed Jonathan for it. Like she wouldn't have freaked out if Jonathan hadn't been in the picture, see what I'm saying?"

"Yes, I think so," Ava said. She was getting a clear picture that Banks didn't think very straight and clear about much at all.

"Every time he looked at Jonathan after that, he would have been thinking if it wasn't for him, Des would still be there. He might have somehow slipped Jonathan more sleeping pills somehow, and I don't know how, maybe put them in a drink he had or something, and then he drowned him while he was in the bath. After that, if I know Banks, he started getting paranoid. Probably worrying about getting caught and going to prison for the rest of his life. He might have even been feeling guilty. Either way, I think he couldn't stand it any longer and decided to kill himself to keep from ever owning what he'd done, the monster he'd become."

"And you think he decided to overdose to kill himself, as a way to commit suicide?"

"Absolutely. It makes sense to me. Not much makes sense right now, but that theory is the one that sticks and won't go away. It always comes back to Banks and his screwed-up perspective. So, what do you think, Agent James?"

Ava tapped the end of the pen against the tablet and shook her head. "Right now, I don't know. But thank you for calling and giving me this insightful theory. I just don't know why you didn't mention any of this while I was speaking with you today."

"Because it was just a bunch of disconnected thoughts at the time. There was nothing to convince me that my best friend had possibly murdered two people and then taken his own life. That's something I fought against believing. No one wants to think their best friend is a murderer."

"Right. Okay. Well, is there anything else you want to tell me?"

"Not really. I just wanted you to hear the theory before I convince myself it's stupid and push it aside."

"I really appreciate that. You call back any time if you think of anything else. Okay?"

"Yeah. I can do that."

"Thanks," she said and disconnected the call.

She looked over the notes and replayed the conversation in her mind. He had sounded nervous at the beginning of the conversation, but by the end, his tone had completely changed. It was more confident and held more authority. As if he thought he had accomplished something important that he had been worrying about.

He'd been worrying about telling a federal agent about his theory, sure. But there had been something else there. Something in his mannerisms from earlier in the day, and something behind that theory. It wasn't often that someone would just toss their best friend under the bus like that. Especially when said best friend was dead from a likely suicide.

But that little hint of doubt wormed its way into her mind again. She finally turned for the shower again.

"What about the trace DNA we found?" she asked aloud, as if the water could give her an answer. "Where did Banks get the drugs? And how did he get them without any of his friends seeing or knowing about them?"

Banks' body had no track marks. If he had been a regular user, there would have been the telltale scars left behind on his arms or other parts of the body that would be a little more difficult for anyone to see.

"There was only the mark from that one needle," she murmured. "The fatal injection."

Of course, she would have to wait for the toxicology report before she could be sure what was in his system and what had killed him. He might have been taking oral drugs that no one knew about. Maybe that's what caused that one injection to be fatal.

The most important thing Ava got from her conversation with Kalen was that he was very eager to turn her attention toward suspecting a dead man had murdered two of his friends and then committed suicide.

It was too convenient for Ava.

Seemed as if Kalen might have something to hide.

Why would he think Desiree was dead already? Did he know more than he was admitting? He said Banks was his best friend, but he'd eagerly thrown him under the bus as the killer. There hadn't been even the slightest hesitation in doing so, either.

Even with all the help he'd given, it just made Kalen look like the guilty party in Ava's mind, and he moved even further up on that suspect list. As of that moment, he took first place on that list.

CHAPTER TWENTY-SEVEN

The next morning, Ava took several minutes during the briefing to recap what Kalen had told her the previous night. She had taken the time before going to bed to enter the conversation into the computer and put it in evidence. Before the meeting, she printed out copies of that document and passed them out to everyone on the team.

"I think it's very important that if any of the lake house friends call any of us, we *need to listen and take notes*," Ava insisted. "If you have a recorder, use that. Just don't let the conversation slip by without noting the details."

"But none of what we record will be admissible in court if anything ever goes to court," Santos pointed out.

"That's why you always ask their permission. Make sure they understand that you want to record the conversation so that you don't forget any important details," Ava said.

Sal nodded and gave her a small smile of approval.

"But what if they say no?" Santos asked.

"Then don't use the recorder," Ava shrugged. "Just write down what you can at the time, and we'll use it for our own records, just like this. If you interview them later on, ask to use a recorder and then ask them to repeat whatever they told you on the phone. Just always remember to get them to *say* they are consenting to being recorded."

Everyone nodded, and Ava handed the meeting back over to Sal, who stood up and presented a large whiteboard with various tasks, lists, and notes on it.

"Alright, I need you all to be completing tasks and marking them off the board. This is one of the oddest cases we've covered as a team so far. There are a lot of moving parts, and I need everyone to focus on doing their job. No getting sidetracked and going down rabbit holes even though I'm certain it would be easy to do. We have two deaths and a missing person. We're working the missing person as if she is an endangered adult as of right now because two of the people she was staying with are dead."

"But they were accidental, right? Maybe one suicide," Santos said.

Ashton nodded. "That's what we were told."

"But we aren't sure what's happened. There's no evidence to the contrary. Yet," Sal said. "That's why I want everybody giving a hundred percent. Overtime is a given, obviously. Don't stop working just because the clock says it's five or six. You know the drill."

"What do you want me working on first?" Ashton asked.

"I want you to find background information on our vacationers. All of them. We need backgrounds on the property owner, too, and any information you can get on her other properties. Being in New Zealand, she's not a suspect at this time, but I want to be thorough, so find out what you can *after* you get full backgrounds on the eight friends. There are families who want to give their boys burials, who need closure, and who want justice served if there's foul play involved. They need answers, team. Let's get them."

"And there's a family who wants desperately to know where Desiree is, also," Ava added.

"Desiree is our main focus for the time. She's missing, and she's possibly in danger. Even if her disappearance had nothing to do with the deaths, where is she? Did she leave angry and upset and have some sort of medical emergency? Did she come across the wrong person or people in her bid to get away from the argumentative boyfriend? Or did the boyfriend harm her and she never left, or ran off as the sheriff says? We need these answers, and the best thing we can do for now is put together the timeline and the evidence and statements we have so far."

Sal moved across the room and flipped the whiteboard over, and everyone worked together to put the timeline in order.

"When will we have the tox reports on our deceased men?" Metford asked.

Sal shook her head. "These things take time. Just like the autopsy reports. A week minimum, and maybe longer. In the meantime, we need to keep working and gathering any shred of evidence we can."

Metford nodded. "Planned on it. Just wondering how soon we'd know for sure if the deaths were related or not, and whether they were accidents or suicides, or if there was foul play."

"Right, I guess I need to address that theory. We're all thinking there might have been foul play involved in the deaths of Jonathan Williams and Banks Becker, but we can't have any opinions one way or the other right now until the evidence bears that out. Do you hear me, team?" Sal asked.

In turn, they all agreed.

"Good. Remain unbiased and form no opinions. That's how you collect viable evidence and don't miss things. It's when you make up your mind that murder was involved that you start missing things you deem inconsequential because they don't fit your view of the situation. We can't bend the evidence to fit the theory we like best, or the one that makes the most sense to us. We have to change our theories according to the evidence we gather. Like I said earlier, no running down the rabbit holes and getting sidetracked."

They all nodded and looked chagrined. Ava had even been guilty of letting her opinion get in the way of how she handled the statements she'd taken the day before. It was supposed to be innocent until proven guilty, and she'd allowed her mind to take far too many leaps and jumps.

Proven, she reminded herself. *As in, evidence to support the charge of guilt.*

But she couldn't just go looking for evidence to support that idea. She had to collect it in an unbiased way, or it might screw up any future court proceedings that might take place. If that happened, there might never be justice. There might be three families out there suffering needlessly forever, never getting any answers, and never getting the closure they deserved.

"Ashton, you have your assignment. I want you riding that computer until it's done. No field work, no helping out the others, nothing. Just concentrate on the backgrounds and property info," Sal said.

"Yes, boss," he nodded, closing his file and heading toward his computer station.

"Metford, you and Ava are doing a great job. I want you to stay with her. You two are going to be interviewing anyone and everyone who had anything to do with the friends at the lake house. You will do the second round of interviews at the hotel and check on the shoe prints with the boys in the lab. Anything you think needs looking into, run it by me to make sure I've not already done it. Got it?"

"Yes, boss," Metford said.

"Got it," Ava echoed him. She and Metford hadn't had time to speak about what he'd said at the hotel the day before, but since they were teamed up for the duration of the case, they would eventually find time, she supposed. It would be good if she could get him to come clean and just tell her what his problem was with her. Whatever his problem was, it was likely that it was also Santos' problem with her.

"Santos, you're with me for a while," she said, nodding to Jillian.

"You got it, boss," Santos said, giving a tight, small smile.

"We've been here five days already," Sal announced. "No doubt, we'll be here quite a bit longer, but let's make it as short a time as possible while still being thorough. Grab yourselves an early lunch and get to work." She turned, motioned to Santos, and they walked out together.

"We getting lunch?" Metford asked Ava.

Ava looked at her watch. It was already after eleven. "The meeting didn't feel like it was that long," she said.

"That timeline took forever and three days to fill out. So much shit to put in there," he grumbled.

"We're essentially working three separate cases," Ava said.

He nodded and exhaled deeply. "I'm starved. So, are we getting lunch like the boss suggested, or are you doing something else?"

"We could stop somewhere quick, I suppose, but I want to go to town and talk to the owners of the pizza place where the friends ate several times."

He shook his head once sharply and then nodded. "Alright. Food first, though. I work better when my stomach isn't gnawing on my backbone."

"Don't we all?" she quipped, heading out the door.

CHAPTER TWENTY-EIGHT

Ava and Metford sat outside the Wendy's just off the main street of County Crider. It was only a five-minute drive from the hotel, and it was in a place that wasn't very busy. It wasn't her first choice for a lunch spot. Ava typically preferred to eat at places that weren't necessarily chains, but with the amount of traveling they'd been doing lately, and the hit-or-miss quality of the local diners between Jackson Wyoming and County Crider, it was nice to have somewhere convenient that she could sort of expect to be familiar.

"Nuggets and a salad," Metford remarked with a shake of his head. "What did you do, have a crisis of conscience about all the bad-for-you food you've been eating since I've known you?"

"At least I'm trying to eat a bit healthier," she defended herself. "Sure beats the grease-feast you have over there."

He tapped his chest. "Hey, I'm healthy as a horse."

"Going to be big as one if you keep eating like that, too," she said, laughing.

"It's good protein, thank you very much. Gotta build up these gains. I will still be able to chase down just as many—and maybe more—bad guys than you. Just try to keep up." He crammed several fries into his mouth and nodded.

"It won't be hard to keep up with you when you're being hauled away on a stretcher because you had a heart attack in the field, Metford."

He chomped on the big bacon cheddar cheeseburger and then held it out as if offering it to her. She chuckled and shook her head. In return, she held out a nugget to him. He laughed.

"No thanks. I think I have enough here to do me at least until dinner time." He wiped his mouth. "How in the world does that fill you up? Seriously, we're boots to the ground most of the time. That wouldn't give me enough energy to run half a block."

"Maybe women are more efficient at utilizing food energy." She shrugged. "I don't know."

"But you're still a little hungry after you eat that, right?"

She shook her head. "Not really."

He laughed. "Want half my bourbon bacon cheeseburger? I ain't going to ride your ass for not eating healthy." He nodded toward his own food. "Obviously."

She chuckled and shook her head. "No, I think this will do until dinner." She grinned. "Of course, I might have double portions of everything then."

He laughed. It was good. Hopefully, whatever tension had flared up in them before would no longer be an issue.

Her phone rang, and she fished it out of her jacket pocket. "I have to take this," she said, shoving her food onto the dashboard and getting out of the SUV. "Uncle Ray, what's up?" she asked, her heartbeat speeding up a bit.

"Hey there, kiddo. You too busy to talk right now?"

"Nope. Lunch break with a coworker."

"Oh, early lunch?"

"Yeah. I'm finished with mine, though. Just waiting on my partner to finish his," she fibbed.

"I'll keep it brief, then. It's an update about your mother."

Ava's vision trembled and her heart beat erratically as if it had forgotten its rhythm. "Mom? What is it?"

"Ava, I am pretty sure she's back in the country."

"What? Already?" Her heart thudded hard, skipped again, and then set a frantic pace that shook her with every beat.

"Yes. I'm almost certain she came in on a container ship from the Port of Barcelona and disembarked at the Port of New Orleans," he explained, his voice low and even.

"Those are strange ports," she mused.

"Yes. But they also weren't being monitored closely because they aren't even on the radar for human or drug trafficking. That makes it even more interesting that we received an anonymous tip about a container carrying drugs and a hint about one that had humans when it came in."

"Why do you think my mother came in that way?"

"Because I believe she's the one who called in said anonymous tip, for starters. And, another agent thought he saw her at the port. It was enough to spark a search for her in New Orleans by the Bureau."

Ava paced to the edge of the small parking lot and stared into the wooded area beyond. "Okay, what happened to the people who were in the container? The trafficking victims?"

"We don't know. Apparently, they were taken immediately to a different form of transport. We put out the word, set up soft roadblocks, and the airports will report any suspicious activity straight to us, but I'm not holding my breath for any useful information from those sources. Most likely, the victims were split up and loaded into different modes of transport, depending on where they were going."

"And smaller groups would draw less attention," Ava supplied.

"That's right. Whoever we're dealing with here, they aren't new to this, and they're smart about it. They're leaving behind no evidence to lead back to the people who really run the ring."

"What about the drugs? Any idea where they were headed?" Ava asked. Sometimes the victims and the drugs were going to the same place, but it was unlikely in this case since the drugs had been left behind. If they had been going to the same place, they would have been picked up at the same time, by the same people, and handed off at a later stop to distributors. Fewer moving parts, less risk.

"Confiscated. They're running tests to figure out who it belongs to. They'll find out if there's more on the streets here and where, and from that, they can trace it to its source in the US, at least. Might be able to get that person to rat out one of the higher-ranking members, or at least a supplier. That'll get us a step closer to shutting down one small line of drug trafficking for a while, anyway."

"But it probably won't get us any closer to finding Mom," Ava said, closing her eyes and turning back toward the SUV. "Why is she still off the grid? Why doesn't she just call or text or something?"

"Well, I don't know for sure, but I do know Elizabeth. She's doing all this for a very good reason, I'm sure. The only thing that would mean enough for her to do all this would be finding who took Molly. What happened to you two back in Prague has haunted her for all these years, Ava. Given the chance to stop those people once and for all, she'd do it if it harelipped hell."

Ava chuckled. "Harelipped hell, huh? You really have a way with words, Uncle Ray."

"I try. Seriously, though, she's got a good reason. I'm sure of it."

"Yeah, I know she does, but I would just like to know she's okay." The Prague incident changed so many lives forever. It haunted everyone involved. It had changed the entire course of Ava's life, and it seemed it might have also changed the course of her mother's life as well.

"What about you, kiddo?" he asked. "You okay?"

"I'm good, Uncle Ray. I'll be better when all this is over, though."

"I have to go, then. Gotta get back to wrangling bad guys," he said.

"Same," she replied. "One thing about it, we'll never run out of work, will we?"

He laughed. "Nope. Never. I'll talk to you later. Take care," he said.

"Alright. You, too," she said, pulling the phone away from her ear only a moment before the line went silent.

"Who was that?" Metford asked as she got back in the car.

She smiled. "Oh, nobody important."

CHAPTER TWENTY-NINE

Ava and Metford returned to the hotel that afternoon to interview Nova and Trevon yet again, and Ava was set to go to the lake house after that. Everything was on a crunched time schedule, but she didn't mind. The busier she was, the less time she could spend dwelling on where her mother was, or if she was really back in the US. If Uncle Ray said he thought she was, then she probably was. But that only eased Ava's mind a little. She could still be in danger. Serious, life-threatening danger. And she probably would be for the rest of her life. No one could interfere with the big trafficking rings and ever be safe again.

"Agent James?" Metford said insistently, as if it was the third time he was saying it.

"What?" she asked, snapping out of her own thoughts. She looked from him to Nova and realized that she had missed something fundamental. She shook her head. "Sorry. I was thinking."

"Well, you zoning out and thinking doesn't make me feel any better about this situation at all," Nova muttered. She gave Ava a scathing look. "Didn't you hear anything I just said?"

"I'm sorry," Ava said, shaking her head and feeling stupid for zoning out like that.

"I asked when we were going to be through here. When will we be able to go home and get on with our lives? We have jobs, bills—"

"Rent to pay so we don't lose our apartment," Trevon said.

"And it might sound crass or bad of us, but that's just the way it is, *Agent* James," Nova finished with more than a little attitude.

"I told them I didn't know when we'd be done with the investigation or when we would be able to let them go home," Metford said.

"We really need you to stay a little longer," Ava said.

"But we haven't been charged with anything. Nobody told us that we *had* to stay here for so long," Trevon said, sitting forward in his seat and looking incredulous.

"No, you haven't been charged, but—"

"But nothing," Nova cut her off. "We have lives. How are we supposed to live if we lose our jobs and our home?"

"I don't like the idea of being homeless," Trevon added.

"Hey," Ava said sharply, looking from one to the other. "One of your friends is missing and two others are *dead*. Doesn't that mean anything to you? I thought this was a group of best friends," she said.

"We *are*," Nova shot back. "Or, at least, we were. And we had nothing to do with the deaths or with Des going missing. The more I think about it, the more I think the sheriff might have been right. Maybe she just left." She shrugged and looked at Trevon.

He nodded. "I don't know where she went, but obviously she didn't think much of us if she left without a word and never even tried to let us know where she was or if she was okay. That's my feeling about it. I'd never leave without telling at least one of my friends where I was. I might not give them a heads-up before I left, depending on the circumstances—"

"But we'd damn sure let them know when we got somewhere. Just to let them know what happened and that we were safe. That's just human courtesy." Nova leaned forward. "And we were supposedly besties. That ain't how I would treat my bestie."

Ava clamped her teeth together. What was wrong with these people? Did it not affect them on a deeper level that they were now missing three of their best friends? Two of them were dead under horrible circumstances and the other was missing without a trace. Maybe they weren't as good of friends as they all made out to be. When Ava had gotten away in Prague and Molly had not, she had thought it would end her. Her soul had been crushed into dust. Not knowing if Molly was alive or dead was the worst pain, fear, and guilt she had ever experienced. She would have gladly remained sequestered for as long as necessary, no fuss about it. She would have done *anything* to help the officials find and possibly save her best friend.

And rent had been the last thing on her mind. It had never once occurred to her how she would live, how she would manage, or what she would do if she didn't return to her job back home. She wouldn't have cared, if it had crossed her mind.

But she reminded herself that in so many ways she was lucky. She was *privileged*. She had a robust network to help her and a family well-connected enough to not have to worry about it. Maybe that's why her mom's disappearance was cutting so deep, even more than Ava had thought. Her mother had always been there for her, and now she wasn't, and that uncertainty cast a dark cloud over Ava's thoughts.

She was sympathetic, she really was. But did they not realize the gravity of this situation?

"Listen, no one has been charged with anything, but we can make it so that you can't leave town until the investigation is over. We don't want to do that, but we can if we need to," she told them.

"So, is that like a threat, or something?" Nova asked hotly.

Trevon nudged her leg and shook his head. "That would go in the official record, wouldn't it?"

"Of course, it would," Ava said flatly.

"But if you stay willingly, we won't need to do any of that," Metford said.

"Well, y'all need to hurry it up. I'm telling you, I have a life to get back to. Now, there ain't no helping Banks and Jonathan. And I'm real sorry they're dead, but keeping us here until we are bankrupt, jobless, and homeless won't help the case any because we already told you all we know," Nova said in a slightly calmer voice.

"We'll stay," Trevon said. "We'll stay, and we'll help any way we can, but like she said, we already told you everything we know."

"Thank you for understanding. We're moving this along as fast as we can," Ava said. "But we need to be extremely thorough, and if we rush to suit you and your lives, well, it might compromise the investigation."

"And that would mean a lot more intrusion into your lives later," Metford added.

Nova sighed dramatically and flapped a hand at them. "Fine. Are we done for the day? Or would you like to hear what we did at the lake for the hundredth time?"

Ava stood there for a few seconds trying to determine how to proceed, but she knew better than to venture any further down this path. It would just be a waste of time. "Again, thank you both. We're done here for the day."

Metford was out of his seat and heading for the door before Ava even picked up her notepad.

As they walked away from the rooms, Ava's phone trilled. "Lab found a possible match to one of the prints outside the window of the lake house," she reported to Metford.

"Whose shoe matched it?" he asked.

"We have to go to the lab and get the results. He didn't say which shoe matched it."

"Damn, I hate mystery and suspense," he grunted.

Despite the tense situation they'd both been in, she chuckled. "So, that's why you became an agent? Because you just can't stand solving mysteries?"

"I prefer it when the answers are right in front of me," he said. "Way easier all around."

The police station wasn't too far away from the hotel, so Ava and Metford headed right over to check out what the lab had uncovered for them. The place was small, and didn't have near the resources of an FBI evidence lab, but it would do, and the evidence analyst seemed to know her stuff. Ava took the report and read over it with Metford. They looked at each other and nodded simultaneously.

"I knew something was off with him," she muttered.

"He seemed awfully eager to throw his dead best friend under the bus, for sure. Now we know why," Metford concurred, flipping the corner of the report.

"What do you say we move Mr. Kalen Hamilton right to the top of the suspect list?" she asked with a cock of her eyebrow.

He nodded. "I'd say that's a good idea. Put him right where he belongs."

"Let's head to the lake house. We're supposed to meet Sal and Santos there after lunch," Ava said.

"But first, food, right? It's almost noon." He held up his wrist to show her the time.

"Where do you put all that food?"

"Hollow legs maybe," he said.

Ava reconsidered the dynamics of the circle of friends as she drove in search of a lunch spot. It was a strange dynamic, to say the least, but she thought it might have been in transition as they were all getting ready to start their adult lives out in the real world. That kind of change has a way of shifting one's perspective and realigning their goals.

Did that shifting dynamic have something to do with the deaths and the disappearance? She was careful not to latch onto the idea, but she couldn't completely dismiss it, either.

CHAPTER THIRTY

Sal was standing in the front yard of the lake house with her hand shading her eyes against the bright afternoon sun when Ava and Metford approached from the driveway. Santos gave a head nod in greeting.

"What have we got, boss?" Metford called over.

Sal shook her head and dropped her hand. "Sadly, not much. I want to do another search of the property inside and out. All the buildings, around the lake, and even inside the wooded area over there where there's a footpath. Ava and I are going in the house to look around again."

"What are we looking for?" Santos asked.

Ashton stepped from the other side of Sal's SUV and walked over to join them.

"Wow, you got off computer duty?" Metford asked.

"I was a good boy and the boss decided to let me come play with the rest of you," Ashton replied.

"Look for anything that seems out of place. Anything. I don't care if it's just a stray strand of hair stuck on something. Bag and tag it. Random pieces of cloth, cigarette butts, all the same stuff the forensic team would have been looking for."

"If they already searched the place, why are we doing it again?" Metford asked.

"Because I am hoping we can find *more* evidence. Maybe there's something small, partially hidden, or seemingly insignificant that they missed. They're human, too, and it's possible that they overlooked something that we can use. Be especially thorough close to the lake. If something was in the water, it could have surfaced by now. Debris has a way of being deposited on the shore. And the forensic team didn't do a thorough sweep of the wooded area, so, Metford, if you would…"

Sal motioned toward the tree line beside the lake. "After you finish around the lake and buildings, take Santos and Ashton and follow that footpath. See where it goes. Look for shoe prints, footprints, anything we might be able to use to track Desiree."

"You got it, boss," Metford nodded, looking determined.

Ava thought he seemed more professional and eager to please in that moment. Sal had given him a position of authority in a way, and that was probably the reason. Was Sal testing him to see if he could handle it? She had done it in such a way that it was smooth, seamless, and natural as if it were just everyday business, but Metford had taken notice. And so had Ava. If Santos registered it, her face didn't show it. Maybe Sal had done it to see how Santos would react. She had not acted favorably toward Ava after Sal had given her an office. That had offended the heck out of her for some reason. Ava was eager to see if she would react the same way with Metford having a bit of authority.

"Alright, team, let's get a move on. Gloves, bags, labels. No goofs," Sal said, motioning for them to get to work. "Come on, let's see what's left inside, see if we can get a feel for what could've happened here."

Ava nodded and fell in step beside her. "Three different incidents at three different times in the same house," she mused aloud.

"I know. Doesn't get more convoluted or crazier than that." Sal cut the seal on the door and opened it.

The interior was cool. The central air had been left on along with the ceiling fan in the living room. It paddled the air slowly, sending a constant, slight breeze out in all directions. Ava and Sal stopped just inside and shut the door behind them.

"Why the hell did they even stay here after Jonathan died?" Sal wondered as they each pulled on their nitrile gloves.

Ava thought about it for a moment, putting herself in their position. What would she have done in that situation? "Maybe they were hoping Desiree would reappear. If she did come back, maybe they didn't want her to be greeted by an empty house."

"Would you have stayed?" Sal scanned the house from the entryway, hands on hips.

"I don't know. I mean, if Desiree were my best friend and she was just gone one day… I *might*. But the thought of staying after my best friend's boyfriend accidentally drowned in the *tub*?" Ava shook her head. "I just don't know."

"I might have slept in my car in the driveway," Sal said. "Not in the house, though."

"Wouldn't they have all been on high alert after Jonathan's death? I mean, their nerves would've been completely jangled, right? How did they even fall asleep after that? How did they fall asleep and not notice that Banks Becker was shooting up enough drugs to kill himself?"

Sal's forehead wrinkled and she looked down the right-hand hallway toward the room where Banks' room had been. She shook her head. "That's a good question. The only answer I have is that they were all up here drinking and smoking pot until they were so out of it that they didn't really comprehend what was going on."

Ava shook her head. "But that's not how they seemed when we got here."

"Nope. It sure isn't, but I don't have any other answer. Maybe they were playing puff-puff-pass after Jonathan's death to calm their nerves and that's how they fell asleep."

"Banks could have slipped away from the group and decided to shoot up after everyone else was asleep," Ava said.

Sal nodded. She stepped toward the living room. Ava turned toward the kitchen and went to the back door.

The door looked solid and had the regular lock and a deadbolt. Nothing looked forced or tampered with as Ava inspected it. There was a single dark thread caught on a nail that stuck out from the molding around the door. She bent to get a better look. She gently removed the thread from the nail and bagged it. Had forensics really missed that? The molding was white, and she had seen it by accident.

"Found a thread on a nail by the back door," she announced to Sal as she entered the living room holding up the plastic evidence bag.

Sal took note of it and nodded. "Maybe they missed that one. Good catch." She turned toward the master suite where Desiree and Jonathan had stayed.

In the bedroom, Ava looked up to the spot where the adhesive had been found. "Did we ever figure out what that adhesive might be used for?"

"Lab should be getting back to us on that soon. I told Ashton to hand it over to them and focus on our part of the investigation, but he did make a list of possible uses, which most of them were things you can guess. The list is so extensive, though…" She shook her head. "It could've been used for damn near anything."

Ava moved toward the bathroom. The tub drew her attention. How did a man drown in that tub? A child or a very petite woman, she could see that, but not a grown man. She stood over the tub, looking from one end to the other. Maybe the sedatives relaxed his body enough that he simply slid under the water. In her opinion, that was farfetched, but she wasn't an expert. Still, it just felt wrong.

The bottom of the tub was mostly dry, but not completely. Her eyes shifted to the faucet. There was no water dripping. She rubbed the faucet with her finger and it came back dry. She looked up at the shower head and ran her finger around it. Dry. Her gaze fell to the shallow, small puddle of water near the center of the tub. It had been ten days since they had been there. The house had been sealed almost the entire time.

"Sal?" she called.

"Yeah," Sal answered from the doorway.

Ava pointed. "The tub is wet."

Sal moved to look. She ran her finger around the faucet and the showerhead. "Dry," she said. "Now that's odd."

Ava's eyes roamed the entirety of the tub and the tiled walls. She leaned over the tub and looked into the drain. "Hair," she said, reaching in for it. "Dark, but I can't tell if it's brown or black," she said, putting it into a bag.

Sal was in full disbelief mode. She shook her head and pointed to the drain. "No way. Did forensics seriously not find that in their sweeps?"

"Has the house been sealed ever since they left?" Ava asked, sealing the bag.

"Yes, it has."

"No one was allowed in here for any reason?"

"No one. You saw me cut the seal on the front door. I personally checked the seals on the other doors as soon as I got here, and they were all intact."

"Were the windows sealed?" Ava asked.

Sal shook her head. "No."

"Should we go check outside the windows to see if there are any new prints? Maybe someone came in through a window while the house was sealed."

Sal nodded. "Probably some damn teenagers up here screwing around on a dare, or just because they're bored."

Ava followed her out of the room. As they headed for the entryway, Ava looked into the kitchen. The sunlight had shifted and was illuminating the floor in a stretched rectangle just in front of the door where she'd found the thread. And right in the center of the rectangle, as if it was being framed, was an alarming sight.

"Sal," she said. "Wait. There's a boot print in the kitchen."

Sal immediately turned and entered the kitchen as Ava pointed it out. "Looks like the left foot. A work boot." She took out her phone and started typing. "I'm pulling up the files and reports from forensics. I don't remember pictures of any boot prints from inside the house."

Ava bent at the waist and inspected the print, being careful not to touch it. The heel had been smudged, and she suspected that happened as she had walked to or from the back door. Turning, she spotted a partial print just a few inches away. It was clear enough to see that it was from the right foot.

"There's a partial from the right foot." She pointed it out to Sal.

"Well, here is a picture of the kitchen from the reports. I just zoomed in on the floor, and guess what?"

Ava stood straight. "No prints."

"No prints, and all the forensics, officers, anyone who came in here wore shoe coverings."

Ava nodded. "You going to take the pictures, or should I?"

"I got it," Sal said.

They had believed that things couldn't get any more confusing and weird with the lake house case, but they had both been wrong. Ava didn't believe it was just teenagers breaking in because they were bored, either. Why would a lone teenager wearing work boots enter a house clearly marked with police tape and seals? Not that it was impossible or unheard-of, but there was no other evidence that anyone had been there except the hair from the bathtub. It just happened to be the tub where a man had died. Did a teenager really break in just to take a shower?

Again, it just felt wrong to her.

She and Sal decided to look through the rest of the rooms before going outside, but there was no other evidence that anyone had been in the house.

CHAPTER THIRTY-ONE

METFORD TOOK HIS ORDERS SERIOUSLY. THE LAKE HOUSE WAS A bad deal all the way around, and he suspected that everyone on the team felt the same about it—there was foul play involved. Usually, he took things at face value until he had clearly defined reasons to do otherwise. He took his orders, did his job, and went on about his life. That was how he kept sane and still did his job every day. He didn't strive to be an over-achiever or the bright and shining star of any team. He simply wanted to do his job, catch bad guys, and make the world a little safer.

"I'll take the shoreline. Why don't you take the buildings?" he said to Santos.

She nodded. "Yep," she said, turning on her heel and heading off.

Was she pissed because the boss had put him in charge of the search area? Probably, but he didn't much care. They'd talk about it later, and he could sway her back to being passing pleasant at that time.

"Hey, Ashton, take the pavilion and the yard."

"On it," Ashton replied, turning toward the pavilion.

Ashton was just Ashton. Politics and hierarchy within the team didn't seem to ruffle his feathers at all. Metford liked working with him, but he wished the man had a bit more of a personality. He supposed that lack was the result of sitting in front of a computer for most of his adult life. That was a solitary job that required little human interaction. Ashton could be forgiven his awkwardness in social situations on those grounds, Metford supposed.

There was precious little in the way of evidence on the shoreline. Metford walked lightly and bent at the waist for most of the circuit. As he completed the round of the lake, he ended up back at the small grilling area near the beginning of the dock. There were two PBR beer cans crushed in the sand. He bagged them and set the bags on the wood of the dock.

Santos finished checking the outbuildings in no time. There was hardly anything in them, and Metford had given Ashton the pavilion and yard, so she didn't have anything to do. Well, she wasn't going to do anything more. If Metford had wanted her to help Ashton when she was finished, he should have told her so.

First, Ava had been chosen as the teacher's pet even though she was obviously far too young and lacked the years of experience Santos and the others had. That wasn't right, in her opinion. Maybe five years down the road, it would have made sense.

Then, just as she was getting a handle on being overlooked the first time, Sal had put Metford in charge of the search. Not that it was any kind of big deal. Forensics had already been over the place with a fine-toothed comb, so to speak, but Metford? Really? Hothead, sarcastic, been kicked off several teams already Metford?

A flare of pain rippled through Santos' head from her left temple to her right. She paused and pressed her fingers against the sides of her head and waited for the pain to pass, then readjusted her sunglasses before heading toward the wooded area.

Just inside the tree line, she turned around. Metford was still dicking around at the grilling area, and Ashton was practically crawling on his hands and knees around the perimeter of the pavilion, raking through the dirt and debris at the edge of the concrete. She scoffed and shook her head as she turned to head deeper into the woods.

The path was narrow but well-defined. It looked to have started its life as a deer trail, but over the years, people had made use of it and the dirt was hard-packed. She walked along the path for a few minutes until the tension that had built in her shoulders and neck eased a bit. Nothing to write home about, but any bit of relaxation after getting so upset over the whole Metford-in-charge ordeal was progress in her book.

Soon, she looked around and realized that she couldn't see or hear the guys anymore. The path had meandered steadily deeper into the woods, and she stood in a quiet, nicely-shaded area listening to the wind sighing through the trees. She inhaled deeply and smiled.

The fine hairs at the nape of her neck prickled and her eyes flew open. Something wasn't right. Something was wrong. Her gut twisted and her pulse sped up. She saw nothing out of the ordinary, but something had put her on high alert. That meant something *was* up. She'd not made it to her age by ignoring her body's signals, and that one had never been wrong in thirty years.

She pushed away from the tree where she had been leaning and took a cautious look around, squinting for anything in the distance. The dark lenses of her glasses didn't help make anything clearer.

The creepy feeling crawled down her spine and sent tingles down her sides.

She closed her eyes and pulled off the sunglasses as she braced for the bolts of pain that would shoot through her skull upon opening them. She had no other choice, though. She couldn't see far enough in the dim woods with the glasses on, and she needed to know what was giving her that feeling of impending doom before she moved.

When she opened her eyes, the familiar fiery rods of pain jammed into her brain and tried to split her skull. She sucked air sharply between her bared teeth and forced her eyes to focus on the darker patches of woods around her. Even when the worst of the pain had dulled, she saw nothing. No movement or animals, nothing but her and the wind.

After a moment, she jammed the glasses back on her face and took a couple of deep breaths. Somewhere in the distance, a dog barked. She listened. It barked again but sounded even farther away.

That's when she realized what had set her anxiety into motion. The *lack* of animal sounds in the woods. She turned slowly, straining her ears to hear any sound other than her own breathing and the wind walking through the trees.

No birds. No squirrels. No small animals of any kind stirred. She couldn't even detect crickets, beetles, or tree frogs. It was as if someone had turned off the track for ambient noises and only left on the wind machine.

For the woods to be so silent, there had to be a predator around somewhere. She let her hand fall to the butt of her gun, feeling reassured that she at least had that for protection.

As was her nature, Santos didn't retreat. She wouldn't run away just because she knew there was a predator out there somewhere. It didn't matter that she might be its next target. She wouldn't run, wouldn't hide, and she would face whatever crossed her path. She hadn't run away from something scary that was trying to hurt her since she was ten. She had run; her older sister had urged her to, and she had listened to Marie as always. Marie had died that day, and Jillian had sworn that she would never run away again. So far, she had kept that oath.

The farther into the woods she walked, the more intense that feeling of being watched, of being *stalked* became. At one point, the path had a slight turn, and she could tell she was headed back toward Crater Lake. It was a relief. The feeling subsided as she drew close to the edge of the woods again.

She could see the house even though she was still several yards from the outlet. She had entered the path near the lake and had walked what felt to be a long distance, but the other end of the path was right at the house, only a few hundred feet away from the lake.

The path was much wider at that end. Two, maybe even three people could walk side-by-side without much trouble. Santos headed for the opening in the tree line and stopped short when she spotted a drag mark in the hard-packed dirt of the path. It was on the right-hand side.

Careful not to disturb the marks, she stepped to the side so the sunlight could hit them. They looked to her like drag marks from shoes. There was nothing anywhere around the spot to bag, but she placed a marker in front of the spot, took a photo, and went to get Sal.

Ava and Sal were at the back of the house checking the last of the windows for signs that someone had climbed in or out of them. They saw nothing that would scream someone had used a window as an entry point. The only place they saw any boot prints at all was outside the back door leading into the kitchen. There was a patch of dirt that had several different shoe prints, and the area was listed as the entry point for most of the forensics team, and it seemed to be used by the tenants more than the main door at the front of the house.

So, where had the muddy print in the kitchen come from? Had it been one of the team who had a careless moment and stepped inside without the shoe covers? Neither Sal nor Ava thought that was possible because of the picture in the file, but they had no clear answer either.

"Hey, boss," Santos called over, coming from the side yard.

"Yeah, what have you got?" Sal asked.

"Not sure. I was checking that little walking trail you told us about and I found drag marks of some kind right over there." She jerked her thumb in the direction of the trail entrance.

"How far in?"

"About twenty or thirty feet, I guess. It's not far. Maybe even less. It curves back and forth quite a bit in that area. It's wide at the beginning and then narrows before heading deeper into the woods, and it's narrow up at the lake side."

Sal traded a quick glance with Ava before looking back at Santos. "Did you walk the whole thing?"

"Yeah, the main path anyway. There's another path that leads off that one, but it goes deeper. There could be more paths; I wasn't trying to end up on the Appalachian Trail, so I wasn't really looking for side trails."

Metford trotted from the dock toward them. Ashton was near the trail entrance as they approached.

"Find something, Santos?" Metford asked.

She shrugged. "Drag marks in the dirt."

"I was wondering where you got off to," he said, his face a ruddy color that meant he was agitated.

"Yeah, you said to check the buildings. There wasn't anything in them, so I went on the trail just to check it out; see what it was like."

"Nova said that Desiree took it a couple of times by herself from the lake because she and Jonathan were arguing," Ava offered, stepping up beside Metford.

He nodded. "Yeah, and she also said that Banks had scared the hell out of Desiree once when she took it."

Sal and Santos walked ahead as Santos showed her the marker. "There it is. I don't know, but to me, it looks like it could be drag marks from somebody's feet."

Everyone gathered around to inspect the marks. Sal took pictures for the file and then used the flashlight on her phone to look through the undergrowth and deadfall nearby.

"Could be from anything. There's nothing around it that would make me think it was a person that made the marks," Sal said.

Santos shook her head. "It's obviously a freshly-disturbed patch of ground, but not like it happened today or anything. And look," she said, bending and pointing to smooth, roundish indents in the middle of the tracks. "Right there. If she was unconscious and being dragged, it's like she came to right here and started fighting, drumming her heels against the dirt." She moved a foot farther ahead and pointed again. "And then, right here, she's unconscious again and being dragged without a fight. See how the marks just sort of fade out and back to the hardpack?"

"I see that, and I agree. Whatever happened here was recent enough that it could have been exactly as you said, but we have nothing to tell us this was made by a human, let alone the one we happen to be looking for. It'll be entered into evidence with pictures and notations. Good find, Santos."

But Santos wasn't happy about it being basically dismissed for the time being. She pursed her lips into a thin white line and put her hands on her hips. She shook her head and took up the rear as the group moved out of the woods again.

"What did you find, Metford?" Sal asked as they stepped back into the yard.

"Just a couple of PBR beer cans crushed into the sand at the beginning of the dock. I bagged and tagged them because I don't think they were there when forensics did their sweep. If they were, I can't find them in the file pictures."

"Ashton?" she asked.

"I didn't find anything of any consequence. I sifted through most of the dirt and sand around the pavilion for any small personal items that might have been dropped or lost there, but there was nothing. Just tiny bits of trash here and there. The place is very clean to be a rental."

"Yeah, we noticed that, too," Sal nodded.

After they looked at the beer cans and confirmed that they were, indeed, Pabst Blue Ribbon cans, Sal looked at her watch.

"Okay, let's all take a nature walk," she said, smiling at the group. "Let's go hiking, team." She pointed toward the trail entrance. "That's where the trail starts?" she asked Santos.

Immediately, Santos perked up a bit. "Yes, ma'am. We can only walk single file for a long way, though."

"Lead the way," Sal said. "Keen eyes, please, team."

Ava took up the rear position as everyone else filed into the woods. She wanted to have time to really look around off the sides of the trail without someone behind her to rush her.

Santos stopped to point out the meandering side trail that went up a rise and disappeared. Ava had an odd feeling that they weren't alone, but pushed it aside as no one else seemed bothered by the feeling. It was probably a squirrel watching them from a tree branch.

Sunlight dappled the ground, and Ava looked down at something blue and shiny. She bent to see another crushed PBR can. "Found another beer can. PBR, just like the ones at the dock." She pulled it out from under the broad leaves of a plant and bagged it.

"Someone had a penchant for the cheap stuff," Ashton commented.

"And it wasn't our college grads," Sal said. "They liked the expensive stuff even though somebody's bank account was taking a beating from buying it. They never bought the cheap stuff the whole time they were here."

Even though it wasn't close to time for the sun to set, the light was fading fast in the forest. The team emerged from the woods and gathered their evidence bags, placing them in Ava and Metford's car for transport to the station where the rest of the evidence was being held.

In all, it had been a decent day, and despite all the new questions that arose from their search, Ava thought they had made progress. She hoped against all odds that they would find Desiree alive and well. It would be nice to have one silver lining in the black cloud of the lake house case.

CHAPTER THIRTY-TWO

The next morning, Ashton was putting the finishing touches on the background files for the college graduates and on Harper Kelshaw. He had done research for hours after they had returned from the lake house the previous day, and with his computer savvy, had set up the system to gather more information for him overnight.

"Ashton, why don't you give us the highlights?" Sal asked.

"Okay. Sure, yeah," he said. "I didn't print out the files for each of you. There is one hardcopy for the caveman filing system, but the files have been uploaded so you can access them on your devices." He grinned. "From anywhere, and you don't have to keep up with papers."

"Okay, stop," Santos chuckled. "We get it; digital makes more sense."

Ashton nodded. "Exactly." He took a deep breath. "Okay, I found some interesting information on our graduates. They really aren't your typical college kids who just float through life and live to party."

"That's such a jaded opinion of college grads, Ashton," Metford said.

"Well, we know it's true that most cases we have that involve college grads, we find that they were real party animals. Not so with this group at all. Take Desiree Smith and Jonathan Williams, for an example. They graduated near the top of their class, didn't have any crazy discipline records or anything like that. One or both of them definitely seemed to come from money. They owned one vehicle and it was paid off, and it looks like they had a pretty large nest egg saved up. They were a serious couple, planning on getting married. They were in couple's therapy, though, so it stands to reason that they were having trouble before the vacation. She had a degree in accounting and was set to start a good career on the West Coast with Vogel Accounting. That's a top-tier accounting firm. They don't hire slackers," Ash told them.

"What about Jonathan?" Ava asked.

"Jonathan Williams was getting ready to start a job at Berber, Ingram, and Bancroft, also in sunny California. It's a top-tier marketing agency, prestigious, and Jonathan would have been chosen because of his grades, and based on several face-to-face interviews. B.I.B. also does not have a reputation for hiring slackers or anyone who can't pass a drug test. And they administer those quarterly, from what I've learned."

"No wonder Jonathan was obsessive about only taking the meds prescribed to him and nothing else," Ava mentioned.

"It would have been worth his while to remain a straight arrow for that career," Santos added.

Ash nodded and turned to the next file. "And then we have Nova Taylor and Trevon Marcus. They don't have the amount of money Jonathan had, but they do well. They're a serious couple as well. They both have degrees in the marine field, and both are set to start jobs in a couple of weeks at the North Carolina Marine and Mammal Center. The Center does research, rescues, conservation, and has a department for marine and mammal rehabilitation. They're a big deal. Nova is going to be a laboratory research assistant, but only because there wasn't an available position for a lead. Trevon is going to be a field research supervisor. These aren't entry-level positions. They already have an apartment ready to move into as soon as they start their jobs. They paid the deposit and the first month's rent in advance. The utilities are scheduled to be turned off at the current apartment and on at the new one on the same day. They definitely think ahead and plan, but..." he said, scrolling through his files. "They were under light surveillance in college. The local PD suspected they were selling marijuana."

"More like smoking it. *All* of it, from evidence at the lake house," Metford cracked.

"That's enough," Sal warned. "We're not here about the marijuana or the drinking. We're here to find Desiree Smith, and although the drinking and smoking might have contributed to her leaving, we need to keep it at that. Don't form opinions based on what these kids were doing on vacation. Unbiased, remember?"

Metford cleared his throat and nodded. "Yes, boss."

"Did they ever get into trouble for selling or smoking?" Santos asked.

"No," Ashton said. "It was just a suspicion. Nothing ever came of it." He cleared his throat and sighed. "Akira Lin and Cai Huang… they're a different story. Both of them came in on full scholarships. Super smart, got excellent grades, and both acquired bachelor's degrees in art. Cai's was a BFA in film studies, to be specific. They both took a mythology course, too, which focused on mythology, religious beliefs, iconography, and ritual practice."

"What use would that be in the real world?" Metford asked and immediately shifted his gaze to Sal and shrugged. "Just asking."

"Well, that's where the rest of their information comes into play," Ashton said. "Seems like they don't really have any clearly defined goals for their lives. They live together, do live-action-role-playing games—mostly the Medieval magical games like you find at Renaissance Faires—and they support themselves mostly by making content for their YouTube and Patreon pages. They both have nearly a hundred thousand subscribers to their YouTube channels, and their Patreon pages have a couple hundred members each. That's paying patrons. Most of their videos are ghost-hunting videos and abandoned buildings, but there are some that document their LARPing. They have written a few books about the paranormal and the LARPing community, which received poor reviews but still sell enough to have a slight residual income even from that. They have money rolling in from several sources. Advertisements, product sponsorships, that sort of thing."

"So they really don't need to have a life goal. At least, not right away, I guess," Santos said.

Ashton shook his head. "They're bringing about five grand a month apiece from the online sources."

Metford whistled and shook his head. Ava was shocked, and even Sal's eyes flew wide.

"You think that's surprising, just wait. By all accounts, Banks Becker was a bit of a jerk, a troublemaker. You all remember how he was apparently causing friction in the group."

Everyone nodded.

"Well, even he was a good student and was responsible in his personal life outside of school," Ashton said. "Comes from a pretty well-off family. He was set to join the Air Force in the fall. Had his sights on being an astronaut."

"Did you find anything that suggested prior drug use?" Sal asked.

Ashton shook his head. "Nothing at all. Even when he broke his arm three years ago, he refused the narcotic painkillers the doctor prescribed him. Wouldn't take them. Said he could handle it with OTC pain killers. Completely clean record. Not even a traffic violation or a parking ticket."

Sal shook her head and chuckled.

"Hey, now, boss," Metford said. "Remember what you told me."

"You're right, you're right," she admitted, turning back to Ashton.

"Kalen Hamilton excelled in his studies. He was a loner and quiet by nature, but never caused any trouble or raised any eyebrows. Same as the others—paid rent and bills on time every month, no priors for drugs, did have a ticket last year for running a red light, but he paid it immediately, and there's been nothing on him since. He got a degree in business management and has been preparing to open his own business in Fairhaven at the end of this summer. It's going to be a sweet shop that serves ice cream and different kinds of desserts."

"Now, that does not shock me. He just seems like the type that would own a little business in his hometown and be happy as a pig in mud about it," Metford offered.

Ava agreed. If any of the friends seemed like the hometown type, it was Kalen.

"What about Harper Kelshaw?" Sal asked.

Ashton scrolled a few pages on the screen and then nodded. "She has no priors that relate to this case. Just some minor traffic violations. She moved from New Zealand to live the American Dream, but it hasn't been as easy as she thought, I guess. The lake house wasn't up to code a few years ago and she got cited for that. Had to shut down rentals until she got it up to par again. It cost her quite a bit to get that done, but she has income from other rental properties. That helped fund the renovations at the Crater Lake property. I searched through her online sites and found where some customers complained about having to argue with her to get partial refunds, and full refunds for various reasons."

"Any major issues they complained about?" Ava asked.

"Not really, from what I gather. Maintenance things in these old houses. There were some other petty complaints that people filed with the police department. Mostly complaints about noise at some of her rental properties, which was caused by tenants, not Ms. Kelshaw. All in all, her record in the US is straight. She seems legit. I have a list of her properties, and that list is attached to her background file."

"So, Ms. Kelshaw has no criminal record in the states," Sal said. "What about ties to anything or anyone drug-related? The slightest tie to *something*, no matter how tenuous, could change the dynamic of this investigation."

Ashton nodded. "I understand. I found no ties at all. She just seems to be a woman trying her best to make something of her life. She seems to be doing pretty well for herself, considering she also doesn't have any outstanding bank loans or big windfalls. It means she's grown a lot slower than she could have, but it seems more sustainable."

"Her financials didn't show any sudden large sums of money—like for the renovation—that might indicate she borrowed from loan sharks or whatnot?" Sal asked.

Ashton shook his head. "Nope. It looks like she used income from her other properties to finance it. That's why it took her so long to get it done and re-list the lake house."

Ava was impressed. So many people didn't have the time, or wouldn't take the time, to do things the smart way. Instead, they jumped in with both feet and borrowed money from whoever would loan it to them and damn the consequences. Personally, she had never seen a single instance in which that played out well for the borrower.

CHAPTER THIRTY-THREE

Ava and Sal had gone over the timeline after the others headed off into the field for the day. Sal paced the length of the two whiteboards she had pushed together in order to fit all the information on the timeline. She shook her head and heaved a sigh.

"What are you thinking?" Ava asked.

"Hell, I don't know what to think. I know what the evidence says, but I also feel what my gut tells me." She kept her gaze fixed on the board as if staring at it harder would make it give up some evidence that just wasn't there.

"Sucks when the two aren't in agreement, doesn't it?" Ava clicked her pen and looked from Desiree's name on the board to her name on the tablet in front of her. The file was extensive, listing known friends, coworkers, and family. Sal had made a call to Fairhaven and asked for the reports from the agents who spoke with Desiree's family. It hadn't arrived, and they were on day twelve of their investigation.

"Ashton and one of the deputies are calling around to Ms. Smith's friends and coworkers again. It seems that she didn't have a very big circle of people who knew much about her or her personal life for some reason."

"Maybe she was a bit anti-social," Ava offered. "She did have a degree in accounting."

Sal grinned at her. "Are you stereotyping accountants now?"

"No, I'm just being realistic. There are certain people who are just hardwired to be more reclusive, and most of the time, you can tell by their chosen careers. Accounting isn't exactly a social career. It's work you do mostly alone. That means you would go nuts if you were a social butterfly and you took an accounting job."

Sal nodded, eyebrows raised. "I can't say you're wrong. What kind of insight does that give about the boyfriend? He was going to be a marketing consultant."

It was Ava's turn to grin. "Well, I would say that makes him the type of person who loves to put out an image to the world. Someone who wants to control everything, every little detail, bending the truth or even outright lying to maintain that image," she said. "It means he would be very particular to be seen and perceived a certain way, and he'd do anything to protect that perception. Makes sense that he'd be with someone reserved like Desiree. If they were having friction in their relationship, it probably stemmed from that kind of clash of personality styles."

"Wow. Impressive amount of insight. How old are you, again?" She chuckled.

"I like learning. I read a lot," Ava said, cheeks flaring with heat.

"I like that about you, Ava. Just be careful not to burn yourself out. You're always burning the candle at both ends."

Ava wasn't about to admit that she was studying psychology in her spare time. She thought profiling was intriguing and wanted to learn as much as she could in that field. It could only help her when she was solving her own cases. She nodded but said nothing.

"Now, what about Harper? Has she contacted you since the last time we texted her?"

Ava shook her head and tapped her phone. "She has been silent, but she said her mother had to be cared for around the clock. Her father isn't able to do it, and he needs help himself. They are both elderly, so…" Ava shrugged.

"Maybe the truth, maybe not, right?"

"Pretty much, but I tend to believe her. I mean, she moved to the US from there. If she wanted to move back, she could just do it."

Sal nodded and started pacing again. "Just spitballing here, but if you were in her position, wouldn't you want to be here?"

"I would want to be, but if I was the sole caregiver for my parents, I don't know that I would just up and leave them to come back unless the authorities said I had to."

Sal nodded. "Get hold of her and ask her to come back. I would be more comfortable with her and her story if she came back. If she's here, where I can go and physically speak to her, I would be able to gauge what type of person she is and get her off my mind as far as this case."

"You think she had something to do with all this? I thought that was *not* the road we were going down."

Sal let her hands thump against her hips in exasperation. "I know. Accidental drowning. Suicide by overdose—or accidental overdose. And a missing person. Unrelated according to the evidence."

"Has the lab finished with the boot print, beer cans, hair, and thread from the lake house?"

Sal shook her head. "No, and it's making me crazy. I know it's a small town and all, but I wish they would get a move on."

They bounced ideas for another half-hour before they started circling back around to being completely stumped as to where Desiree might have gone.

"I'm calling it lunchtime," Sal sighed, dropping her pen on the desk.

"Want to go to a diner in town?" Ava asked.

"Good food?"

Ava shrugged. "Gotta be better than the Wendy's Metford keeps wanting to eat."

Sal chuckled. "Yeah, he says the new burgers are really good."

Ava groaned. "I'm tired of the fast food. I can practically feel the grease coating my veins. I'm ready for some real food."

Sal laughed. "And food from a diner is real food? More real than fast food."

Ava nodded and stood. "Definitely. I don't cook much at home. Mostly just premade dump and heat boxes or microwave stuff." She shrugged and grinned sheepishly. "I know. That's not real food, either."

Sal shook her head and grabbed her bag. "Come on. Diner food is apparently as close to homecooked as either of us get. I'll drive, you text Harper."

Ava nodded and smiled. It was good to know she wasn't the only one who worked all the time. She got in the car and pulled up Harper's contact information and shot her a text.

Before they reached Claudia's Dine-In, Harper had replied.

"Harper's upset because she will have to return. Says her mother is very sick and her dad needs help. They have no one else. She's an only child," Ava said, reading the message aloud.

"Just tell her we need her here." Sal pulled into the parking area and turned off the engine.

Within a couple of minutes, Harper replied.

"She says she needs to find someone else to care for them until she can go back," Ava said.

"Okay. I am going to go in here and have lunch. We can deal with this afterward." Sal opened the door and got out without waiting for a reply.

Ava read the messages again. She felt sorry for Harper. Being the only child of an elderly couple who needed constant care couldn't be easy. Especially not when Harper had moved away from them years ago and come to the US on her own and became an entrepreneur without any help. Why had she made the decision to leave her family and go to a country where she had no one? Had there been family problems? Maybe. Was going back to care for them Harper's way of trying to mend their relationship? Or, perhaps, did she just feel duty-bound to care for her parents?

Or, maybe there was no problem at all and you're just reading way too much into the situation. Harper obviously cares for her parents, or she wouldn't be in New Zealand, half a world away from everything she's made for herself, Ava scolded herself.

What would she be willing to do for her own parents in that situation?

Ava looked up in time to see Sal open the door of the diner and motion to her. Ava nodded and held up a finger. She would be there in a minute.

She read the messages again. They seemed genuinely emotional and sincere. She shot Harper a text that might come back to bite her in the ass later, but she would answer for it if that happened. She couldn't just leave the woman hanging while she went in and enjoyed a nice meal.

I'm sorry for all your troubles. We'll continue with the investigation, but we might have to ask you to return if anything comes up that can't be handled long-distance. You should go ahead and retain someone to stay with your parents to be prepared. We'll try to make it work for as long as possible. I hope your parents get better soon. Let me know as soon as you are back in the US.

Her thumb hovered over the send button and she looked to Claudia's Dine-In again. The flickering blue neon name in the window held her attention for far too long. She jumped when a car door slammed to her right. A group of teenagers piled out of the car, laughing and goofing as they went inside.

Ava looked at her text again, nodded, and hit the send button before she could change her mind. She silenced that conversation and got out of the car, hoping that Sal would tell her to send a similar message to Harper after lunch, and hoping she didn't take it upon herself to text the woman.

All through lunch, Ava couldn't get her mind off her mother. She would do anything for her mother. If Elizabeth was sick and needed constant care, Ava would give up her career and all her worldly belongings to be there for her.

Likewise, if she got the call that Molly had been found alive and she needed someone to stay with her around the clock, Ava wouldn't think twice about doing it. There would be no thinking, no decision, nothing. She would be there.

She owed Molly that much. She owed her more than that. She should have found a way to take Molly with her when she ran, but she hadn't. She had left her wounded best friend and saved herself.

Ava's stomach clenched and her throat tightened. She forced a neutral expression so Sal wouldn't see her guilt. That guilt wasn't for the world; it was hers and hers alone.

If Uncle Ray was right and Elizabeth was back in the US, it was likely that Molly was, too. If Ava's theory that she was tracking Molly was right. And really, what else could have caused Elizabeth to disappear and go globetrotting off the grid? Ava thought Elizabeth harbored more than a little guilt over Molly, too.

She alternated between being super hopeful and reminding herself not to let her hopes get too high. The lead might go absolutely nowhere. It might be another dead end. It also might take much longer than she and Ray hoped.

She settled for keeping her head as level as possible and burying herself in work to keep her mind busy. If that meant burning the candle at both ends and running the risk of burning herself out… so be it. She didn't see another way to get through it.

CHAPTER THIRTY-FOUR

The team met up after lunch at the hotel. Ashton pointed out Harper's home address. She had two acres set in a rural area. The house was multi-level and modern, according to the file Ashton supplied.

"Should I let Ms. Kelshaw know we're going to her house?" Ava asked Sal.

Sal shook her head. "I already gave her the heads-up and told her we wouldn't be entering the house. We're sticking to the outside. She gave her blessing."

A tingly sensation ran over Ava's body. It was the unfamiliar feeling of almost being caught doing something naughty, and she knew it stemmed from the message she had sent to Harper without Sal's approval or even her knowledge. Apparently, Harper hadn't mentioned it, though, or Sal would've called her out on it first thing.

She nodded and put her phone in her pocket.

"Let's go, everybody," Sal said, flicking her hand toward the door.

Metford got into Ava's car, and to her surprise, Santos climbed into the backseat.

"Ashton is driving the other car," Santos said. "His driving scares the hell out of me."

Metford laughed and nodded.

Ava chuckled uncomfortably. "I don't think I've ridden with him."

Santos scoffed. "Better adrenaline rush than a rollercoaster at a shady-ass carnival."

"Is this going to be more hiking, you think?" Metford asked Ava.

She shrugged. "Beats me. Haven't seen the property."

"Boss was changing shoes in the other car," Santos said.

Maybe it was rough terrain, but Ava didn't know how Sal would know that unless Ashton had said something. Even with satellite imaging, Ava couldn't tell the lay of the land, just that it was very rural and sat at the end of a long, narrow road that might have been a paved county road or a gravel one. She had only seen the screen for a few seconds and had not thought to pull it up on her tablet or phone.

They drove for thirty minutes before they started getting into truly rural terrain. Neighborhoods thinned and houses became fewer and farther between until there were long stretches of nothing but crop fields and forested areas. As they drove deeper into the country, the houses that did pop up every now and then were getting older and older. The last house they saw before turning onto a private road on the left was an ancient-looking Victorian farmhouse that sported three broken windows on its facing side. Its paint was peeling and the porch shunted to the right. The yard was mostly dirt patches with just a few tufts of grassy weeds sticking up in random places. A German Shepherd lay in one of the dirt patches under an old oak tree. He raised his head lazily and watched the cars pass.

"Creepy places out this way," Santos muttered. "Looks like a setting from a Stephen King book."

"Well, we *are* in Maine," Metford pointed out. "But that doesn't look so bad. There's nothing wrong with that place."

Santos grunted and crossed her arms. "Nothing right about it, either."

"I dunno, I think it's quaint," Ava offered.

Metford gave her a skeptical look. "Quaint?"

That set Santos chuckling, but Ava shrugged. "Just needs some love. You have to admit, the windows were pretty nice. Or, would be, if they had panes in them."

"Yeah, I guess so," Santos admitted. "You won't catch me out on that porch, though."

The private road followed a curving path up a gently sloping mountain. The forest grew denser on each side, and the temperature dipped a few degrees. They rolled down their windows. The air was fresh and smelled of clean green things, and Ava found it relaxing. Sounds, even the normal noises from the vehicle, were damped as if she were hearing them through a blanket. It was nice, and for a moment, Ava was a bit jealous of Harper.

The house was almost half a mile from the beginning of the private drive. It sat on a rise with the mountain rising sharply just behind it. The levels had been built as if following the dips and rises of the land on which it sat. To the left of the house, there was a cobbled path that wended its way through a flower-and-tree garden and up to the top of a hill, where there was a small waterfall.

"Was there a creek down the mountain?" Metford asked, pointing out the waterfall.

"I didn't see one," Santos said.

"Well, there has to be one. Maybe it just goes farther into the woods and we couldn't see it from the car," Ava said.

Santos let out an impressed whistle as she looked up at the magnificent house. "How much money does she make from rentals?" she wondered.

"Look at that storage house," Ava pointed. "That's bigger than my house back home."

Sal and Ashton were already ahead of them, walking the perimeter of the house and stopping every few steps to peer into windows.

"Hey, look," Santos said, moving quickly to the side of the storage building. Propped up against the wall was a screen as if from a window.

Ava and Metford followed her.

"That doesn't belong to any of the windows in this house," Ava noted as she pointed up at the extra-large windows of the house—none of which had screens on the lowest levels.

"Doesn't look that way, does it?" Metford asked.

"The missing screens at the lake house?" Santos asked, pointing to the screen again. "And look at the bottom corner. Ripped."

Ava got her phone and snapped several pictures for the file. "It might be one from the lake house. If it is, the rip explains why it's here."

Metford looked at her questioningly.

"For repairs," Ava said as if it was obvious.

He scoffed and shook his head again. "I would have repaired it at the lake house. Why transport it all that way just to prop it up here?"

"If the perp was a peeping tom, maybe it made it easier to peep without the screen in the window," Santos offered.

"That's it, Santos," Metford nodded. "The boyfriend was peeping on the missing woman."

"He got bored with peeping and snatched her," Santos continued, laughing low.

Metford stood extra straight and tall, acted as if he was straightening his shirt, and nodded. "Well, there are just some things you don't outgrow," he said, imitating Antonio Rutherford.

"Yes," Santos said, doing her best to imitate the man she'd never met. "Especially when my Mommy used to get them for me when I was younger."

Metford and Santos broke into callous laughter.

Ava was unimpressed and walked away from them shaking her head. Some things shouldn't be used for entertainment. Especially when it was someone's pain and grief. Antonio had been in genuine pain for the loss of his mother, and Ava's heart had broken for him. Such a strong man who obviously took great pride in his accomplishments and did everything he could to be an upstanding person brought nearly to tears as he recalled losing his mother. That was a pain that would probably not diminish much, if at all, as the years passed. As much as she hated to think it, one day, Metford and Santos would be brought low by such tragedies in their own lives. Would they look back at that time on the callous, inconsiderate way they'd used a man's pain for entertainment?

Sal stood above them on the concrete veranda that ran the length of the house, hands on hips, shaking her head. Her expression was sour. "Hey!" she yelled sharply. "Metford, Santos, put a lid on it. That'll be enough. Stop with the juvenile imitations and stop shooting in the dark with theories. I already told you that's how cases get screwed up. If you two want to be riding a desk for the rest of the year, just keep at it."

Metford and Santos immediately dropped their heads and the act.

"Now, can we please get back to work?" Sal asked.

"Yes, boss," Santos said.

"Sorry, boss," Metford muttered, walking away from Santos and toward the cobbled path.

"Yeah, sorry," Santos echoed as she turned her attention to the edge of the property where it met the woods.

Sal descended the steps to where Ava stood.

"Thank you," Ava said.

"Mm. Sometimes those two get under my skin," she confided.

"I just can't figure any of this out. It's like we *are* just shooting in the dark and hoping to hit the right target. The only real leads we have about Desiree point to Kalen and possibly Nova and Trevon."

Sal shook her head. "Stick to the hard facts. Evidence that would hold up in court. As far as Nova and Trevon, all you really have—all any of us really have that points to them—are feelings and opinions. Every person registers and copes with grief and tragedy in different ways. Sometimes, those ways seem odd or off-kilter to us. But only when we compare them to our ideal of *normal*. Just because they act as if they don't care... well, we can't arrest anyone because they don't care that a friend is missing and two others are dead."

Ava nodded and ran a hand over her face in exasperation. "I really want to call in a professional search team to scour the woods around the lake house for evidence of Desiree while we focus on the friends. Maybe the search team will find something, and maybe we can find a hole in one of the friends' stories. Or maybe one of them will have a crisis of conscience and spill the tea about what really happened up there at Crater Lake."

Sal was silent for several minutes, and Ava was sure she was going to shoot down her request for the search team.

"Let's give it a little more before we call in the search team. Just because her parents haven't heard from her doesn't necessarily mean we're looking for a body. We don't even have the autopsy reports back yet on the men. If, and that's a really big if, the theory I know you can't get out of your head is right, then it would behoove us to wait so we have a better idea of what exactly we are investigating."

Ava nodded. "So, you think the same thing. You think the deaths and the—"

"No, no. We're not discussing this here or anywhere else. I just think it would be a good idea to wait at least until we have more information. After we get the reports, we will decide on the best course of action."

Ava nodded once. "Right. Of course." But she knew she had been on the right track thinking the deaths and the disappearance were connected, and that one or more of the group of friends knew something and was involved.

CHAPTER THIRTY-FIVE

SEVEN DAYS, AN ENTIRE WEEK, AFTER AVA'S TEAM ARRIVED AT County Crider, each member of the team was showing signs of exhaustion. They hadn't had time to fully recuperate from the Wyoming excursion before rushing to Maine. Going so long without seeing home or sleeping in one's own bed was disheartening at the very least, but when there was seemingly no real progress in the case they were working, it was more than simply disheartening; it was depressing and exasperating.

Tempers had shorter fuses, patience was nearly non-existent, yawns and glazed eyes abounded, and no one had a sense of humor. Not even Metford's trademark sarcasm survived past the fourteenth day. He showed up to the morning meeting with bloodshot eyes and a pale face, nursing a large coffee.

"You okay?" Ava asked him before the meeting started.

He nodded a couple of times. "Headache and a whole bunch of don't-wanna-be-here-anymore."

Ava grunted in affirmation. "Maybe it won't be much longer."

He scoffed. "Yeah, we're going to magically solve all three cases before the end of the day."

She pursed her lips to keep from engaging him further. It would only draw out his Little Debbie Downer side even more, and she didn't think that would be good for him, her, or the team. Sighing, she walked to the other table and sat to wait for Ashton to show up. He was never late for anything, and she thought he was probably finally feeling the effects of fatigue just like the rest of them.

A few minutes later, with everyone present, Sal started the meeting only to be interrupted by a notification from her phone. She held up a finger to the team and turned her attention to her phone. Suddenly, she was heading to the end of the room where the printer sat. It whirred to life and spat out several sheets of paper, which she snatched immediately and began reading. She separated them into two stacks and moved back to the group.

"Well, we finally have the autopsy reports for our two deceased men," she started. "The files are being uploaded as we speak, but in the meantime…" She handed the first stack of papers to Ava and the second stack to Santos. "Look over them and pass them around."

Ava's heart pounded. Finally, the moment of truth. The reports would hold the information to either disprove or prove that her theory had been correct about the deaths.

Jonathan Williams' report seemed normal for the first bit, but then it changed. He had only his sleeping pills in his system, and at only a slightly elevated concentration. From the notes, it seemed instead of taking two as he was prescribed, he probably took four. That was only a double dose and nowhere near a fatal amount.

The most interesting information came later in the report. The medical examiner had found and noted bruising and light abrasions on Jonathan's forearms, shoulder blades, and his heels that were found to be consistent with defensive wounds. There was also a small, round, very light bruise just below each collarbone in nearly the exact same location. The means and manner of that bruising was undetermined. The death was ruled suspicious, which meant it was no longer considered an accidental drowning.

Had Kalen been correct in thinking Banks slipped Jonathan extra sedatives? Did he think that Banks might also have held Jonathan under the water until he drowned?

Ava held the paper as if she were still reading, but in reality, her mind was playing out scenarios. Her brain was spinning with ideas of what could have left the small, circular bruises just below Jonathan's collarbones. The one image that kept coming to mind was of someone standing over him, holding him under the water with their hands on top of his shoulders. The thumbs would press in just below the collarbones.

With her question burning to be asked, she passed the report to Ashton and waited for Bank Becker's report to make it to her.

Banks had an overdose of pentobarbital in his system. That was it. Nothing else. There was only trace amounts of THC in his system from the marijuana, which didn't exactly match what the others had said about him smoking pot with them. The pentobarbital had killed him very fast and that's why the needle and band were still intact on his arm.

"What's pentobarbital?" Metford asked.

"Damn," Ashton muttered, shaking his head as he looked over Banks' autopsy report. "That's the only drug used in state-sanctioned euthanasia," he said in a low voice, still looking at the paper.

"What? So, Becker got his hands on pentobarbital and gave himself a lethal dose?" Metford asked incredulously.

"No," Sal said. "The death has been ruled homicide, Metford. Didn't you read it?"

Metford inhaled deeply. "I skimmed. I have a migraine, boss."

"Now's not the time to be skimming for any reason. Get something done about the migraine. We're now investigating both deaths as homicides."

Adrenaline fluxed through Ava's system at the words. "That means we're also connecting Desiree's disappearance with these two deaths?"

Sal was silent as she considered it for a moment before nodding. "It would be unprofessional to do otherwise, I believe. We've all thought about it, and now we have proof that at least one of the men was murdered by someone who had access to pentobarbital. How he was given the fatal injection without acquiring defensive wounds is still unknown."

After the bombshells, Ava followed Sal outside. "Sal, could I speak with the medical examiner?"

Sal looked her up and down suspiciously. "What's up?"

"It's just a theory I want to run by him about those collarbone bruises on Jonathan."

Sal nodded and gave Ava the number for Dr. Eli Griffith. "I don't know how busy he is today, but he was extremely busy when I was first in contact with him. It seems there are other cases going on here besides ours."

"Thanks. I'll call and find out." Ava walked back inside and headed to the conference room. Dr. Griffith didn't make her stay on hold for long.

"Hello, Agent James. This is Dr. Griffith. How may I help you?" He sounded pleasant but dull. Not disinterested, but as if he were a low-energy sort of person.

Ava laid out her theory about Jonathan being held down from the front until he drowned.

"That could very well be what happened, but there was no foreign DNA found on him or under his nails as if he were warding off an attacker and fighting for his life. A drowning man is one of the most violent. The panic and terror wipe out everything but the pursuit of survival."

"But that could be explained by the sedative in his system making him groggy and unable to fight back like normal, right?"

"I suppose it could explain it. I'm looking over my notes, and I see that the level of sedative was nowhere close to being fatal. He'd been prescribed that medication consistently for eight months. If he suddenly took a double dose, it would make him very lethargic and sedate. Now, the other man, there's no doubt that was homicide. Someone knew what they were doing by giving Mr. Becker that large a dose of pentobarbital, and it was someone who had access to it in the first place. That's not a drug that you can buy off the street corner to get high, and you definitely can't just pick it up over the counter. State executions use it, and veterinarians use it."

"I didn't think so. We're looking at two homicides here, is that what you think, Dr. Griffith?"

"I think that's very possible. More possible than accidents."

Ava thanked him and got off the phone. Her theory had been right, at least, to a point. Strangely enough, it didn't make her feel better. If anything, it made her sadder to know someone, or multiple people, had planned the deaths. And what of Desiree? Had she suffered a similar fate? Or was her fate worse? More like Molly's fate?

She hurried to catch up with Sal. It was time to request the search team again, and she needed to know their next move as far as the friends were concerned.

CHAPTER THIRTY-SIX

Santos and Ashton went with Ava and Metford to the hotel to interview the friends yet again about the deaths.

Before they went in, Ava stopped them. "Remember, we need to find out if any of them had access to pentobarbital. Find out if they work with, or have worked with veterinarians. I'm pretty sure none of them have ever been involved with the drug in the capacity of state executions, but don't just rule it out because it seems unlikely. Start out soft, just ask general questions about injectables and then ask about working with animals. As a last resort, tell them what the drug is and see how they react."

"We already know Trevon and Nova work with animals," Metford pointed out.

"They've *studied*, and earned the paperwork that says they're qualified to work with them, but I don't know how much hands-on experience they've had, if any," Ava reminded them. "But it's definitely worth asking about. Santos and Ashton can take Cai and Akira, and whichever of us finishes first can talk to Kalen. I'll text you when I'm done," she said to Santos. "You text me when you two finish with Cai and Akira."

Santos nodded. "Got it."

They all went in and knocked on their designated doors.

"Oh, you two again," Nova groaned as she let the door open to the wall. Again, she turned her back and just walked into the room.

Ava tried not to bristle, but it wasn't easy.

"I trust you know your way in," she said.

She took her usual seat at the window, curling her feet into the seat with her and looking slightly annoyed. Trevon sat on the bed with the headboard at his back. He barely glanced in their direction. His attention was on the television where a nature documentary was playing.

"I don't know," Metford said, stepping around Ava. "Mansion like this would be easy to take a wrong turn in." He managed a sarcastic grin as he plopped into the same chair he had used last time.

Ava pushed the door shut and gathered herself as she walked to the table. "It's nice to see you again," she started, trying to be civil.

"Mm."

"Mr. Marcus, could you join us, please?" Ava asked.

Trevon used the remote to turn off the television, but he didn't move from the bed. "Better?" he asked, giving a half-smile.

Taking a deep breath, Ava nodded. "Thank you. We're here to ask you about some more things."

"And I thought this was just a social call," Nova said, shaking her head as if it was the dumbest thing she'd heard in ages.

"Ms. Taylor, you studied marine sciences, right?" Ava asked without looking up from her tablet.

"Ooh, and they do their homework," Nova said, chuckling dryly. "Yeah. If we ever get to leave this dump, I have a cushy lab job lined up at a marine center in North Carolina. You know, somewhere I can put my hard-earned degree to good use."

"I think that's great," Metford said. "Did you do any hands-on classes? You know, like classes where you actually got to work with animals, or did you just read about them?"

"No, man," Trevon said, sitting straight on the side of the bed, his eyes angry. "We did work with animals. We interned in a marine center in Maryland for a while. Our third year, we both worked in a veterinarian's office way the hell out in the country, and we both volunteered at a shelter and at an aquarium. Is that enough detail for you about our studies?"

"Yeah, because if you need to know the exact dates we worked and the times we took our rare lunch breaks, I'm sure we can get that information for you. I know it must be very important to the case at hand," Nova added, looking smug.

"Did you ever assist in euthanizing any animals?" Ava asked suddenly, trying to catch their reactions.

Trevon and Nova looked as if someone had slapped them.

"No," Nova finally said. "We wouldn't have, even if it had been required. We want to help *save* animals, not kill them. Jeez," she said, her voice sounding thin and breathy.

"Really?" Metford pressed. "Seems that would be something you'd have to do to have a well-rounded course of study."

"Conservation, lab research, marine and mammal *rehabilitation*," Trevon said as if he were explaining something very complicated to a toddler. "There's way more advanced degrees to get before you're even halfway qualified for that stuff."

Metford looked at Ava and shrugged.

"So you wouldn't have had access to pentobarbital?" Ava asked.

They shook their heads, both looking equally confused.

"What's that?" Trevon asked.

"It's the drug that killed your friend, Banks Becker," Ava said, watching closely for their reaction.

"We already told you that none of us ever took hard drugs. Never. Only weed on special occasions and alcohol. The alcohol was a lot. There doesn't need to be a special occasion to drink. But none of us would have ever injected anything, I'm telling you. I'm positive. Why would we have risked our futures for it? Banks was supposed to be going into the Air Force at the end of summer." She paused. Tears glistened in her eyes. "Do you know how excited he was about that? He talked about it all the time. Since our sophomore year." Her voice cracked and her chin quivered.

Trevon took her hand. "She's right. He was an ass sometimes—hell, most of the time—but he was a pretty straight arrow. He smoked, but swore that this summer was the end of that because he didn't want to risk his career. Always was talking some shit about being an astronaut someday." He looked to the floor and squeezed Nova's hand.

"Pentobarbital isn't exactly a drug people use to get high," Ava said.

The couple looked at her, confused again.

"Then what is it?" Trevon asked.

"Veterinarians use it to euthanize animals," Ava said.

"And they use it in state executions," Metford added.

Nova's hand flew to cover her mouth and she turned wide, stricken eyes to Trevon.

"How the hell did Banks get a hold of it?" Trevon asked, brow furrowing deeply and drawing down over the bridge of his nose.

"That's what we are trying to figure out," Ava said.

"Jesus, Trey, they're saying he was murdered, I think," Nova said, turning to Ava. "That's what you're saying, right?"

"Yes. I'm sorry, but that's how it looks. We need to ask if you two would consent to a polygraph test," she said.

"Absolutely," Nova said with no hesitation.

"Yes, of course," Trevon nodded. "We didn't have anything to do with his death, and we'll do whatever it takes to help find whoever did."

"Polygraphs aren't admissible in court, though," Nova said.

"No, but we use the results to further our investigations," Ava told her.

"We'll get the tests scheduled and get back to you," Metford said, looking to Ava and standing.

She stood and closed her tablet. "We'll see ourselves out."

Before the door shut behind them, Nova broke down into sobs.

Ava texted Santos to let her know they would speak with Kalen and meet her and Ashton back outside in twenty minutes.

"I take it we're also talking with Mr. Hometown," Metford commented.

"Jeez, stop. I don't want to be explaining it to Sal when you screw up and call him that to his face and he complains about you."

Metford chuckled and held up his hands. "Alright, Agent Killjoy."

Kalen still seemed every bit as nervous and anxious as he had on their previous visit. The dark circles under his eyes were proof that he had not been sleeping so well, either. Ava suspected the friends were all as tired of being away from home as she and her team were, but with the added stress of losing three friends in such a short time.

"I have no idea what that even is," Kalen said when asked about the drug in question.

Ava explained it to him, and his reaction mirrored Trevon and Nova's. Raw shock and disbelief.

"Who would even have access to it, then? Certainly, none of us. Not Banks, either." He took a ragged breath and looked out the window. "Are you saying someone murdered him? Or could he have..." He let his words trail off and shook his head. "He wouldn't have taken it no matter what he thought it was. Banks didn't like needles. Whined like a bitch when the doctor had to give him a shot for anything. Besides, they wouldn't let him in the Air Force if he was a junkie, right?" His breath hitched and he looked back out the window.

Ava gave him a moment before continuing. "Mr. Hamilton, would you agree to a polygraph?"

He turned to her wide-eyed and shook his head. "Why? I didn't kill anyone. I didn't do anything wrong. Why should I take a lie detector test?"

"We're just trying to rule all his friends out," Metford said.

"No. I won't take one. I don't trust those things. Too many reports of people being wrongly accused because of them. No. And you can't force me to take one, either. I know for a fact they aren't admissible in court." His tone rose as if he were getting frantic.

Ava held up a hand and nodded. "You're right, Mr. Hamilton. It's totally your choice, and if you don't want to take a polygraph, you don't have to. That's your right. We'll leave you alone for now, and be in contact if we need anything further from you." She stood and walked out the door.

Ashton and Santos were just coming out of Akira and Cai's room.

"Well, they're going to take a polygraph," Ashton said.

"And a little warning about how easily they veer off-course and into the realm of the paranormal would have been exceptionally nice," Santos added.

Ava chuckled. "Do they still think ghosts did it?"

"Current theory is a spectral entity," Santos said. "Whatever that means."

"So they didn't know anything about the drug?" Ava asked.

Ashton shook his head. "No, they were both genuinely shocked and truly upset by the revelation that their friend had been murdered."

Ava nodded and headed toward the door. Progress was slow, but it was happening finally. She could at least be satisfied with that.

The bad thing was that she couldn't help but think that Kalen was the most likely suspect in the murder and that he knew where Desiree was. Had he also killed Jonathan? Maybe. It was the most likely scenario.

Why would Kalen have killed the men? Maybe he was secretly in love with Desiree. Maybe he harbored ill will toward all of them because he was so different and didn't really fit into their group. People had become killers for less.

CHAPTER THIRTY-SEVEN

Two days later, Ava and Sal went back to Kalen's room at the hotel to speak with him about his past.

He opened the door, and the dark circles under his eyes had become darker, his face paler and his cheeks more sunken. His gaze darted from Ava to Sal and he licked his lips nervously as he stepped back and motioned them inside.

"Mr. Hamilton," Sal started. "We need to ask you some questions about your past."

"Okay," he said, sitting stiffly in a chair. His face was fixed in an expression of expectation.

"It seems that some of your past..." Sal let her voice fade as she looked toward the window and spread her hands. "It seems that some of your *indiscretions* were a little harder to find out than others."

He nodded stiffly.

"We talked to three of your old college buddies," Ava told him.

He blinked at her but said nothing. Tiny beads of perspiration glistened at his hairline.

"They told us some very interesting things about you, Mr. Hamilton," Sal said.

"Like that you used to deal drugs," Ava added. "All kinds of drugs. Their words, not mine."

He swallowed hard and his throat made a little clicking noise. His fingers were laced together so tightly that his knuckles were white. He shook his head.

Ava nodded. "Yes. That's exactly what they told us, Kalen. Said you mostly dealt in pills and powders, but you'd been known to deal with liquids, too. Would that have been injectables?"

He shook his head again and opened his mouth to say something, but didn't.

"Now is the time to come clean, Mr. Hamilton. If you gave Banks the pentobarbital… well, maybe you didn't know it would have deadly results," Sal said as if offering an explanation.

"No, I didn't give it to him. I never dealt in anything that was to shoot up. Not that I know of, anyway. It was easy money, and it was mostly harmless drugs. Just party drugs, or drugs like Adderall that helped people study so they could pass an exam or something." His eyes rolled back and forth like those of a scared animal.

Sal shook her head. "Nope. We're not buying that you didn't know what you were doing was harmful."

"I picked the shit up from a location, I delivered it to another, and at the end of the month, there would be an envelope of cash waiting for me in my mailbox. Easy money, and I never took the stuff myself and I never gave any of it to my friends. Ever."

"Kalen, we know you probably didn't mean to hurt Banks," Ava said.

Tears streamed down his drawn cheeks. "No, no. I never did anything to him. He was my best friend. I swear to God, I don't know anything about what happened to him. And I know what I did back then was stupid. I was an idiot. For money. All for money. How do you think I afforded to even come out here for an entire month?" he pointed out. "I don't have money like Banks or Jonathan. I didn't get a huge sign-on bonus from a job like Trey and Nova did. I had to do what I could to get by. I don't want stupid mistakes from my past to ruin my future. You understand that, right?"

He broke out into a desperate smile and held his hands out toward Ava across the table. "You believe me, right? I even told you what I thought might have happened. Not that I want that to be the truth, but

Banks was really in love with Desiree, and I don't know what he might have done if things had gone off the rails in that part of his life. If he did kill Jonathan, or Desiree, even by accident, he might have killed himself because of the guilt."

"And that would be awfully convenient, wouldn't it, Kalen? If the killer killed himself in the end. That's *not* usually how these situations tend to work out, though," Ava assured him.

"I came clean about the poltergeist pranks I pulled at the lake house, didn't I?" He nodded dramatically. "I did. But I also told you that I didn't pull all those pranks."

"Why don't you tell us about the pranks that you *didn't* pull, Mr. Hamilton," Sal suggested.

"Yes, of course. There were several. Like when Nova woke up and found Desiree and Jonathan's window open that first night. That wasn't me. I was the first one asleep that night. I was exhausted from the ride up there and the heat. Three beers and I was sleeping like a baby all night. And the night Akira and Cai found their window open. They thought it was Nova pranking them because they had laughed at her and called her a chicken. Nova swore it wasn't her, though, and now, I believe her. We were all in town together at least twice and went back to the house together only to find that Desiree and Jonathan's personal belongings had been moved around and were missing. Days later, those things would show up in random places. I didn't have anything to do with that, either. Personal things were off-limits for me. I just didn't think it would be right to touch their personal things, you know?"

Ava scrutinized his behavior and the look in his eyes. He seemed to be telling the truth, but some people are good liars. If he wouldn't consent to a polygraph, she would have no way of knowing if he was being completely truthful or not.

"Okay, if I give you a list of all the pranks I pulled, and all the ones that I know for sure weren't me, you could talk to Akira and Cai. Find out how many of the pranks they were responsible for. Do the same with Nova and Trevon. Whichever pranks are left unclaimed were probably done by the killer. I think someone was toying with us up there the whole time. At the time, we all just tried to brush it off. We were only interested in having a good time, and didn't want to think that someone might have legitimately been in the house with us or intending to harm any of us."

Ava and Sal shared a look and Sal finally nodded.

"Alright, Kalen. You make us that list, and we'll see where it goes from there."

He heaved a relieved sigh and smiled. "Thank you. You'll see I'm right." He seemed to relax as he got up and took a notebook from his bag on the floor at the end of his bed. "What about that shoeprint? Did you ever find out who it belonged to?"

"I'm sorry, Mr. Hamilton," Sal said, standing. "That information is given out on a need-to-know basis, and you don't need to know. Not just yet anyway." She motioned for Ava to follow her and headed for the door. "You make that list, Mr. Hamilton. Be very thorough. Very detailed. We'll be back to collect it later."

He nodded and gave them a wan smile as Sal closed the door.

CHAPTER THIRTY-EIGHT

Later in the day, Ava sat at a table in the conference room with hardcopy files spread out before her. There were so many moving parts that she had to force herself to focus on only one case at a time. Since Banks' death had been ruled homicide, and Jonathan's was suspicious, there was even more pressure on the team to find Desiree. Each time Ava tried to focus solely on the missing woman's case, though, it somehow meandered into the others. They were tied together and she needed to figure out how.

She pulled out the original evidence list from the lake house. It didn't include the newest findings because it had been printed before the hair, thread, boot print, and beer cans had been entered into the system. With a sigh, she folded the paper in half and placed it to the side. She needed to print out the new list. Turning to her tablet, she brushed the paper and it fell to the floor. When she picked it up, she saw that a partial fingerprint and the adhesive residue from the master suite were right at the top.

After a call to the lab, she confirmed that the residue still had not been processed. There was no telling what it was doing there or what it might have been used for. They did have one piece of useful evidence: a partial print lifted from the mirror did not match any prints from the friends or the owners.

"So, who's print was it?" she asked Brianna, the technician who'd been processing the evidence.

"Well, we don't know. It could have been there forever, you know. The house is a rental property," she answered, sounding annoyed.

"Well, there were other prints in the house—partials, too, right?"

"Yes."

"Did it match any of those prints?" Couldn't the lab techs ever just give pertinent information without having to be drilled with questions?

"No, it didn't match anything we have. Not in the databases. Not in the evidence from your current cases. Nothing."

"Thanks," Ava said. "When do you think you will have a list for the adhesive?"

Brianna huffed, not bothering to mask her irritation. "Listen, we already told you that the list of possible uses for that tape is practically endless. It can be used for *anything*. We have to prioritize and get answers for the things that we can actually get answers for. That adhesive residue? It's going to take a while. A long while. We're swamped with evidence just from this lake house case alone, and we're doing the best we can to get it analyzed. I'll call you when we get the answers you want for the residue."

"Thanks," Ava said, disconnecting the call angrily.

Sal approached the table. "Getting anywhere with all this?" she asked, eyeing the scatter of paper files.

"Partial print matches nothing. Maybe it belongs to the ghost that was haunting the place," she said sarcastically.

"Hey, wouldn't that be something?" Sal raised her eyebrows.

Ava nodded. "I'm spinning my wheels here, Sal. I need to know what that industrial tape was used for and I need to know whose print that was on the mirror, but I've got neither."

"You think that's where your answers will be?"

She nodded again. "I feel it in my bones."

"Remember, stick to hard evidence. You've done great with that so far, always pulling yourself and the team back when you start to deviate. It's a good job you've done. Keep at it."

"Yeah, I'll try." Ava noted that Sal wasn't just acting differently lately, now she even *looked* different. It wasn't anything overt like her hair was a different color or her clothes were different. It was more in her actions.

Small changes that were snowballing and turning into larger changes that were more easily noticed.

Sal tapped the table with her fingertip and gave a small smile. "I'll be back later. Call or text if you need me for anything before then."

Ava nodded. "Will do."

Sal walked out. She'd been going off by herself more often lately. At first, Ava thought she was only going out to gather more information about the case or maybe to talk to the local police, but she never returned with anything tangible. There was no new information, no new evidence, no new interviews—nothing new at all had been entered into the system.

Was Sal dealing with a personal matter that was drawing her attention away from the case? A few times, Ava had started to question her friend about it, but it never seemed to be the right time or place to broach the subject. Besides, Ava didn't like it when people pushed her for information she wasn't ready to give out. When she was ready, she would give it to whom she pleased. Maybe Sal was the same way, and Ava wanted to give her privacy. If she needed advice, help, or just someone to listen, she knew she could talk to Ava.

Ashton walked into the room with his tablet open in front of him. How did he even see where he was walking with that thing constantly in his face? Ava held up a paper and waved him over.

"Hey, Ashton," she greeted him.

He veered toward her and lowered the tablet. Barely. "What's up?"

"You think you could do me a favor?"

"I'll try."

"I talked to the lab and they're being super slow getting with the adhesive residue. Do you think you could make me a list of its most common uses? I don't want the whole speculative list of what it could be used for, just the common sense kind of stuff, like what someone would typically use it for. It's expensive. I don't think anyone would buy something like this to use just to hang a poster or tape up a fake vine."

He shook his head. "You wouldn't think so, but you really never know. I can get you a list, though, that's no problem." He flipped the cover closed on his tablet. "And I can get if faster than the lab any day of the week."

"Awesome. You're the best, Ashton."

Metford groaned and stretched in his chair at the next table. "Can I go chase a bad guy now?" he asked.

Ava chuckled. "As soon as we figure out who the bad guy is, I promise you can."

"I've made zero progress on these interviews. They were hard enough to live through in person, but having to read the transcripts is like cruel and inhumane treatment." He stood and stretched again. "I think you're right on that tape. It's a smart move to figure out what it was doing there. I'm no decorator or anything, but I don't think it was used for that, either. It's just weird that the rest of the stuff in that house was pristinely clean and then there was a piece of tape and the residue on the wall."

She nodded. "Yeah, weird to me, too. The owner hires cleaning crews to come in after tenants leave. Antonio said they do that even if it's just a weekend rental. The crew is very thorough. They even wipe the top of all the mirrors, every light fixture in the house gets cleaned, and even the plants."

He chuckled. "Well, they were fake as hell, though. Dust loves fake vines and plants."

She scoffed and nodded. "I guess. I wouldn't know from personal experience, though."

"Me neither." He looked at his watch. "Think we have time to run over to that Wendy's and grab a burger?" He grinned sheepishly and tilted his head toward the door.

"You have an addiction, Metford."

He shrugged. "I know. I need help." He took a step toward the door and looked at her questioningly.

She stood and shook her head again. "I see an intervention in your future. The near future."

"What about your own part in this?"

"My part? No, no. I'm innocent in this. You are the one who can't go a single day without having to grab two of those burgers and wolfing them down in one sitting. I'm telling you, Metford, you're going to be sorry one day. You'll eventually be a wheezing, obese glutton with clogged arteries who can't even walk a flight of stairs without risking a heart attack."

He gave her a cockeyed grin. "And you, Agent James, are an enabler, so you will be guilt-bound to help me wheeze my way through life." He got in the passenger seat and closed the door. "Besides, I don't think I have to worry about any of that."

She started the car. "Really? Why not? Because the Mighty Metford is resilient to the mundane illnesses of us mere mortals?" Were she and Metford finally moving past their differences? Dare she think they were *bonding*?

He laughed. "Nope. Nothing so fancy, even though I wish. I'm an FBI agent who goes out chasing down the guys that everybody else runs from. We catch serial killers, psychotic murderers, and just plain evil people, Ava. I don't think cholesterol will be what takes me down."

It was warm and bright outside. A few thick white clouds floated along the horizon like ships stalled on the shore of a faraway dream. It was easier to think about the clouds and the sky and the weather than about what Metford had said. It made it easier to make-believe that he was wrong and that she, at least, lived a perfectly normal life like the billions of other normal people in the world.

CHAPTER THIRTY-NINE

The day had finally arrived for the FBI search team to arrive. Ava had been up since before dawn waiting anxiously for them. Ten days. That's how long it had taken to finally get them there. She hoped like hell it wasn't too late for Desiree. If the woman was still alive, and she was smart—which apparently she was, she had the degree to prove that—maybe she had found shelter somewhere in the woods and was waiting to be rescued.

There was the question of provisions, though, and Ava knew the outlook for Desiree Smith was grim. It wasn't impossible that she was still alive, just improbable.

Hours later, the search team arrived. Sal and Ava met them and gave them the information and instructions. The search team leader was a real hard-ass. Cooper Alto was a middle-aged Italian who still spoke with a New York accent even though he had been out of the city for two decades. He still had the big city manners—that brusque attitude toward everyone, and especially toward a female agent who deigned to give him orders. He didn't like the dynamic, and was quick to show it.

He grated on Ava's nerves and threatened to send her temper into overdrive with his chauvinistic attitude. He was smart about his quips, though. He said and did nothing that would get him into much trouble with his superiors. The actions and mannerisms were just that of a hard-ass, by-the-book agent, but his words always seemed to be a dig at women in general, and there wasn't a female on his team. Ava knew without asking that was by design.

"Ava, why don't you go back to the conference room at the hotel and work the files some more?" Sal asked in a way that was more of an order than a request as soon as they were out of Agent Alto's earshot.

Ava pursed her lips. She wanted to stay, but she didn't want to seem argumentative. Especially in front of Alto and his team. It would only undermine Sal's authority even further in his eyes. Ava nodded and shot Alto a sour look behind his back before turning to leave.

Back at her table, Ava took out Jonathan Williams' autopsy report and focused on just what was on that paper.

If someone smaller and weaker than Jonathan wanted him dead, they could have slipped him the extra sedative in a drink or even in his food. That would have made it feasible for that smaller person to overpower him in the tub and hold him under the water long enough for him to drown. It only took one inhalation underwater to kill a person.

In the group of friends, only the women were smaller and weaker than Jonathan. The men were all of comparable size and strength. Banks was even more muscular and seemed quite scrappy. It made sense, given that he had been preparing to start a career in the military.

It was enough to make her take a second look at all the women in the group. Nova, Akira, and even Desiree. If Desiree and Jonathan had fought and she had left to get away from him, there was a chance that she had been injured and spent her time away brewing over it. It wasn't impossible for Ava to envision an abused girlfriend exacting revenge and ending up killing him.

"Metford?" she said.

From the next table, he turned to her. "Yeah?"

"Want to go back to the hotel with me for more questioning?"

"Not really," he said, sighing as he stood to join her.

"Santos," she said, turning to the table where Santos sat looking through photos from the lake house.

"Yeah? Got something?" Santos stood and walked over to join them.

Ava told them her theory. Metford looked confused but nodded.

"You're right. That would explain Jonathan's death, anyway, but what about Banks? What happened… did this woman seduce him into shooting up? And how did she get the drug anyway?"

"I don't know," Ava admitted. "One thing at a time. Right now, I just want to go back and question the women."

Metford and Santos followed her to the car.

"Can we talk to Nova last?" Metford asked. "You know she's going to be worse than ever when you throw this new theory at her feet, right?"

Ava shook her head as she knocked on Nova's door. "Best to get it over with as fast as possible."

Nova opened the door and didn't even bother with her usual sarcasm or annoyance, she just walked away from the door and sat in her usual chair without speaking. Trevon roused from the bed where he'd obviously been napping. He glared at them and slid off the bed and headed for the bathroom.

"Nova, I need to ask you about your relationship with Jonathan Williams," Ava said without sitting.

Nova scoffed and bobbed one shoulder. "What about it? She was my friend's fiancé. We were all friends." She rolled her eyes and leaned her head back, closing her eyes and pinching the bridge of her nose as if in pain. "I have a headache, so, if you could step on the gas pedal, I'd really appreciate it."

"You and Mr. Williams got along?"

"Yes, we did." She lifted her head.

"Were you upset that he wasn't treating your friend right?" Santos asked.

Nova shifted her gaze to Santos and shook her head and then nodded. "I'm sorry, is it wrong to be upset when one friend treats another like shit? What's this all about?" She looked back to Ava.

"Did Jonathan get more aggressive or violent with Desiree at the lake house?"

Nova didn't answer. She sat perfectly still, assessing each of them for several seconds. "None of us liked how he treated her. Again, what's this got to do with anything?"

"There were bruises at the bottom of his collarbone. You know, like someone might have been holding him down in that tub. Someone smaller and weaker might have slipped him some extra sleeping medication so they would be able to overpower him. Could I see your thumbs, please?" Ava asked.

Nova shook her head in disbelief and shoved her spread hands toward Ava. "Whatever gets you out of my face for the day, lady. Already gotta see you tomorrow for that stupid lie detector test."

"Agent. It's Agent James or Ava. Not 'lady,'" Ava said, leaning to examine the shape and size of Nova's hands and thumbs. "Thank you. We might need to return to get impressions later." She turned to leave.

"That's it? You're just gonna come up in here and say some stupid shit like that, take a quick look at my hands, and then leave?"

Trevon came out of the bathroom.

"You don't need to look at his thumbs, too?" she asked, pointing to her boyfriend.

Ava looked pointedly at his hands. "No, they're far too large to be the killer's." She turned and the three agents filed quickly out of the room. She shut the door securely behind them.

"Told you," Metford said.

"And now it's over," Ava pointed out. "We don't have to deal with her for a whole other day."

"Whoopie."

"You think it was her?" Santos asked.

"Don't know. Her thumbs actually look thinner than the bruises, but an eight-by-ten glossy is all I have as reference. I just wanted to see if she would show me her hands willingly."

Santos grinned and nodded. "That was slick. She did it willingly, so it probably wasn't her."

"And she never flinched when I told her we might get impressions later." Ava knocked on Akira's door.

Cai answered. "Come in," he said immediately, showing them in congenially.

Akira sat on the foot of the bed, her legs crossed. She had a sketch pad on her lap. She looked up and smiled wanly at them as they entered. Putting the pad aside, she turned and got off the bed. "I was sort of hoping it was our food. I put in the order like three years ago."

"Sorry to disappoint," Ava said. "I just need to ask you about your relationship with Jonathan Williams. Did you two get along?"

Akira's gaze slipped toward Cai and then quickly back to Ava. She nodded and tucked hair behind her ear. "Yeah. We were all friends, you know."

"Were you closer to Desiree or Jonathan?" Santos asked.

Akira shook her head and scoffed. "Well, Des, naturally, but she was a package deal. To be her friend, you just sort of had to accept Jonathan, too."

"So, you didn't like him much?" Santos asked.

Akira wrung her hands and gave a nervous grin. "He was mean to Des, and I didn't like that. None of us did, but..." She looked to Cai and back to Ava.

"But what, Akira?" Ava asked.

"None of us wanted him *dead* just because he was a jerk to her. We all sort of figured that she would get her head on straight sooner or later. If she got sick of the way he treated her, she'd leave. She wanted to make it work between them, though. She really loved him."

"Did that bother you?"

She shook her head. "I thought it was nice that she was willing to try to make it work. So many people just walk away when something gets tough nowadays."

"After she disappeared, did you think he might have caused it?"

She shook her head, but not with conviction. "If I had thought Jonathan did anything to her, I would have called the cops, *pronto*. What's this about, anyway? I've already told you this before, and the local cops, too."

"There were bruises under Jonathan's collarbones as if someone might have held him down in that tub."

Akira gasped and shook her head. "That's awful. Who would do that?" She looked to Cai, who moved to her side immediately and put his arm around her.

"Because of the extra dose of sleeping pills in his system, we're thinking it was someone smaller and weaker than him," Ava said.

"You think Akira did that to him?" Cai asked, his eyes wide.

Ava shrugged. "We're just going where the facts take us." She looked at Akira's stricken face. "Would you mind letting me see your thumbs, Akira?"

She and Cai exchanged a look and then she held out one hand. The other, she kept securely around his waist.

Ava leaned close and looked, nodded. "The other one, please."

After a moment's hesitation, she presented the other hand, fingers splayed. Ava looked at it and then nodded again.

"Thank you. We might be back later to get impressions of your hands." She turned to leave.

"Wait, don't you need like a warrant or something to get that?" Cai asked.

Ava smiled at him. "Just like with the polygraph, not if you give consent willingly. If you have nothing to hide, there's no reason to withhold consent."

Akira nodded. "I don't mind. I'll do it if it'll help find who did these terrible things to our friends. I already agreed to the polygraph tomorrow."

"Do you need to see my hands?" Cai asked suspiciously.

Ava glanced at them and shook her head. "Your thumbs are too square-tipped to have made the bruises, and besides, I don't think you would have needed to drug him to hold him down. You're about the same size as Mr. Williams."

Cai looked confused but nodded.

Outside, Metford shook his head. "Cai isn't the same size as Jonathan." Santos shook her head.

"But did you see how blocky his fingertips were?" Ava asked.

"They were, but I didn't notice until you mentioned it," Santos said.

Ava nodded. "No way those thumbs would have left only the little light, circular bruises I saw in the photos."

Ava wasn't exactly working on the most scientific level, but she thought she had made progress again by working the human and emotional side of the case. Science could do little to gauge a person's reaction to certain emotional stimuli. She didn't think either woman had anything to do with Jonathan's murder or they wouldn't have been so willing to hold out their hands for inspection, and they would likely have argued about the impressions.

But Akira had hesitated. Did that mean something?

CHAPTER FORTY

Ava made it to the police station as Kalen left. She went inside and found Sal.

"I figured you'd show up," Sal said.

"Yeah, had to come find out how the friends did on their tests. I just saw Kalen leaving with the cop. He looked mad."

Sal nodded. "He's upset. He still didn't want to come in, but I finally persuaded him."

"How'd you do that? He was adamant he wasn't doing the test," Ava said.

"Told him I could tear his life upside down with all the information from his past if he didn't do it." She looked around. "Not the most admirable tactic, but it worked."

"So, how'd they do?"

"They all passed the pertinent parts with flying colors." She nodded toward the door. "Everyone but Kalen Hamilton, that is. He definitely knows something and is hiding it."

Ava's heart raced and anger rose in her chest. "I knew it," she said angrily. "I knew he had something to do with all this. Why'd you let him walk?"

"Well, for starters, he's only going as far as the hotel. And we can't arrest him based on the polygraph results. We don't have any hard evidence against him."

"We need to really turn up the heat on him, break him. I don't think it would take a lot, either." She snapped her fingers. "Let me bring him back to the station for questioning, maybe let him sit in a cell for a few hours until I have time to get to him, you know, let him worry."

Sal shook her head. "No evidence, no cell, Ava. That's how this works and you know that." She turned Ava toward the door and held up a finger. "We're in a cornfield here, wait until we're outside."

Cornfield was Sal's way of telling Ava they were surrounded by big ears that might overhear things she'd rather they did not.

At the cars, Sal looked around. "We go dragging him in here and tossing him in a cell right now, it could screw up the entire case. Do you want to see a murderer walk because we got ahead of ourselves and didn't follow procedure?"

Ava shook her head. "Of course not. You know me better than that," she defended.

"Alright, then. Let's do this by the book. And I mean by the book. Take no liberties at all with the interpretation of rules. Just follow them to the letter, and make sure the rest of the team does the same. Can you do that?"

Ava nodded. "Yes, I can." It felt like she was being tested, or that she was being given a heads-up about something, but she didn't know what.

"Good. Now, go get the evidence on Mr. Hamilton. Get the hard evidence and get it quickly… and *by the book.*"

Ava nodded. "Yes, ma'am."

Sal nodded and gave her a small smile. What was that look in her eyes? It was uncharacteristic for her. Not the usual hard glint or confidence she usually had during the last leg of an investigation. It was softer, and it made Ava feel peculiar. Something was definitely going on with Sal. Again, it wasn't the right time or place to ask, either.

Ava got in her car and headed to the hotel. The team had missed something in the evidence, failed to link something that needed linking, and it was up to her to figure out what so a man wouldn't get away with murder.

As she pored over the files and photos, taking notes obsessively, Ava heard thunder mere seconds before lightning ripped across the sky.

Stuttering light, bright enough to hurt, came through the windows followed by a super loud whipcrack sound. Five minutes later, Agent Alto entered the conference room. His clothes were dripping wet and his cheeks were ruddy.

"We're calling it a day. Be back tomorrow morning, weather permitting," he announced, looking directly at Metford. "Didn't get more than a quarter-mile before the storm rolled in."

Metford looked up and shook his head. "Boss should be here in a few minutes. Until then, she's in charge." He pointed to Ava.

Alto blinked slowly and inhaled deeply as he turned his eyes to Ava. "I trust you heard what I said."

"I did," Ava said, fighting the urge to be a jerk to him.

He nodded once, curtly, and left.

"Wow, he's such a cuddly muffin," Metford remarked. "And he *likes* you, Agent James." He chuckled. "Can't believe you didn't just take him to school over that attitude. You certainly don't care to rip into me."

"Yeah, but he's not worth the effort. I know a lost cause when I see one," she said, looking back to her papers.

"Aw," Santos cooed. "I think she's saying you're not a total lost cause and waste of effort, Mettie."

He nodded and put a hand over his heart. "I know. Ain't that a revelation. Hey, Ava, you care to meet my family on Thanksgiving and tell them the news? And maybe even let the Bureau know?"

Ava grinned and shook her head. "And here I was holding out hope all this time that I was right about you." She motioned toward her files. "Why don't you make yourself extra super useful and help me out here? Put your nose in the files and let's see what we can find. We missed something that implicates Kalen Hamilton, and I need to find what it is. You too, Santos, unless the boss has you doing something else."

"No, I'm still logging details from the nine million photos of the house and surrounding property. I'd jump at the chance to do something else for a while," Santos said.

Ava nodded. "Great, because I could use the extra eyes and opinions."

The three worked together for several hours before calling it a day. Ava didn't go out for dinner. She let Santos, Metford, and Ashton go while she retreated to her room with a box of donuts and two large coffees. Sugar and caffeine were her go-to for that little added burst of energy and concentration. It was going to be a long night, but she was determined to find evidence on Kalen.

CHAPTER FORTY-ONE

At two in the morning, Ava reached for another donut. Her fingers hit the bottom of the box and searched blindly as she continued to scour autopsy photos again. Finally, she looked at the box. It was empty. So was the second coffee cup.

She groaned and let her head flop back against the wall. Her neck was stiff and her back muscles burned. She let the tablet slip to the cover on the bed and closed her eyes. They had missed nothing. There was nothing there to pin on Kalen.

If there was nothing in their files, nothing from their investigation that would connect Kalen to the deaths and disappearance, she would have to figure out some other angle to hit it from.

"The search team," she said aloud, sitting straight. "I'll go with them in the morning."

She met Sal at seven the next morning in the conference room.

Sal grinned and held up a cup of coffee. "You're here earlier than usual," she said.

Ava tipped her own cup in Sal's direction. "Cheers. Yeah, I was up until two going over all the files and evidence, personal notes, and making new ones."

"Dedicated as usual. What did you find? Anything to link our Mr. Hamilton to the deaths or disappearance?"

Ava shook her head. "Santos and Metford even helped me for several hours. There's nothing new. We didn't miss anything. The only thing I got that was sort of new was the idea that maybe someone smaller and weaker, like possibly a female, drugged Jonathan and then held him under the water. It made sense with the bruises we found. We went to the hotel and questioned Akira and Nova, but I don't think they did it. Now that they passed the polygraph, I'm convinced neither of them did it. That still leaves me with nothing. If Kalen did it, his hands would have left larger marks, I believe. Just like with Cai, his fingers are broad on the ends. Too blunt to have left those small bruises."

Sal nodded. "So, where to go from here?"

Ava grinned. "Well, that's why I'm here. I wanted to know if it would be okay if I went with the search team today."

"No, I really don't think that's a good idea at all, and I don't have to explain why."

"You don't, but what if I promise to hold my temper in check, just overlook Alto's prehistoric attitude, and do what I'm here to do?"

Tilting her head, Sal scrutinized Ava and tapped one fingernail against the side of the paper coffee cup. "I don't know. He's really bad. And it's not so much your temper I worry about, it's your mouth. I know how sharp your tongue can be, and a man like Alto… well, if you cut him with your words, he'll just get worse. That could compromise our investigation."

Ava shook her head. "I swear on my life, I'll just let his words fall on deaf ears. I need this, Sal. I can't sit here and go over the files again. I'll claw out my own eyes. I know most of it by heart, and there's no good I can do from here. I need to feel useful and like I'm making progress."

Sal held up a hand. "Okay, okay, but the instant you think you won't be able to keep your mouth shut and your temper in your pocket, I want you out of there. No matter what. The investigation comes first. Got it?"

Ava didn't mind letting her relief and gratitude show with a big sigh of her shoulders. "Thank you, Sal." She turned and had to fight the urge to run out the door before Sal could change her mind.

Alto watched her approach with cold, disinterested eyes, hands on hips. "Agent James, may I help you in some way already this morning?

Agent Rossi already gave me the instructions for the day. She didn't wait until the last minute, either. She sent them via text last night."

"Yeah, she's good that way, isn't she? Really got it together." She grabbed one of the reflective vests from the back of the truck and put it on.

"What are you doing, Agent James? Are you confused about your own orders for the day?"

She shook her head. "Nope. Not at all. I'm going to accompany the search team today."

"No," he snapped, waving a finger back and forth in the air. "No. I don't need another person out there to worry about. Me and my five agents are plenty enough. It's not like we're searching the Amazon. It's Bumbee Ridge, for God's sake."

Ava smiled and nodded. "Yep, in County Crider. I know." He was not going to make it easy for her to keep her promise to Sal, but she set her determination like stone and kept her measured, neutral smile.

"I don't know what you're playing at here, but don't get in my way. This is still my search team and I'm still in charge. You're only here until I say otherwise. Got it?" He glared at her, the small muscles in his face tensing.

Ava nodded. "I got it. I won't get in your way."

"Come on, team!" he yelled, his baritone voice cutting through the chatter of the agents and the noise of the excited dogs. "We got us a guest today, but she won't get in the way. Let's get walking. I'd like to make it far enough today that we actually have to use the quads and trailers to get there tomorrow."

Ava followed the team into the woods. They didn't walk single file on the path, but spread out, putting about ten feet between themselves. Each agent had a dog on a leash. They had marked the area already searched with tape and spray paint on trees, and Alto had the grid map at the lead so he could guide the group.

For the first half-hour, Ava didn't have much of a complaint about the search team's progress, but once she realized they weren't paying any attention to possible evidence on the ground, she started getting frustrated. She had come prepared with gloves and plastic evidence bags. The search team members had the same gear, but none of them wore gloves or took the bags out.

She stopped and picked up a hair ribbon that one of the agents had stepped on. Cramming it into a bag, she hurried forward, trying to look ahead of them, but it did little good. By the time she yelled to point out a piece of a strap that looked like it was from a belt, a dog and an agent had already trampled over it.

"Dammit!" she yelled, rushing forward to grab the piece of belt and ram it into a bag.

"Something wrong, Agent James?" Alto asked with a smug grin.

"Your agents aren't even paying attention to the evidence on the ground. They are trampling over everything, and so are the dogs."

He shrugged and chuckled. "I'm sorry, but we're here to find a missing girl, not act like the good fairies of the forest picking up trash." He walked toward her, letting the other agents go on ahead. "And if you want to play trash lady, feel free, but if you want us to be picking up forest litter, we won't. That's not our job. Call a cleanup crew."

Ava struggled to not just go nuclear on him. "Agent Alto, there might be something in the evidence your men are walking all over that could bring a murderer to justice and save a woman's life."

He scoffed and shook his head. "Nothing can save her life. You're not dumb; you know just like I do that girl is dead or she would have been found already. It's been two weeks. Now, if you don't mind, we are moving on."

She stood with empty evidence bags clenched in one gloved hand, the other curled into a fist. If she hadn't made a promise, she might have told him what she thought of his brutish tactics, but she had made that promise, and she did want Desiree found whether she was alive or not. Her family deserved closure and justice.

CHAPTER FORTY-TWO

Tagging along for a while longer, Ava saw that something was going to have to be done to change the way they were searching the forest. She picked up an unopened Berry Fruit Blast Goody's Powder package that had very recently been in the mouth of one of the big bloodhounds, or that had been slobbered on by one of the dogs. She flung the single-serve package from her glove into a bag and stripped off the gloves with a frustrated grimace.

"Agent Alto, stop the search party, please!" she called out loudly as she jogged toward him.

He turned and scoffed. "No way. I told you already—"

"I remember what you said, but your team is walking over and ruining evidence that we need. I need you to stop until I can get some help in here to walk in front and collect it *before* the dogs roll it around in their mouths and the men squash it into the ground underfoot."

"I'm sorry," he replied, giving a dry chuckle and shaking his head. "You don't give the orders around here. This is my team, and I'm in charge of the search." He made a shooing gesture. "Find your lane and stay in it, agent."

"I am asking you very politely. I'm not giving an order. But you really need to stop. Just take a break and rest the dogs until backup gets here. Please." It was almost physically painful to force herself to be pleasant to the man.

"You do what you have to do, and I'll do the same. I can't delay the search for half a day just because you asked nicely. We'll take our lunch break, but then we're moving on whether or not your backup gets here."

She called Sal to let her know they needed to be out in front of the search crew to gather evidence *before* it could be trampled and chewed. Any prints that might have been on the packaging of the Goody's Powder had surely been rendered useless by the dog's saliva. Same for any DNA that might have been there.

Thirty minutes later, Alto whistled and yelled at his team.

"Whoa, wait a minute, Agent Alto," Ava said, holding up her hands in front of him. "Come on, I'm sure they're almost here. Five more minutes."

He shook his head. "Sorry, little lady. I'm not taking orders from you today. We have waited long enough. I told you thirty minutes," he commented as he looked at his watch, and continued, "and that's up now." He motioned for his men to start moving forward again.

Ava was in a predicament. She had tried explaining the situation to him, but the man wouldn't listen simply because she was a woman. She had tried to keep the peace for the sake of the case and was still trying to play nice to keep from compromising the investigation. But then, Alto's actions were compromising it already, and he didn't seem to care one bit.

She stepped in front of him again, anger visible on her face. "Alright, that's it. I *am* ordering you to stop this search party now. You will wait, or you will be explaining why to your superiors." She grabbed the evidence bags and shook them in front of him. "They're killing me. Almost every piece of this has been trampled, nosed, licked, and scooted through the dead leaves and squirrel shit. Probably none of it is viable now. Because of your obstinance."

"How about this? I'll call it a wrap for the day and take my men right the hell out of here. How's that sit with you? Then you can explain why we up and stopped for the day. I don't take no browbeating from the likes of you, *Agent* James." He took out his phone.

"The likes of me? Seriously?" Ava asked, growing angrier by the second. "How about you make good on your little threat and just see where that lands you?"

"Agents!" Sal yelled from fifty feet away. "Stand down, both of you." There was no denying the authority in her tone. There was no anger, just authority—something Ava hoped to master one day soon.

That day wouldn't be as long as she was facing Cooper Alto, though. He just brought out the worst in her.

"Agent James, what's going on?" Sal stood facing them.

Ava started to explain, and Alto cut in, talking over her. After the third time, she turned on him.

"Do you mind, agent?" she shot at him. She turned back to Sal. "This is what I'm dealing with." She continued to try to explain the situation.

Sal held up a hand when he tried to cut in again. "I'll hear your side, too, agent. You'll have your chance to talk in a minute."

Ava finished but her cheeks still burned with anger. She walked over to join Metford and the two officers from the local sheriff's department while Sal spoke with Alto.

It took about fifteen minutes for Sal to de-escalate the situation, and she was not happy as they moved ahead of the search team. She gave Ava a hot look, and she knew she had pissed off the boss. There was nothing to be done except take the consequences when they arose.

When they were a hundred feet ahead of the search party, Sal walked over to Ava. "You know, you can't go pulling rank to try and get your way, Ava."

"That's not what I was doing."

Sal held up a hand and shook her head. "You were yelling at him. You were mad enough to throw a punch. I'm not sure if you would have or not had I not shown up when I did, but he was calling his superiors. He had witnesses to the way you were acting, which was unprofessional. If you want people to do as you say, you have to act with authority, not with temper tantrums. Understand? He was getting ready to bring a shitstorm down on your head that you might not have been able to get out from under for years. Now, as your boss, I'm telling you to never let that happen again. Ever."

Ava felt completely chastened and gave a slow nod. "Yes, ma'am. I'm sorry I let my temper get out of control."

"You should ride a desk for the next month because of it, but I don't think that's where you will be of the most benefit, but don't think for a minute that I won't put you on desk duty if anything like this comes up again."

Ava nodded, angrier at herself than at Alto at the moment. She'd been stupid and lost control at the worst possible time. She even hated to admit that Alto was right. It had been three weeks. Rain had spattered the whole place. For all she knew, all this evidence could have been left by anyone from town. She'd just been too tunnel-visioned to see it clearly.

She turned to take a deep breath and look into the woods when she saw what looked like a bear wallow. In the center of it, there was a woman's scrunchie. She gasped and pointed excitedly to it.

"A scrunchie," she said to Sal.

They went over and stood at the edge of the wallow.

"Let me get some pictures before we disturb the area," Sal said.

"It looked like a bear wallow to start with, but I don't think that's what it is," Ava said, squatting to get a closer look at the disturbed leaves and grass and deadfall.

"Nope," Officer Beau said with confidence. "They don't make wallows out in the open like this. Looks more like a person bedded down, or otherwise pressed down the leaves and undergrowth. No bear fur in it, either."

Ava nodded. It was good to have someone along who understood wildlife and the woods a bit better than she and the team. "Could it be where a deer bedded down?"

He shook his head. "No. No animal did this," he said confidently.

Sal nodded for Ava to collect the scrunchie.

Seeing the scrunchie in the bag made Ava feel better. She barely cringed when she heard Alto yell at his team to get them moving again. Her team was far enough ahead that they could get more evidence that would be useable. She stood and looked around for anything else in the area before moving forward again.

Just like everything else in this case, she didn't know if it would be of worth. But at least it was something.

CHAPTER FORTY-THREE

"Hey!" Metford called out. He was only a few feet from the scrunchie site. He pointed. "Got a driver's license under the dead leaves here," he said.

"Get a perimeter up around this site. Don't let that search team near it," Sal ordered.

Officer Beau caught the roll of yellow tape Metford tossed to him. He and Officer Fulton strung it around tree trunks and bushes nearby.

"Is it Desiree Smith's license?" Ava asked, moving toward it.

"I didn't move it. It's facedown," Metford said.

Sal took photos and then nodded. Ava flipped it over with one gloved finger and then lifted it by the edges. "Scarlett Tomalin, Maine. Twenty-five. Expires next year," she read from the front. Scarlett was a pretty woman with dark brown hair and eyes. "Five-feet-seven, 120 pounds."

"Sounds a lot like the description of our missing woman," Sal mentioned.

Ava nodded. "A whole lot."

"Bag it. We'll run a check and find out who she is and why her license is out here in the middle of nowhere," Sal said, ducking to go under the yellow tape. "Let's keep going and stay ahead of the search team. God knows what that area would have looked like after they tramped through it."

Metford shot a conspiratorial look to Ava as they and the officers moved out to Sal's right, forming a search line.

"Ahead," Sal said. "Looks like a campsite."

The campsite sat to their right in a little alcove formed by the lay of the land and an outcropping of large, grey, moss-topped rocks. The brown tent was only really big enough to house one person, and had one flap tied back. It had been secured by standard pegs in the ground. Vines had grown and wrapped around the peg ropes. Forest debris littered the floor inside the shelter.

In front of the tent there was a blackened area surrounded by stones and covered in black soot and burned wood. The storm had come through the area, scattering the sooty ashes over the front of the tent and a nearby stump that had been used as a makeshift table. A pack of cigarettes lay in the center of the stump, crushed, wet, and ruined. A beer bottle lay on its side near the edge of the stump.

"Get a perimeter up. Make it twenty feet farther out all the way around than you normally would. I want all this secure," Sal ordered.

Metford and Beau worked to cordon off the area while Ava and Sal took photos and searched for more obscured evidence.

"There's too much to bag and tag, Sal," Ava said as she squatted at the edge of the tent and lifted the front off the ground a bit.

"We'll have to get a team out here to do it right. Forensics." She continued to take pictures. "Where'd that young officer get off to?"

Ava looked around. "His name's Fulton, and he was just right there on that rise a minute ago."

They continued photographing and searching for another half-hour before the search team passed them. Ava looked in the direction of their noise but only saw one agent's head as they passed in the distance.

"This was a good spot for a camp, I guess. Mostly hidden," Ava said.

"Yeah, and we could be wasting our time here."

"No, I think she was here. I bet that was her scrunchie we found back there, and she ended up here. There's long brown hair caught on the zipper of the tent. We may find her safe and sound yet," Ava said, allowing her hope to rise again.

Sal merely grunted. "Or maybe it's Scarlett Tomalin. Or someone else entirely."

Ava hated to admit it, but she was right.

A few more minutes passed and then Beau whistled to draw their attention. He pointed toward the trail. "Sheriff Anderson's here."

Ava looked at Sal. "Did you call him?"

"No. Must have been that Officer Burton," Sal said.

"Fulton," Ava corrected, looking around for him. "I still don't see him. Maybe it was him."

Sal shrugged. "Neither here nor there. This is still our investigation."

Ava hoped the sheriff was more amicable than Alto had been. As he came into view with Fulton by his side, Ava nodded in acknowledgment. He raised a hand.

He moved under the yellow tape, looking before he took each step. "Looks like you found a lifer-camp," he said, his sharp eyes scouring the area.

"A what?" Ava asked.

"Ah, what we call lifer-camps. Some of the homeless use the woods as their home. Not a whole lot we can do about it, but come spring, we always find one or two that didn't make it through the blistering deep-freeze." He shook his head. "Damn shame."

"I thought maybe we had found where Desiree had been taken to," Ava said.

"Taken to? Nah, it's likely she was here, though. Fulton said you found a hair tie thing back there a ways. She probably ended up bedding down here when she found the tent. Still say she left to scare her boyfriend. Make him think she was gone for good." He looked around shrewdly and shook his head. "She might have run into trouble out here seeing as how she wasn't equipped to stay more than a few hours or one night. A young girl can find herself in real trouble out here real fast."

"Yes, that's what I was thinking," Sal said. "This camp has obviously been here for a good while, and it hasn't been used regularly in a long time from the looks of it. If someone had grabbed her and brought her here, it would have been because that person knew about this campsite, which implies that it would belong to that person. There's no sign of that here. If she was here, it was purely by chance."

The sheriff nodded, satisfied that at least one of the team agreed with him. Ava didn't agree. Why was Sal just giving up on Desiree? Why wasn't she at least trying to hold out some bit of hope that the woman might still be alive? And why did everyone still think she had run away of her own free will? It didn't make sense. All the more reason for her to figure it out.

"We'll search more thoroughly tomorrow," Sal announced. "Let's get ready to move back out, everybody."

"Yep, the woods get dark a lot sooner than the rest of the land," Sheriff Anderson said. "Best get out while the getting is good."

Ava looked over the campsite a while longer, but she caught up with Sal and the sheriff before she risked having to walk out of the woods with Alto and his team.

CHAPTER FORTY-FOUR

Early next morning, before even the morning meeting, Sal and Ava took the scrunchie with them to the hotel. It was turquoise-blue satin with tiny yellow flowers embroidered all the way around it. If it had belonged to Desiree Smith, one of her friends might recognize it as such.

"You're sure that's not one she could have just walked in and bought from a hundred different stores?" Sal asked as they made their way to Nova's door.

"No. I searched online, and the only place I could find any design like it was from a specialty shop in the North Mall back home in Fairhaven. It comes in a three-pack. One of the trio is pearl white, the other has a net ribbon around it that has diamond-shaped jewels on the ends of the tassels," Ava explained. She had spent three hours last night scouring the internet for women's hair accessories trying to find the exact design but hadn't found the exact match. "Even the one I found wasn't exact. The flowers aren't the same, and the one in the mall only has three flowers that look more like sunflowers."

"Wow, that's a lot," Sal muttered, knocking on the door.

Ava shrugged. What could she say? It wasn't in her nature to be anything less than painfully thorough. Some would probably call it obsession, but she liked to believe she was just thorough.

Nova took one look at Sal and gave a small smile. "You're a new face around here. Come on in." She walked away as usual. "Does this mean that you have some new information?"

Trevon took a seat beside Nova. "What did you find out? Who killed Banks and Jonathan?"

Sal shook her head and nudged Ava to show the scrunchie. "Unfortunately, we still don't have the answer to that, but we did find this. I was wondering if either of you—"

"God, that's Desiree's scrunchie," Nova whispered, reaching for the bag.

"Please don't take it out. It's evidence," Sal said.

"Where'd you find this?" Nova asked, tears shimmering in her eyes.

"Are you sure it's hers, babe? I don't recognize it," Trevon frowned.

"Yeah, she wore it to tie up her hair at night. If she didn't, her curls would just turn into knots by morning, and then she'd almost be crying trying to get them out. Said she'd been pulling her hair up at night since she was eight." Nova reluctantly handed it back to Ava. "Where'd you find it?"

Ava cleared her throat. "Pretty far into the woods beside the lake house."

"Oh, God," she said, stifling a sob. "She's dead, too, isn't she?"

"We don't know anything yet," Sal said quickly. "Could she have dropped this when she went on one of those walks on the trail?"

Nova shook her head. "No, she didn't pull her hair up during the day. It gave her a headache if she did. She would've had that in her hair to go to sleep. She would've had it in when she…" She raised her hands and shrugged. "When she left, when she was taken?"

Sal shook her head. "We don't know that either. Not yet."

Akira said much the same thing, and her reaction was the same as Nova's had been. She was horrified to know the scrunchie had been found in the woods so far from the trail. She also told them that Desiree had bought that scrunchie from a flea market back in Fairhaven where a woman handmade a lot of women's accessories. Desiree was just that kind of person. She would buy from the flea market to help support locals rather than ordering online or going to the mall.

In the hall, Sal turned to Ava. "Well, we don't have to wait for the lab results to conclude that the hair tie belonged to our missing woman. I say we stop and talk to Mr. Hamilton before we leave."

Ava nodded. "That sounds right down my alley, actually."

Kalen opened the door looking like a deer in headlights. Ava thought it might be his default setting lately.

"May we come in, Mr. Hamilton?" Sal asked politely and with a smile.

"Ye-yeah," he stammered as he moved aside. "Sure. But if you're here to harass me about that polygraph, you can just forget it. I told you I don't trust those things, and you threatened me into taking it. Made me super nervous, and you see what happened because of it."

"No, no, Mr. Hamilton. We're not here about the polygraph," Sal told him. She reached for the bag containing the scrunchie and held it up. "I just wanted to come by and ask if you recognized this."

He looked at the scrunchie and shook his head. "Should I? I know what it is, but I don't use anything like that." He ran a hand up the back of his hair. "Not long enough. And I don't have a girlfriend at the moment who would wear it."

"It's not familiar to you at all?" Ava asked.

He shook his head. "No, it's not. You want me to take another polygraph to prove it?"

"You think you could pass it this time?" Ava remarked.

He huffed. "What do you want? I don't know what else I can do here."

"Did you hurt Desiree Smith?" Ava asked. "No polygraph, no more trying to tiptoe through the tulips with you. Just tell us straight up. Did you hurt Desiree?"

Kalen's face underwent a plethora of changes as if he were fighting with himself to maintain his cool. "No, I didn't hurt Des. I wouldn't hurt her. I had no fucking reason to hurt her," he nearly yelled through gritted teeth. His hands were balled into fists at his sides, and his eyes flared angrily at them.

"There's no need to get so upset, Mr. Hamilton," Sal said. "We're just trying to do our job."

"Yeah, and our job is to find out if you did something to Desiree. Or did you do something to Banks or Jonathan? Maybe it wasn't the woman you hurt; maybe it was the men who were crazy about her," Ava pursued the line of questioning.

Kalen went very still and then his face reddened as he shook his head. His hand shot out and batted a bottle of water across the room. Ava flinched as water sprayed out the top of it. "I. Did. Not. Hurt. *Anyone!*" he screamed. Just as suddenly as his temper had flared, he seemed to deflate and sink to a chair. He covered his face and sobbed. It was a long, loud, whining sound followed by tears. "I didn't hurt anyone. Why don't you people believe me?"

"Because you haven't been honest with us, Kalen," Ava said.

"But I have," he whined, looking at her with a wounded expression.

She shook her head. "Only after your omissions were found out and thrown in your lap."

He bared his teeth, grabbed two handfuls of his own hair above each temple, and voiced a grating, wordless scream.

Sal held out both hands. "Mr. Hamilton," she said loudly and firmly. "I'm going to have to demand that you calm down or we will have the officer outside take you into custody."

He stood and leaned toward her. "If you could arrest me, you would have already. You're trying to make me admit guilt when there's none to admit." He immediately sank into the chair and started crying again.

He had them there. Without saying anything more to him, Sal and Ava left.

"He's guilty of something," Sal said later in the car.

"I know," Ava said, still frustrated with the situation and still trying to process the man's mood swings. "He might be quiet and unassuming, but he's got a volatile, quick temper, too. I could see him lashing out and hurting someone during those episodes."

"Yeah. Not hard to imagine. We will continue the search for evidence against him. Now I think we'll find Ms. Smith's body, not Ms. Smith."

"You didn't think she was still alive, anyway, did you?"

Sal shrugged. "It was fifty-fifty until just a few minutes ago. I want the evidence to convict him. That means we need to get to it before the search team does."

"They might trample over top of her and any evidence of what's happened," Ava muttered. She pictured perfectly what would happen if Alto's team stomped so brutishly all over the scene. "Even if she's alive, they're liable to botch the scene so bad we couldn't get a conviction."

"We're going to the woods again. We need to get ahead of them again so we don't have to worry about it."

"Are we calling in Metford and the officers?" Ava asked.

"No. Just us this time."

An hour later, Ava and Sal were passing the cordoned-off campsite and heading into new territory. The search team had only been unloading their quads when the women arrived. Sal had paused only long enough to tell Alto what they were doing and that he should keep the team behind her and Ava.

But the further they pressed into unknown territory, the more doubtful they felt.

"Screw it," Sal said, pulling out her phone. "I'm calling in the whole team and the sheriff. This is a hell of a thing to screw up just because I got in a hurry to try and get evidence against one man who might or might not be guilty." She put the phone to her ear.

Ava was shocked but also pleased that Sal had the presence of mind to step back and assess even her own actions. She was an excellent leader, and she knew that she was susceptible to making mistakes just like everyone else. That was yet another lesson for her to file away.

The quads rumbled closer and soon came into view. Sal told Ava to stay put, and she went to Agent Alto. There were no raised voices, but Ava saw that Alto was not happy. He talked a lot with his hands, but it did him no good in the end. Sal was used to dealing with men like him, and she stood her ground unflinchingly.

Everyone was stalled out until the rest of the team and the sheriff arrived with two of his deputies.

Within twenty-five minutes, they found another campsite. Ava, Sal, and Santos were at the front of the line when it came into view. They all three stopped and looked at the makeshift site, and all three yelled at the man standing stock-still near the tarp that had been strung between trees for a makeshift shelter. He had been camouflaged in his neutral-toned clothing until he stepped slightly toward a tree to hide himself.

The man froze for a split second and then bolted into the woods. By then, the others had seen him, and they all gave chase. The uneven forest floor was dangerous. It seemed to be a sentient thing that was determined to slow their pursuit. With each stumble and obstacle, the man got farther and farther away.

"Get the dogs up here, Alto," Sal barked into her walkie. "We're losing him!"

Ava could barely understand her as she yelled into the handheld and ran at the same time.

Ava cursed as she whipped her head wildly left and right. "Footsteps," she said, pointing, and they followed their direction, but it was no use. The man seemed to vanish.

By the time the dogs got there, they were able to follow his scent to an opening in the forest, and then they lost him. Or, rather, they found too many trails for the team to follow. It would be useless to go off on a wild goose chase down each scent trail.

"Whoever he was, he's made many trips in and out of these woods." Sheriff Anderson huffed with the exertion of the chase. He looked around the woods and shook his head.

Sal called off the search for the man. "Get back to the camp. Maybe we'll find out who he is."

As they scoured the site, Ava found a pair of filthy work boots sitting near a log. "Those might match the prints we found in the kitchen of the lake house, Sal."

Sal nodded. She took pictures. "Metford, bag and tag them."

"Here's a leather strap," the sheriff called. "It's buried in dead leaves, but doesn't look all that old."

Ava moved to his side. "That is a leather strap from a woman's sandal." Was it the killer's campsite? Had they been wrong about the friends? About Kalen?

Sal moved over to the strap and took photos. "That is the strap off a sandal," she confirmed. "Good eye."

Ava squatted beside her. "What if this is the killer's campsite, Sal? What if we were wrong all along? What if Kalen really is innocent and the real killer has been staying here?"

Sal shook her head. "No. I don't think so. Doesn't make sense."

But to Ava it did. It made perfect sense. "We have to follow the hard evidence."

Sal closed her eyes and nodded. "I know."

"Jackpot," Metford called. "Boss, you're going to want to have a look at all this stuff. Somebody is seriously messed up."

Ava's heart dropped. As much as she wanted to catch the killer, she always hated sifting through the evidence of what the killer had done.

CHAPTER FORTY-FIVE

THE NEXT MORNING, THE TEAM WENT TO THE LOCAL SHERIFF'S office where the previous day's findings had been stored in boxes. It was a scary amount of evidence.

Six bras, each of them a different size, had been found in varying states of decay. Three of them had tested positive for human blood. Nine women's blouses, again of different sizes and styles. They had also been found in varying states of decay. Two pairs of panties. Twelve driver's licenses, most from Maine. Several tubes of lipstick, three women's sandals—one missing its strap—and a handful of jewelry had been found in a small cave and were in the best shape of anything they'd found except for the licenses, which had been stored in the log by the boots.

Sheriff Anderson blew air between his lips and looked at the mounds of evidence sadly.

"I think it's obvious that someone has been killing for a while and using that area as a base of sorts. Both of those campsites were strategically placed," Ava said. "And look, there's a man's wallet with his license and cards still inside. The license expired last year. There's a man's comb and a razor. A man's belt. It wasn't just women he targeted."

"Just mostly women," Sheriff Anderson said, sounding defeated. "There have been a lot of missing women reported over the last two years. That's one thing we've been so busy working on. I'm trying to get some closure to the families, but I keep hitting dead ends. For a town this small, it's very strange to have so many women go missing in such a short time."

"Have any of the missing women been found?" Ava asked. Was she still holding out hope for Desiree? Even in the face of all the evidence they'd found?

He nodded. "Out of twenty-seven, eight have been found alive. They left for various reasons, but all left of their own volition and free will. Truth be told, I chalked up over half of the missing women as just that—runaways. I even suspect there might be a prostitution or drug ring taking young women from the area. You know how those things work, and they're getting worse every single day. I just couldn't explain all the disappearances, but..." He waved a hand to indicate all the evidence.

Ava took the stack of licenses. She took the top one and entered the information into the police database computer. A woman's picture popped up with a report that had been filed two years earlier. She had been reported missing by her sister and mother.

"Bailey Kemp, York County, reported missing two years ago by her sister and mother," Ava said. She took the second card and entered the information. "Kinsley Knoles, reported missing eighteen months ago by her mother. She's from Somerset." She picked a card at random. "LaFayette Washington, Penobscot County, reported missing—"

"From County Crider three months ago," Sheriff Anderson said. "I remember her family and how torn up they were over her disappearance. She was here for a visit with her aunt and cousins before going back home to start college. I'm still working that one."

"Mei Hon, from Washington County, Virginia, reported missing from here two years ago," Ava said. She put her hand on the remainder of the cards. "I would bet that a lot of your missing persons can be solved right here."

"Sad as that is, I think you're right, but we still don't know for sure if they're alive or dead. There are no bodies yet, and before I can give those families closure, I need either the people alive and breathing, or dead."

"There's no denying what's right in front of us, boss," Metford said.

"Yeah, we're definitely dealing with a serial killer," Santos said.

Ashton nodded in agreement.

Sal nodded, too. "Looks like the case has taken a severe left turn from the way we were working it."

Ava let her gaze roam over the roomful of evidence again, and her heart pained. Why would someone take so many lives? Why the need to snuff out the lives of *young* people?

"That ring," the sheriff said, moving toward the table where a silver ring glinted in the bright light. He picked it up and studied it a moment.

"You recognize it?" Sal asked.

"Carrie Vayle. Local girl. Just turned eighteen this month." He put the ring down. "She was reported missing by her father at the beginning of July. She was a troubled young woman, always in trouble at school, always getting picked up by the officers in town so they could take her back to her daddy. He'd be worried sick, and then he would turn to mush because she was alright and back home. Poor man is going to be devastated. He just lost his wife a couple years back to cancer. Been taking care of the family business and three kids by himself ever since. Damn shame."

It was a damn shame. All of it. That there was a need for people like Ava, Sal, Metford, Santos, and Ashton was a shame. Having to look for bodies instead of breathing people was a shame.

CHAPTER FORTY-SIX

Sal took the team back to the forest so they could go to the makeshift campsite again after seeing all the evidence in the room at the station.

"There's more here," she said to them. "I'm sure of it. We just have to find it."

They were walking toward the site, and Ava was on the lookout for any movement as she recalled how easily the man had hidden from them right in plain sight the day before. She saw nothing, but from farther up the rise, a man on Alto's team did see something.

Alto yelled, alerting Sal and the team that they had a visual a few hundred feet straight ahead of the campsite. The search team had to backtrack and come down from the rise as it was a sixty-foot drop on the other two sides.

Ava and Metford took off at a dead run at the same time. Santos and Ashton were on their heels. The only sounds in Ava's ears were the rushing of air in and out of her lungs, the steady beat and pulse of her heart, and the blood coursing through her veins. There was nothing else. She alone existed as she ran. With her senses heightened and adrenaline speeding her response time, she easily spotted obstacles, trees, low branches, dips in the topography, and small drops. Each time she leaped over or across something, there was a second or two of pure silence and weightlessness in which she felt unreal and yet more alive than ever.

Movement ahead drove her harder. She pumped her legs a bit harder and faster, urged her lungs to pull just a little more air with each inhalation. Then a dog ran past her, breaking her concentration for a fraction of a second, but it was enough to cause the whole thing to crumble. Another dog darted between her and Metford, its leash flapping out behind it and whipping in its wake.

Ava's rhythm disintegrated and she realized she needed to slow down. Her lungs burned, her heart raced out of control, and sweat poured from her head and face. She lost a bit of momentum, and she jogged and then walked and then stopped, panting for breath as the dog handlers trotted by. Metford shook his head.

"Damn dogs. I hope they catch him," he grunted, arming sweat from his face.

"I wish the German shepherds were after him. They'd tear him a new ass," Santos said from behind them.

Ava kept walking in the direction the dogs had taken. After a minute or two, she started jogging and kept a decent pace until she saw the edge of the forest. She stopped, confused. There was a paved road only a few feet away.

"It's the end of the woods," Ashton said.

Hands on hips, Ava walked to the edge of the forest. There was a small ditch separating the forest from the graveled shoulder of the road. She shook her head.

"Lost the scent!" one of the handlers yelled to Alto.

"He probably caught a ride from somebody," Ava said, turning away in disgust.

"Hey!" a handler shouted from farther down the road. "I got tire tracks here in the dirt of the wash-out."

Metford and Ashton ran to set a perimeter around the tracks. Ava, Sal, and Santos walked to the tracks. The previous storm had washed dirt across the road, and it was thick on the shoulder. The tracks were at the shoulder and turned out onto the road.

Sal took photos from every angle. Ava was sure they would be useless. What were they going to do without a suspect? Try to match the tread marks to every car in town?

Sal's phone rang, and she answered. After a few minutes, she thanked whomever was on the other end and hung up. "There was blood on the boots under the layer of mud. No match in the system, though."

It was something, Ava supposed. Disheartened, the team headed back to the campsite. Alto and his team came through a few minutes later, and Sal stopped them.

"Agent Alto, I need two of your men to help bag everything at this site and take it back to the station," she said.

He shook his head. "Why my men? They're just as exhausted as the rest of us right now. We have to get the dogs back."

"Two men. My team will be working, too. With two more, we can be out of here in twenty minutes or so. Two men. Your pick. Or, if any of them want to volunteer. You know, just out of the goodness of their hearts because they actually give a damn about catching a serial killer."

Two of his agents immediately stepped forward, handing off their leashed dogs to other agents. Alto shook his head and turned away.

Ava marveled at his lack of sympathy and concern. She thought that men like Alto probably gave agents everywhere a bad rap. He wasn't the only agent who acted like a jackass, but he was one of the worst she had dealt with.

CHAPTER FORTY-SEVEN

Day fifteen came, and Ava was in the conference room with the team. It was quiet. Too quiet as they waited for Sal to start the meeting. Did they all feel that same sinking in their stomachs that Ava felt? Did they all feel as if they had failed not only the grads at the lake house, but all those other victims as well, by letting that man get away?

Sal finally came in with a look on her face that seemed to echo everyone else's. "Alright, team, let's get started. I know yesterday was disappointing, but we are making progress. And this time, it's in the right direction." She picked up a marker and pointed to the timeline on the boards. "Now, we need to adjust this and our files to reflect everything we have learned; all the new information we have." She turned to the first board and raised the pen.

Everyone glanced around silently at one another as if daring each other to be the first to speak.

"Well, don't everyone offer at once," Ava tried. Everyone laughed, but there was no humor in it at all.

It took nearly two hours to correct the timeline and update the files. It was still quiet and the mood was depressed across the room.

"Someone needs to go cut the friends loose at the hotel," Sal told them once they were finished. "We know now that none of them were involved, and there's no need to keep them sequestered any longer."

"Who do you want to do it?" Santos asked.

"I don't care. You all pick. Now, get to it, team." She turned and walked away, leaving them to manage the situation.

Ava stood and walked to a window. Sal walked at a brisk pace to her car, phone pressed to her ear, and a serious look on her face. She drove out of the lot faster than usual. Where was she going in such a hurry? Why had she been so short with them?

"Well, I call 'not it,'" Santos said, sitting back in her seat and stretching her arms over her head. "They're going to react one of two ways, and I don't want to deal with either."

Ava shook her head and looked at Ashton. He immediately started clacking away at the keyboard of his computer as if extremely busy. She looked to Metford. He held her gaze and shrugged.

"Metford, you want to go with me to do the deed?" she asked, half-expecting him to tell her no.

He stood and sighed. "Not really, but somebody has to face the music. I wouldn't feel right leaving you to do it alone."

"I think you just like the tension." She headed for the door.

"Nah, but by the time we get done, it will be close to lunchtime," he said, grinning and rubbing his stomach. "There's a certain burger calling my name."

"God, do you ever get full?"

"I do, but it doesn't last long."

"We need to take their shoes back to them, too," Ava said.

"Are they still at the lab?"

She nodded.

After getting the shoes, Ava drove to the hotel. She was both looking forward to cutting them loose, and dreading Nova's reaction.

She set the box of shoes in the hallway and took out the bags marked for Nova and Trevon. Nova opened the door and immediately saw the shoes. She scoffed and propped against the door.

"Just returning shoes?"

"Could we come in for a minute? We have some good news," Ava said.

Nova huffed and walked away.

Ava put the shoes on the table, and Nova grabbed the bags, yanking them to the floor. "You can't do that. Are you crazy?"

Trevon put a hand on her shoulder. "It's a sign of death to come," he said. "It's a... superstition, I guess."

Ava's shock subsided a bit and she nodded. "Well, I'm sorry about that. I didn't know. I've come to tell you that you are both free to go home, or wherever you wish."

The couple looked at her suspiciously.

"What the hell do you mean?" Nova asked.

"Just what she said," Metford answered. "You're innocent. You can leave whenever you like."

Nova let out the world's biggest huff. "I'm so thrilled that you finally, after fifteen whole days, realize that we are freaking *innocent*. Just like we've been telling you idiots all along. And now what? You expect us to be falling all over ourselves with gratitude? Well, screw that. Kiss my ass, is what I have to say to that." She stood and kicked a bag of shoes toward the bed.

Ava saw Metford bristling from the corner of her eye. She opened her mouth to stop him from saying anything, but it was too late.

"You need to calm down, Miss Taylor," Metford seethed. Ava deflated as soon as the words came out of his mouth.

Nova spun to face him. Her eyes were hard and angry. She was looking for confrontation. "You need to go fu—"

"Nova," Trevon cut in, stepping between them. "Come on, leave it."

Metford took a step back as Trevon moved aside.

Nova shot Metford the bird.

"How would you like to spend some time in a cell for that?" he asked.

"How would you like to have your life turned inside out because of incompetency?" she retaliated, stepping toward him.

Ava stepped up beside Metford. "I think we all need to calm down here," she said, giving a pointed look at Metford.

His face was contorted with anger, but he made a visible effort to calm down.

Trevon led Nova away, but her mouth still spewed every hateful thing she could think of.

Metford stepped away and took a deep breath. Ava took the verbal abuse. She understood that Nova and the others had been cooped up as if in prison for over two weeks while the FBI and local law enforcement looked at them with suspicion. They had lost three members of their group of friends on top of that. It would take a while for them to recover, and in the meantime, Ava thought they had a right to be angry.

In the hallway between rooms, Metford shook his head but held his cool. Ava felt they had surely bonded and built the trust they needed to work successfully together as a team.

The other friends were just glad to be getting out of the hotel and out from under suspicion.

Ava felt better as they got back into the car. Things were finally starting to go right for the investigation, and everyone involved.

CHAPTER FORTY-EIGHT

Sal called while Ava was driving.

"Get back out to the campsite. Sheriff Anderson says they have a man cornered there in a cave. He was at the campsite, says he has a gun and will shoot anyone who comes in the cave. Ashton and Santos are already on their way. I'm too far out to get there. You're in charge."

"We're on our way," Ava said.

"Alright!" Metford whooped after she disconnected the call. "We got the bastard, Ava."

Maybe there was cause for hope after all. Despite everything that had gone wrong during this entire investigation, Ava allowed herself to feel optimistic. "I hope so."

A few hundred yards from the campsite, Sheriff Anderson and four deputies stood in a semi-circle twenty feet from the mouth of a cave. The sheriff waved her over.

"He's in there and says he has a gun," he said.

Ava nodded. "We'll handle it, sheriff."

She approached the cave but didn't try to go inside. "Sir, my name is Aviva James. I'm with the FBI. I promise I'm not here to hurt you. Can you tell me your name?"

"Jeff Kalter. They're saying I did something I didn't do."

"Okay, Mr. Kalter. We just want to know if that was your campsite back there."

"Yes, and now it's gone," he sobbed. "They took everything I had there. Don't even have my shelter anymore. I was going to get the tent from the other site, and that's when the cops showed up waving their guns and screaming threats."

"Well, Mr. Kalter, there's a good reason they did that. There are a lot of things back there at those sites, things that don't belong to you."

"Yeah, I know, but I didn't hurt anyone to get them like the cops are saying. I took that stuff from somewhere else. It reminds me of everything I used to have." Sobs echoed from the cave.

"I don't understand, Mr. Kalter. There was women's underwear there, women's shoes, clothes, makeup. What does that remind you of?"

"My wife and kids." Another sob echoed. "They died in the terrorist attacks on 9/11." More sobs and a sniffle.

Ashton tapped Ava's shoulder. "Can I try to get him out?"

"He says he has a gun. I don't want anyone getting shot." She shook her head.

"I've got on my vest. Let me try."

"Do you have experience with this sort of situation?"

He nodded. "I used to talk down my cousin when he got violent. He had a mental disorder and I was the only one who could calm him down."

"Do you still do it?" she asked, shocked that she didn't know that about him.

He shook his head. "He got shot and died three years ago."

"I'm sorry. I didn't know," she said. "You can try, but don't force anything."

He nodded and moved directly in front of the cave.

"Hey, don't try to come in here. I have a gun. I will shoot you. I don't have anything to lose anymore," Mr. Kalter called.

Ashton took a knee and held up his hands. "I won't do anything, Mr. Kalter. I'm unarmed. I'm just here to talk to you, try to find out what's going on and how we can help you."

There was a pause of silence. "Help *me*?"

"Yes, sir. I heard what you said about your family, and I'm sorry. Truly sorry," Ashton told him. "I lost family in those attacks as well. I know that pain. It never goes away."

"No, it doesn't. Eats your soul away, but it doesn't kill you and put you out of your misery. Just leaves the husk of a body here to linger on suffering."

"You're right," Ashton said. "Mr. Kalter, I don't think you hurt anyone. Did your wife have dark hair and eyes?"

"How did you know that?" His voice sounded thin.

"Was she about five-seven, hundred-fifteen pounds?"

"Hundred-thirty. She thought she was getting fat," he said, chuckling sadly.

"You had a daughter?"

"And a son. They were twins, but he had blond hair like my side of the family. How do you know all this? Have you already run my name, pulled my history?"

"No, sir. I was going by the things we found at the campsite. Your daughter liked to wear T-shirts, and your wife liked blouses that buttoned."

"Yeah," Kalter replied, his voice barely audible.

"You don't have a gun, do you, Mr. Kalter?"

The man suddenly appeared at the mouth of the cave, squinting as he looked around at the officers and agents. He shook his head. "No, I don't."

Ashton stood and nodded, offering him a sympathetic smile. "Why don't you come on down to the station with us?"

Mr. Kalter wore clothes that were just dirty rags. His beard was long, unkempt, tangled like his mop of long, twisted hair, and his cheeks were sunken. The hollows under his eyes were nearly black, and his face bore savage wrinkles. The rags drifted around him like a filthy cloud as he walked out. His shoulders were stooped as if the weight of the world bore down on them.

Ava's heart broke to see him.

"I'll go if someone will get me something to eat and drink. It's been..." he started, then seemed to be counting and finally shrugged. "It's been a long time since I ate anything."

After assuring him, Ashton put him in a cruiser without incident. Ava told them she would meet them at the station with food and drink for Mr. Kalter.

She stopped at a convenience store and bought him a sandwich from the cooler and a soda. After further consideration, she bought several cans of soup, crackers, canned sandwich meat, and all the beef sticks and cheese snacks. She put it all in a large duffel in the car and then drove to the station.

Mr. Kalter scarfed the sandwich so fast that Ava was afraid he would choke on it or get sick and yak it up, but he did neither.

After running his numbers, which they got from his expired driver's license, they found that his story checked out. His wife had taken the kids to see her father at work that fateful day. They had been trapped on the twenty-first floor during the attack.

"I was supposed to go with them that day," Kalter told Ashton. "I didn't. I wanted to get the boat ready for our vacation the next week." He shook his head. "After, well, I stuck my head in a bottle. That's where it's been ever since."

"I'm so sorry for your loss, Mr. Kalter," Ashton said.

"I thought I could… I thought I could hold it together a while, you know? I nearly did. But then the recession hit. I already lost everything, and then I lost everything again. Lost my job. Lost my home. I didn't care about anything anymore. An' even if I did, nobody would talk to me. Nobody would believe me." He took a deep, shuddering sigh. "Been in and out of work for years. People don't even look at me anymore. They'd rather treat me like dirt. Easier to sweep it under the rug than offer a helping hand."

Ashton spoke with him a while longer before asking where he'd gotten the items in question.

Kalter nodded. "From the basement of a business in town where I sleep a couple of nights a month. Only when I'm sure I won't be caught. Business owners frown on homeless people holing up in their basements. Some things I found out in the woods, though. Like some of the sandals and a hair band that I thought Megan would have liked. I could just see her wearing it in her hair. She was the apple of my eye."

Ashton nodded. "I bet she was. Kids are the best things in life. Where was this business? What is the address?"

Kalter nodded as tears slid down his cheeks into his beard. "Love my family more than life itself. I don't remember the address or what business. I go in the back door between two sets of dumpsters and it's always after dark. Three businesses all connected, but only one has a door with no outside lock."

Ashton noted the information.

Sheriff Anderson gave him a card for a shelter in town that offered other forms of help to get people back on their feet.

Ava walked him out. She called a cab to take him to the shelter, pressed a fifty into his hand, and waited for the cab. When it arrived, she placed the duffel of food in the backseat with Mr. Kalter.

He cried when she wished him well and gave him her card.

She watched the cab drive away. When she turned, Metford was standing by the car, arms crossed, wearing a smile.

"That was real noble of you," he said. "You have a heart about you. That's good." He grinned. "I guess."

CHAPTER FORTY-NINE

Late in the evening, after seeing Mr. Kalter off, Ava asked the team to go with her to the lab. They could help sort through and do some of the mundane, time-consuming tasks to help speed the process along.

"I want to go to town and see if I can find the business he was talking about," Ashton said.

Ava nodded. "Alright. He couldn't remember anything specific about it. Probably was drinking when he went there."

"I'll start with the ones closest to the woods."

"Call if you find anything."

As Ava sorted through a bag of what seemed to be mostly old trash, she spotted pieces of a Haribo bag and others from Big Mama sausages. She put them aside because they tickled something at the back of her mind. They seemed important. More important than most of the other contents of the bag.

When she had finished, she called Sal. She mentioned the scraps of trash that had seemed important, but Sal didn't have an answer for her.

"It'll come to you sooner or later. We cut the grads loose, right?" Sal asked.

"Yeah. Metford and I did that first thing after the meeting. We came to help sort the mountains of stuff from the campsites immediately after sending Mr. Kalter to a shelter."

"Since we're clearing people, we need to clear Kelshaw and Rutherford, too. We've only been to the lake house, Kelshaw's house, and I went to the apartment building, but there were two other properties. We need to have a look around them just so we can mark this couple off the official list, too."

"We'll do it tonight before dark," Ava replied, fingering the strip of gold plastic from the Haribo bag.

She got off the phone and went to Metford and Santos. "We need to do one more thing before we call it a night."

"Dinner at Wendy's?" Metford asked. He wasn't joking.

"Afterward," Ava said, feeling the hunger pangs in her gut, too. "We need to go check out the two rental properties Kelshaw and Rutherford were renovating before she left. Sal says we need to just drive out and look around so we can mark them off the official list of suspects. She wants the case cleaned up and streamlined. That means tying up all loose ends so we can concentrate on finding the serial killer."

"I'll call Ashton," Santos said. "It'll go quicker if we go to one place and you two take the other one."

Ava nodded. "Smart thinking, Santos. I'll text you the address."

"Place looks like it will be nice when they get it finished," Metford commented as he and Ava walked behind the two-story brick.

"Nicer, in my opinion. Did you see the size of that living room and kitchen?"

He nodded. "I would have the windows blocked if it was my place."

"Me, too," she said, tiptoeing to look in another window. It was covered with thick curtains.

Ava's phone rang. "Agent James," she answered as she continued to try to peek through windows.

"Ava, we found a body in the basement," Santos said.

"What?" she gasped, stopping and grabbing Metford's forearm to stop him.

"A damn body. A woman's body in the basement."

Her heart surged into her throat and she ran for the car.

"On our way."

CHAPTER FIFTY

The drive was only a few minutes long, but it was agonizingly slow. Ava's heart raced as they sped down the highway. Metford had barely even pulled to a stop before Ava leaped out of the car to join Santos and Ashton in the driveway.

"Show me," Ava said.

Santos led the way. She covered her nose and mouth as they neared the partially open door of the basement.

Ava pushed the door open and pulled her shirt over her own mouth and nose. The stench was unique and gut-wrenching. The high sickly-sweet aroma of human decomposition. Once smelled, it's never forgotten.

Metford entered, shaking his head. "So much for calling it a night," he muttered.

They moved to the far corner where the body lay half-covered with a blackout curtain. The body had been placed close to the wall under a high window. It was out of sight unless anyone entered the room.

"We smelled the decomp and came inside," Santos said, looking guilty.

"The door wasn't pried," Ava noted, still looking at the badly decomposed body of the woman.

"I got in through a window upstairs."

"Did you break it?" Ava asked, hoping not.

Santos shook her head and leaned close. "But I did use a credit card to—"

Ava shook her head. "I'm sorry, I can't hear you, Santos."

Santos looked shocked for a moment and then nodded. "I said it was open."

Ava nodded and looked back at the body. "She's been dead for some time. Probably weeks from the state of her."

Ashton nodded. "I would guess around a month."

"Reddish-blonde hair, expensive earrings and rings. No wedding ring, though." Ava lifted the curtain. It made a ripping sound as it pulled away from the thigh. "Looks to have been a robust woman, full-figured, nice shoes and clothes. She wasn't homeless and didn't shop at Walmart."

Forensics arrived and swiftly did their job. Ava waited outside impatiently.

"We found her ID underneath her with her wallet. No purse, though," reported the forensic tech. Granger was unfamiliar to Ava, but he did his job quickly and efficiently.

"Who was she?"

He held up the plastic bag containing a badly stained ID card and turned it to face a light. "Harper Kelshaw," he said and offered her the bag.

A shock ran through her chest at the name. She took the bag. "How long has she been dead?"

"Weeks, maybe a month. Won't know until the autopsy, though."

"Cause of death?" Ava asked, feeling a bit numb.

He nodded. "Stabbed in the chest, but I don't know exactly how many times, and her skull is cracked in the back. Take your pick, but my guess is that it wasn't accidental or suicide."

"Thank you."

Ava looked at the driver's license and saw the name and address were the same as she had on file. Harper had never gone to New Zealand. Harper wasn't the person she and Sal had been texting and emailing all along.

Ava called Sal to give her the news.

"So, who the hell were we communicating with?"

"I don't know," Ava said. "Can we ping her phone to see where it pinged last?"

"Yes. But the cell coverage is so spotty out here that I don't know how accurate it will be."

"What about her boyfriend?" Ava asked.

"What about him?"

"Wouldn't he have been out here at all since she left? Wouldn't he have known she wasn't in New Zealand?"

Sal was quiet for a bit. "That would be logical."

"Whoever ran from us in the woods that day had to be strong and fast to disappear like that. It may seem out of left field, but what if it was him?"

"You mean you think Antonio is the serial killer?"

"He's the only person left on our list that we haven't extensively researched besides Harper Kelshaw," Ava pressed.

"We have to investigate this as if it's a separate case for now. Remember, by the book. If it's connected, it will show up in the investigation. Let me think about the boyfriend. I'll be back early in the morning. For now, full investigation starts on this new murder."

The Haribo and Big Mama sausage wrappers flashed in Ava's mind again. "That's it, Sal. The Haribo and Big Mama wrappers. He had them in his house. They were on his counter. Metford pointed them out. Antonio said his mother used to buy them for him when he was a kid and he'd gotten back in the habit of buying them after her death earlier this year." Excitement thrilled through her.

"Hold the thought, Ava. Those snacks can be purchased at almost any store. They're literally everywhere. Anyone could have dropped them in the woods."

Ava didn't agree. She thought Antonio had dropped them because he had been there. It wasn't a coincidence that the campsites were so close to the lake house. It wasn't a coincidence that he hadn't noticed his girlfriend had disappeared.

"Can we please ping his phone at the same time we ping Harper's?"

"We'll see in the morning," Sal said.

Ava hung up, a little miffed at Sal's rebuff, but more determined than ever.

"It's got to be Rutherford. I'm certain," she announced to the group.

"Seems to be that way, but we were certain it was one of the group. And we were sure it was Kalen," Metford pointed out. "Isn't the homeless guy either."

"You're right," Ava admitted.

"What do we do?" Santos asked. "Should we roll up and arrest the guy right now on suspicion?"

Ava shook her head. "No. It's been this long. We don't want to give him a reason to suspect us or give him a sudden heads-up. If we make the wrong move too quickly, he could high-tail it out of town. I also don't really feel like spending even more time chasing up false leads and spinning our wheels. Let's get the phone ping first, then go for the arrest. Solid evidence. By the book."

"By the book," Santos echoed.

CHAPTER FIFTY-ONE

Sal worked it out to ping both phones the next day. Ava didn't know if she had done it because she thought the theory was right, or if she was trying to prove Ava wrong. Strings were pulled, favors done, and the pings were traced.

"Harper's phone pinged for seventy hours in the woods behind the house where she was found dead. It continued to ping until the day before Santos and Ashton found her," Sal said.

"What about Antonio's?" Ava asked, anxious.

"It pinged there for a few hours."

Ava pumped her fist in the air. "I knew it. It is him, Sal. We have him in our sights."

"The tech told me that the ping locations couldn't be ruled as absolute or even very accurate," she warned.

Ava shook her head. "Why not? I mean, the phones pinged there, the towers recorded the pings."

"That's just it. There are very few towers out here. They are few and far between, and that broadens the area. The broader the area, the less accurate the ping. It could be off by a mile." Sal dropped the papers on the table.

"What about when we were communicating with Harper? When she was texting us on her phone? She was dead already. Was his phone near hers then?"

"Yes, but again, it can't be trusted as accurate, even though we have our suspicions, there's no hard proof that he was really there. He could've been a mile away, give or take. And remember, technically that's just his phone. We have to prove that he had possession of it at that time."

Ava thought for a few minutes as she looked over the ping locations. "According to this, Harper's phone was in the woods a month ago. She's been dead all that time."

"Yep," Sal said.

"Sick bastard."

"I concur."

Ava took out her phone to check the times and days of her texts with Harper, or whoever was pretending to be Harper at the time. The replies matched perfectly with the times of the pings from Harper's phone in the basement of the house where she was found. Antonio's phone was always there, too. "It was him, Sal. He was pretending to be her the whole time. Just like he did with the friends through the website."

"He was used to pretending to be Harper," Sal said.

Ava put down the papers. "I want to stake out his apartment."

Sal tapped the table with one finger and her brow furrowed. After several minutes, she nodded. "But you can't let him see you and you absolutely cannot go into the apartment building. Not until I get a warrant to search it, and that will only be after I convince someone that he is likely the serial killer."

What was with Sal? Ava knew the importance of doing things by the book, but this was more than enough circumstantial evidence. Hadn't they spent long enough twiddling their thumbs on this one? Even if it wasn't Rutherford, they could get closer to ruling him out if they at least interviewed him again—and then saw what his actions were. Ava didn't understand why Sal seemed to have been dragging her feet the entire time they'd been in Maine.

She wanted to say all those things, but what she actually said was: "Thank you."

"Take Metford with you." Sal walked away.

CHAPTER FIFTY-TWO

After filling Metford in on all the details, he was thrilled to go along for the stakeout. Three hours into the night, he began to fidget in his seat, and Ava was questioning her sanity. Why did it always seem like she got herself into impossibly uncomfortable situations either socially or physically?

"Sitting in a car all night is hard work," Metford complained.

Ava nodded. "I always think it's going to be really easy. All I'm doing is sitting, after all."

"Yeah, but nobody ever tells you about all the times you have to go pee because of all the coffee you drink so you can stay alert."

She laughed. "And nobody tells you how many times the backs of your thighs and lower back will seize up in horrible cramps, either."

"If they did, would it change your mind?"

She shook her head and chuckled again. "Nope. At the time, I'm practically begging to do a stakeout because I'm sure I'm right about someone, and nothing can sway my decision."

"Ten hours later, though," he muttered, twisting to the side and rubbing his lower back.

"Yeah, I know, right?" She arched her back away from the seat. "And no sign of him at all. I don't even think I've seen him walk by a window."

"Me neither. Maybe he's out stalking another victim."

"Let's hope not." She stifled a yawn.

Just before sunrise, Sal texted that she and Santos were on their way to take over for the day.

"Not a minute too soon for me," Metford groaned. "I'll be glad to get out of this seat and hit the sack. I'm beat."

Santos rang Ava's phone.

"What's up?" Ava said into the phone.

"Sheriff just called. Boss is on the phone with Ashton. Meet us at two-eleven North Main Street. Someone spotted a man acting weird and sneaking into the basement of an abandoned business there. He thought it sounded like our man."

Ava glanced up at the one lit window of Antonio's apartment. "On our way." She hung up and started the car. "You heard that, right?"

"I did, but it might just be Jeff Kalter going back there. He said he goes there a couple of nights a month."

She nodded. "But it could be our serial killer, too. That basement is where Kalter said he got a lot of the items at the campsite."

When they arrived, Ashton was just getting out of his car, shaking his head. "I didn't make it over to Main. I only went up Amick Street. One block away," he said, stalking toward Sal and Santos.

Metford led the team through the door. A wide concrete hallway lay beyond with a door to the left. The hall continued past that door and opened into a wide room.

Metford pointed at the door and held up a fist for everyone to stop and hold. He eased the door open and a flurry of movement drew everyone's attention toward the right. Metford rushed in, and the door on the other side of the room flew open. A figure darted through it. Ava and Ashton had already gone into the room and turned to go back to the hallway to prevent the man from escaping.

Santos pushed past them and ran down the hallway to the larger room. The man came into view, saw Santos, and turned to run away from her, but Metford had already closed in on him. The assailant wore a hoodie, making it impossible to see his face in the dim light, but Ava was sure it was Antonio.

The man ducked, and Metford ducked, spreading out his arms to grab him. The man stepped back and threw a punch that caught Metford in the face, sending him flying backward. Santos lunged at the man's side but caught an elbow in the side of the head. She staggered to the side. Ava didn't hesitate. She ran straight for the man's back as he was stepping over Metford's leg. She tackled him hard, riding his back to the concrete floor.

Sal was right on her heels; she pinned one arm under her knees and pressed his face toward the floor with her hands on the back of his head. Ava straddled his hips and wrested the other arm behind his back. Sal then cuffed him.

Ava stood. She and Sal hauled the man off the floor and ripped the hood off his head.

"Antonio Rutherford," Ava said. "You are under arrest."

Ashton helped Santos up. She brushed him away angrily as she held the side of her head. Metford held a hand over his nose and stood. He checked his hand for blood.

"You're going to be charged for assaulting two agents and resisting arrest, Mr. Rutherford," Sal said. "Ashton, get him in a cell."

Ashton took him. The sheriff met him in the hallway and they escorted the man outside as Ashton Mirandized him.

The rest of the team searched the basement. There were clean clothes—two suits, ties, shoes, and underwear—in a plastic zip bag. There was a large black bag containing soiled clothes that had been overturned and partially spilled on the floor.

"That's what he had in his hand when I opened the door," Metford said. He shone his flashlight on the spilled clothes.

"Looks like these are the clothes he wore when he killed someone," Ava said.

Santos put her light close to a shirt. "That's blood, for sure."

"You know the drill," Sal said. "Bag and tag."

CHAPTER FIFTY-THREE

Antonio sat across from Ava, eyeing her with cold smugness. "Mr. Feeks, it would really help your case if you came clean now," Ava said.

"Why did you call me Feeks?" he asked, his smile faltering a bit.

"Oh, isn't that your name? Hendrix Feeks, right?" She smiled and waited.

His face registered annoyance, but he kept his tone civil. "So, you found out my real name. It's not illegal to change your name as far as I know."

She shook her head. "No, not if it's done legally, but you constructed an entirely new identification *fraudulently*, Mr. Feeks." She looked at the file in front of her. "But I suppose that's the least of your worries, considering what we found at your campsites out by the Crater Lake house."

He chuckled. "You found nothing of mine out there."

"Oh, but we did," she said, removing several photos of evidence.

He shook his head and sat back in his chair, unruffled.

She removed a plastic bag containing the ID cards and slid it toward him. "Oh, and these, too."

His face sagged for only a split second, and he sat back again, holding her gaze. "Never seen them before."

"Mr. Feeks, we know about all those missing women. They aren't really missing, are they?"

"How should I know?"

She sighed and put away the ID cards. "Mr. Feeks, as we speak, there is a team at your apartment going through all your personal belongings. They are dismantling your home piece by piece."

He laughed and shook his head. "That's perfectly fine, Agent James. I've done nothing. They can search all they want, and I'll still walk out of here. It's ludicrous that you have me here, anyway."

"We found all your clothes in that basement, too. You know the ones, right?"

He shook his head. "They aren't mine. My clothes are in my apartment." Sweat had popped out on his forehead and glistened in the fluorescent light. His gaze shifted from Ava's to the mirror behind her.

She nodded. "Even the soiled clothes in that garbage bag? Those are yours, aren't they?"

He laughed and shook his head, but the worry in his eyes couldn't be hidden.

"If you had those clothes on… well," she began, then stopped and shrugged. "We'll find out soon enough, won't we? The lab is working on those clothes as a priority right now."

Ava stood. "I'll be back in a few. You want something to drink when I come back?" She cocked an eyebrow at him, daring him to ask for anything, almost wanting him to ask so she could deny him upon her return. Not professional, but she was feeling particularly hateful toward him.

He shook his head. "No thanks."

She nodded and stepped out.

Metford had left her a message, and she called him back as she stood on the other side of the mirror watching Feeks.

"There is all kinds of video equipment in Feeks' storage space in the basement of the apartment building. And rolls and rolls of that industrial tape that we found in the lake house. It looks like he was using that tape to secure small spy-type cameras around the rental house to peep on the occupants."

"Thank you. If you find anything else, call back. He's playing innocent and cool right now. I need something to rattle him."

Ava stepped in and sat again. "Mr. Feeks, I just got a call from one of the agents at your apartment. It seems that the contents of your basement storage area give rise to more questions. Been spying on your girlfriend's tenants? That's not very gentlemanly of you."

He blanched but said nothing.

CHAPTER FIFTY-FOUR

Hendrix Feeks, or Antonio Rutherford, whatever he wanted to call himself, spent the next three days in a cell while the lab collected and ran the prints from all the equipment in Feeks' basement storage. DNA was found on much of it.

Ava walked into the interrogation room smiling smugly, giving him a bit of his own medicine. "Mr. Feeks, your prints and DNA were on the recording equipment. You really can't keep denying this."

"Of course my prints and DNA are on the equipment. It's mine."

"Did I mention that the lab extracted all the videos, too?"

He shifted in his seat.

"You've been doing this for a while, and not only at the lake house." She leaned on her elbows. "Remember Harper? Do you remember stabbing her repeatedly in the chest? Or bashing her skull from behind? What did you do, Mr. Feeks? Hit her while her back was turned, and then stab her to make sure she was dead?"

"Ludicrous." His voice had lost all its force.

"You keep using that word, but we both know it's not ludicrous. Harper... what did she do to deserve that? And from the man she loved, no less."

He licked his lips quickly and shook his head.

"We have your DNA on her body. The blood on the garbage bag clothes is hers. There are no more secrets, Mr. Feeks. Tell me about the missing women and men. Where are they?"

"I... I... I don't know what you're talking about," he stammered.

She shook her head. "No more games, either. We know you're guilty." And he was. But they couldn't connect him to the deaths of Jonathan Williams, Banks Becker, or Desiree Smith. As a matter of fact, they didn't know for sure that the missing women and men were dead. It was all educated guesses that needed concrete facts to back them up. Or a confession, which would be awesome, too.

"What do you want and what can you do for me?"

She shook her head. "We want the locations of the missing women and men for starters. And I'd like to know why you killed Harper and those kids up at the lake house."

He sneered. "Harper was a lovers' spat. The kids at the lake house, though, I don't know what you're talking about."

That made Ava raise her eyebrows. So they had him on one charge. It might have to be enough. "A lovers' spat?"

He nodded. "She wanted to run off to New Zealand to hang out with her so-called friends there. Nothing but a bunch of drunks who spent their days lazing around on the beaches and doing nothing constructive at all. They were a bad influence, and she was starting to act like them. Every time she came back from there, she acted more and more like them. Spending money hand over fist, dressing in clothes that were inappropriate for her age and status in the community." He chuckled. "Ironically, she had agreed to wear an outfit that I had bought for her on the day we argued for the last time. She just wouldn't listen to me. She was determined to go to New Zealand. Again." He shook his head. "Don't you need to be taking notes, or something?"

"No, it's all being recorded, Mr. Feeks."

"What else do you want from me?"

"Locations of the missing people," she said without hesitation.

"Help me, and I'll help you, agent."

"Tell you what, Mr. Feeks," Ava said, standing. "How about I leave until tomorrow or the next day, and you sit in your cell. When I come back, I'll have some more evidence against you."

"You wish," he scoffed.

"The lab should have the prints pulled from those hypodermics the deputies collected close to the campsite. There were two of them. What are they going to find when they run the contents of those needles?" She grinned and turned for the door.

CHAPTER FIFTY-FIVE

Another day passed. As much as Ava wanted to press Feeks for a confession, she forced herself to stay away. Letting him sit in that cell was the best persuasion she had until the lab finished with the needles. If they turned out not to be his, she still had nothing.

Sal came to her. "It seems that Mr. Feeks wants to speak to us."

Ava nearly jumped out of her chair. "Finally. Is he going to confess?"

Sal shrugged. "Just said he was ready to talk."

At the station, Ava and Sal watched Feeks through the two-way mirror. He was pale and drawn, unlike the ruddy-cheeked scrapper they had arrested.

"Ready?" Ava asked.

Sal nodded. "You go in first. If it's necessary, I'll come in later."

Ava nodded and took a deep breath. Was it the moment when a serial killer was going to confess his crimes to her? She hoped so.

Feeks watched her enter and take a seat.

"Still haven't lawyered up?" she asked.

"I have."

Ava shrugged and looked around the empty room. "Where's your attorney? Shouldn't he or she be present?"

He shook his head. "He advised me to do this. Said he could get me a deal if I cooperated."

"Jail doesn't agree with you, huh? Nothing to be ashamed of; it doesn't agree with many people. Now, what did you want to talk about, Mr. Feeks?"

"You wanted locations. Show me the cards, I'll tell you where to find them."

Ava's heart raced and felt as if it tripped over itself as she took out the cards and placed them on the table in a neat stack.

He took them and breathed in deeply. He put down two cards and slid them to her. "Scarlett Tomalin and Janie Tipton. Both in a mine shaft on the backside of a local mountain. I can mark it on a map for you." He pulled another two cards. "Sylvie Masters and Bailey Kemp are in a deep ragged ravine. I can also mark that on a map for you. Scavengers and the elements do away with a lot of evidence, scatter it around and don't leave much, if anything, at the site. So I can't promise how much will be there, but that's where I left them."

Ava's stomach roiled with disgust and anger and horror. He was listing dumpsites and pointing out victims as if it were of no more importance than ordering a sandwich at the deli.

"Kinsley Knoles is in a lake a few counties away. I wrapped her in barbed wire and weighted her with cinderblocks. It's going to be hell getting to her because I put her in the deepest part."

"Barbed wire? Why would you do that?" she asked, unable to keep the disdain from her voice.

"As the body produces decomp gases, the barbs put holes in it so the body won't float to the top." He slid the two men's cards to her. "Leslie Marks and Sean Baxter are resting inside hollow trees at Bumbee Ridge. Two separate trees." He took out two more cards. "LaFayette Washington... I put her in an open grave the day before a burial. The name on the tombstone is Marianna Tilson, aged eighty-seven. She's in Polk Cemetery, a few miles away but still in York County. And Mei Hong," he said, tapping the card. "She's inside the wall of the other unfinished rental house. Not the one where you found Harper." He pushed the other three back to her. "Those are scattered in the woods, and I can't remember where. It's sufficient that I confess, I suppose."

She picked up the cards with numb fingers. She had heard some terrible things in her life, but Hendrix Feeks had so casually admitted to things that would haunt her nightmares for years to come. She put the cards away and stared at him in disbelief. Was she in a nightmare? Could anyone be so heartless and cruel in the waking world?

He smirked at her, and she stood, not breaking eye contact. She waited until his gaze shifted before she turned her back and walked out.

After gathering herself and her thoughts, Ava told Sal she was ready to go back in.

"Mr. Feeks, what about Desiree Smith, Jonathan Williams, and Banks Becker? Where are they?"

He sat motionless for a moment and then grinned widely. "I'm afraid I really don't know what you mean. I did nothing to those kids. I already admitted to the others, why would I lie about this?" He spread out his hands and leaned forward on the table, relaxed.

"Ever heard of pentobarbital?" she asked.

The little bit of color he had left drained from his face. He remained silent.

"That's what killed Banks Becker. A recent college graduate who had good grades and was getting ready to join the Air Force after his vacation. He never used drugs, you know. Smoked a little pot with his friends, drank a lot of alcohol… but he wasn't hurting anyone. And he had accomplished so much, done so much with his life, and he was going to do even more, accomplish even more."

"Tragic," he shrugged.

"Jonathan was going to work for a big marketing firm in California. Desiree had been hired by a prestigious accounting firm there as well. Not slackers. Not hurting anyone. Just kids celebrating their accomplishments and having one last good time before they headed off into their lives as productive adults. They each would have benefited society on so many levels."

Feeks clicked his tongue and shook his head. "As I said, tragic. It's always a shame for one to be cut down in youth. That's what partying and doing drugs and drinking gets you, though."

Ava was frustrated. It shouldn't have mattered. The crimes he'd confessed to were enough to put him away for several lifetimes. This monster would be off the streets for good.

But it wasn't justice for Desiree, Jonathan, and Banks. It wasn't the same at all.

CHAPTER FIFTY-SIX

Two days later, Ava received the lab reports from the hypodermics. She took the reports to Sal.

"They had pentobarbital in them," Sal said.

Ava nodded. "And the prints came back as a match to Feeks. They were his needles. The partial from the lake house mirror matches his."

"It's time to give him another visit."

Feeks looked tired and haggard. Ava was glad to see it.

"Find those bodies?" he asked.

"That's not why we're here, Mr. Feeks," Sal said.

He gave her a scathing look. "Then what?"

Ava folded her hands on the table. "You are being charged with another murder, Mr. Feeks. Banks Becker. There were prints on two hypodermic needles."

"I'll give you two guesses which needles had your prints," Sal said.

He was visibly shaken. "Proves nothing."

"Except that you were in possession of a controlled substance. A controlled substance that killed a young man," Sal countered.

"Oh, and we know what you did to Jonathan, too. You're not too careful with leaving prints, are you, Mr. Feeks?" Ava taunted.

After several minutes of floundering and seeming like a scared rabbit in a snare, Feeks stilled and glared at the two women, nodding.

"You want to know the truth, I'll tell you. I killed them. All three of those useless twenty-somethings who had never put in an honest day's work in their lives. I killed them." He bared his teeth and leaned toward them. "I wish I had run into you two alone because I would love to have your necklace," he sneered, pointing to Sal's pendant necklace, and then turned to Ava to continue, "and your earrings to add to my collection, which I'm sure your grubby agents have ruined by now." He scoffed and thumped back in his chair. "Those college kids were stupid. They thought it was a ghost going through their things and moving stuff around."

Ava glared at him with more hatred than she'd ever mustered before, and for once in her life, she didn't feel bad for feeling it. That rage boiled up in her body until she was ready to snap.

But Feeks didn't care. He laughed heartily as if he'd just heard a great joke. He shook his head. "You know, I stood over one of the women in the living room. She was passed out on the floor, and I stood right over the top of her. That cute but silly little Asian girl? I crawled right into bed and curled against her back while her boyfriend slept off his pot on the other side of her." He closed his eyes and rubbed a hand down his chest as if reliving the memory. "I even went in after you sealed the house and showered in the bathtub where Jonathan drowned."

"How did you get back in the house without breaking the seal?" Sal asked, considerably more calmly than Ava but with the same searing emotion in her eyes.

He laughed and thumped the table. "The master suite's window has no screen. I made sure of that. The window lock was shit. I just cut a piece of pliable plastic from a milk jug. Just slid that in there and wiggled the lock until it was open. Raised the window, and in I went. How did you like those boot prints in the kitchen? I couldn't resist having a bit of fun." He held his belly and laughed again. "Can't feel good knowing I outsmarted you with a piece of plastic."

Ava waited until he had regained his composure.

"What the hell twisted you so bad?" she asked.

"You mean, what turned me into a heartless monster?"

She nodded. "Yeah."

He sighed and looked sad. "My mother died earlier this year. It was a huge blow to me. She was hardworking, straight-laced, gave me all my foundations in life. She taught me to always work hard and to never dilly-dally around, no wasting time, because that was the worst thing in the world that anyone could ever do. You remember, don't you?"

"You're not getting any more sympathy from me, Mr. Feeks," Ava said icily.

"Oh, I know. It was just funny to watch you squirm a little. Anyway, that's why they all had to die. They were all wasting time, playing around even though they were well past the age when that should have stopped. They were laying around, partying… wasting the lives they'd been given." He shook his head. "No good to anyone. Not productive at all. Wasting time and resources that could be put to better use on people who actually have standards, people who do something productive with their lives."

After a few moments of silence, Sal cleared her throat. "Mr. Feeks, where are their bodies?"

He laughed. "Desiree is chained behind the waterfall up at Harper's home. You were there and had no idea you were so close."

"What about what happened to Banks and Jonathan?" Ava asked.

"Of course I killed them. Annoying little shits."

Ava couldn't take any more. She stood and exited the room. Sal sat at the table staring at Feeks for a few more minutes, neither of them speaking. He laughed every now and then and managed to look proud of himself. Sal just looked disgusted.

She joined Ava in the other room. "Well, that's that."

Ava looked down at the ground, barely keeping her lunch down. "Why don't I feel any better?"

"Because sometimes even catching the bad guys reminds us how depraved humanity can be. But that's why we do this job, Ava. To make sure we protect innocent people from monsters like him." Sal put a hand on her shoulder and squeezed. "Let's go home."

Ava didn't say anything else. She went through the motions of packing and readying to leave, but she felt as if she was phoning it in from another planet. It would be good to get back home and have the case behind her.

It would be good to get away from monsters, even if only for a little while.

EPILOGUE

A week after returning to Fairhaven, Ava and the team had their normal celebratory evening at the bar. The case had been closed successfully. Another bad guy was going to rot in jail, and the world was a bit safer.

Everyone seemed more relaxed and settled. Even Sal had returned to being her normal self instead of the tense, curt grump she had turned into in Wyoming.

Ava was finally, truly comfortable with the group for the first time, and she stayed through the entire evening.

Afterward, when they were all leaving, Sal pulled Ava aside. "I need to talk to you in private for a minute."

Ava followed her to the car. "What's up?"

"I was ordered to do research on a human trafficking ring and not tell anyone. I had to keep it a secret. That's why I was so distracted in Maine," Sal said.

"Why are you telling me if it's supposed to be secret?" A human trafficking ring? Should she allow her heart to hope? Or should she be filled with dread? Was she getting ready to receive some bad news or good?

"Because the secrecy was only throughout the research and reporting." She shrugged. "That's over now. The research was for a case that you know about."

Ava's heart thrilled. "Mom?"

Sal nodded.

"I didn't know you had kept up with that."

"I didn't, but it fell to me. Your mom is in the country. She's still tracking the ring and is holding out until she can get the name of the leader. Or, that's what she hopes to do."

"You spoke to her?" Ava suddenly felt crushed.

"No. She left clues that were put together by your uncle, I think. Him or another agent in the know. There's word that Ash Patterson and Jack Kearns are key players in the ring, and the Cornbread Mafia is in cahoots with a much larger organization that spans the entire globe. We have information about the center of the Cornbread Mafia. Their HQ is in Tennessee. Argyle Sams is the leader. Ash and Jack take orders from his second in command, Lyle Edwards. Argyle gets women from all over the South and hands them over to the larger ring. He gets paid for each one. He produces and distributes meth and other drugs from the streets to other countries. There's more, but you need to call your uncle about it."

Ava was overwhelmed. She leaned over and hugged Sal quickly, holding back tears. "Thank you."

Sal nodded, holding back her own tears. "Now, go on and get out of here. You've got a phone call to make."

Ava got into her own car and let the tears fall. On her way home, she let her emotions run the gamut and clear from her system.

She called Uncle Ray and gushed about what she had learned from Sal.

"Now," he said, "open your secure email. All the information is there for you along with a rough plan for how the investigation will progress."

She looked at the screen of her laptop with wide eyes. "Uncle Ray, does this mean I am finally allowed to at least know what's going on?"

"That's what it means, kiddo. You'll have all the information and progress reports as soon as I have them. Totally above board and legal."

Ava was thrilled to know things had gone so far with her mother's and Molly's cases. She was even more thrilled to be allowed access to the cases. She would be able to help. She was sure that was the direction things were going.

After hanging up the phone, she opened a document that was several pages long. It showed how the larger organization connected the smaller ones all around the world. The crimes perpetrated by those people made Hendrix Feeks look like a priest.

The last thing Ava had wanted to do was delve back into the world of hunting monsters. But now, she felt electric. She tasted victory on the edge of her tongue. Now, she knew exactly what she had to do to end the reign of terror of these men for good.

"I'm coming, Molly. I'm coming," she whispered.

AUTHOR'S NOTE

Dear Reader,

Thank you for for reading *The Lake House,* book five in the *Ava James FBI Mystery series!*

Fall is my favorite time of the year and I love being able to sit outside with my comfy sweater, hot cup of coffee, and type away soaking up all the fall vibes around me. I have so many ideas and I can't wait for you to read the books I'm working on currently. I hope you can sit by the fire and enjoy them this holiday season!

If you can please leave me a review for this book, I would appreciate that enormously. Your reviews allow me to get the validation I need to keep going as an indie author. Just a moment of your time is all that is needed to ensure Ava James' series can continue. Ava and the team are counting on you!

Yours,
A.J. Rivers

P.S. If for some reason you didn't like this book or found typos or other errors, please let me know personally. I do my best to read and respond to every email at mailto:aj@riversthrillers.com

ALSO BY
A.J. RIVERS

Emma Griffin FBI Mysteries by AJ Rivers

Season One
Book One—*The Girl in Cabin 13**
Book Two—*The Girl Who Vanished**
Book Three—*The Girl in the Manor**
Book Four—*The Girl Next Door**
Book Five—*The Girl and the Deadly Express**
Book Six—*The Girl and the Hunt**
Book Seven—*The Girl and the Deadly End**

Season Two
Book Eight—*The Girl in Dangerous Waters**
Book Nine—*The Girl and Secret Society**
Book Ten—*The Girl and the Field of Bones**
Book Eleven—*The Girl and the Black Christmas**
Book Twelve—*The Girl and the Cursed Lake**
Book Thirteen—*The Girl and The Unlucky 13**
Book Fourteen—*The Girl and the Dragon's Island**

Season Three
Book Fifteen—*The Girl in the Woods* *
Book Sixteen —*The Girl and the Midnight Murder* *
Book Seventeen— *The Girl and the Silent Night* *
Book Eighteen — *The Girl and the Last Sleepover**
Book Nineteen — *The Girl and the 7 Deadly Sins**
Book Twenty — *The Girl in Apartment 9**
Book Twenty-One — *The Girl and the Twisted End**

Ava James FBI Mysteries

Book One—The Woman at the Masked Gala
Book Two—Ava James and the Forgotten Bones
Book Three —The Couple Next Door
Book Four — The Cabin on Willow Lake
Book Five — The Lake House

Dean Steele FBI Mysteries

Book One—The Woman in the Woods

Emma Griffin FBI Mysteries Retro - Limited Series

Book One— The Girl in the Mist

Other Standalone Novels

Gone Woman
* Also available in audio

Made in the USA
Monee, IL
02 December 2022